GW00793142

The Clock

by
Janet Dove

authorHOUSE™

1663 LIBERTY DRIVE, SUITE 200
BLOOMINGTON, INDIANA 47403
(800) 839-8640
WWW.AUTHORHOUSE.COM

First published by AuthorHouse 06/21/05

ISBN: 1-4208-4564-0 (sc)

Printed in the United States of America
Bloomington, Indiana

This book is printed on acid-free paper.

Cover illustration is by Lewis Dove

Acknowledgements

To my wonderful husband Lewis, for all his encouragement and support enabling me to fulfil my dream.

Thank you Jacqueline for being my confidante and also for your inspiration, and I thank Judith for your help and support.

Thank you, Yasmine and Kristian for believing in me.

Ray's pillow was saturated with the sweat, which seeped from his brow and temples and trickled profusely down his nose and cheeks. An awful drumming noise was hammering and pounding away in his head through the tense darkness of the long, humid night.

He screamed for help as he ran, terrified, through the thick undergrowth and thorny bushes that scratched his arms and legs, threatening at every step to ensnare him. They were after him again, chasing him headlong towards the trap, which he knew very well lay directly ahead of him. Although he knew the terrain well, he felt powerless to avoid the trap, as though his fate was somehow pre-ordained. Somebody, or something, was hurling firebombs in his direction, scorching the damp grass beneath his feet and incinerating the bushes, which crackled into flames and acrid smoke all around him. All he could hear were his gasping breaths from the exertion of running and the blood, pounding in his temples as he ran from his unseen foe. Whichever way he turned, solid steel bars sprang up in front of him, blocking his path and forcing him back onto his original course. There was no escape from these metal bars. Whichever direction he took, they caged him in like a tiger, systematically sealing him into this hellhole as their steely claws slammed deep into the ground before him. It seemed as though someone was anticipating his every move in this deadly game of chess. The strategy for his defeat was utterly cold and clinical.

The thumping in his head began to subside until it finally resolved into footsteps coming closer and closer until he awoke with a start as Sam's soft, warm hand caressed his shoulder……..

CHAPTER I –
Ivy Cottage

The chilly December wind moaned under the eaves of the old cottage, wrapping its icy tendrils around the doors and windows, as if franticly trying to find its way in. It whistled around the thatch and howled down the chimney, but despite its efforts to intrude, the atmosphere within was warm and cosy, as one might have imagined it to be for the past three hundred years or more. The cottage nestled at the end of a winding lane leading up the hill from a charming, unspoilt village in north Essex, which Neil and Madeline discovered during their courting days back in the late 1950's.

They were exploring the immediate area, having enjoyed an idyllic picnic on the village green on a beautiful, balmy summer's day and with all the hope and expectation of youth they began dreaming about sharing their own special place in the country. Of course, they could not have known then what fate might have in store for them as they wandered hand-in-hand down that picturesque country lane but, when they set eyes on 'Ivy Cottage' they were immediately captivated by its 'picture postcard' appearance. It was love at first sight. As they peered in through the gate, the owners, who were busy working in the garden, saw them and invited them in to look around the garden in which they were taking such an obvious pride. The young couple looked at each other and smiled. They knew, without a single word passing between them that they were both thinking exactly the same thing. Somehow, someday they must find a way to make this beautiful cottage their own. Whilst the owners were very friendly and happy to show the young couple around their lovely garden, it was clear that this was their retirement home and that there would be absolutely no chance of them agreeing to sell it.

The approach to the cottage was through a wrought iron gate, set back off the road in the middle of a high hedge, which ran along parallel to the road. The wide gravel drive, flanked by an armada of lavender bushes, led to a small porch over which climbing roses trailed in a profusion of reds, pinks and yellows. Leaded-light windows on either side of the porch gave the house a friendly and welcoming ambience, whilst the upstairs windows seemed to be almost peering out from under the thatched roof. Ivy climbed up the corner of the house and swept round to an archway from which hung an old-fashioned gas lamp. A shingle path led under the archway, along the side of the cottage and round to the back where there was a very colourful and traditionally English country garden, an abundance of plum and pear trees and a small apple orchard beyond. The main drive continued to the right from the front porch and round behind a high laurel hedge to a gravelled area that was large enough to park several cars. Neil casually remarked at the time that they would have plenty of space to entertain their many friends here. However, they knew that for the time being at least, they must content themselves with the idea of living in such an idyllic setting and hope that someday it just might work out for them.

Then shortly afterwards to their complete amazement, their dream came true when they were advised by the local estate agents that the present owners had recently decided to go and live in Australia. Apparently, they wanted to be close to their daughter, whose emigration a year or so before left the elderly couple feeling somewhat empty, especially as there were now grandchildren for them to visit. Neil would never forget how, when they finally went to view the property, a broad grin spread across Madeline's face as they drove up the lane, turned in through the gates and up the drive with the gravel crunching under the car's tyres. How she beamed with delight as they stepped into the large entrance hall with its solid oak floor, its brass ornaments hanging on the wood-panelled wall and the staircase with its beautifully turned wooden banisters. Beside the staircase was a small alcove leading to a spacious farmhouse-style kitchen with a large table and heavy rustic chairs, which the owners agreed to leave for them. Madeline loved cooking and was very excited at the prospect of preparing meals in this large, well-equipped kitchen complete with an original kitchen range and two butler's sinks. A serving-hatch opened into the dining room, which they would put to good use in the years to come. They immediately felt very much at home in this house. Another door led off to the left into the sitting room with its charming ingle-nook fireplace, topped by a huge oak beam and adorned with horse brasses, family photographs and numerous ornaments and souvenirs of visits to exotic places around the World. The owners appeared to have travelled extensively and it looked as though they always brought mementos of their trips back with them. Neil was amazed to see how unusually spacious it was for a cottage of this period and it appeared to have everything they could possibly have hoped for, and more besides. Madeline practically floated from room to room as she murmured about how the wonderful atmosphere would be an inspiration for her writing. She was so enthusiastic, having long dreamed of writing a novel and she felt that this setting would be ideal for her to turn her dream into reality. The upstairs rooms were gorgeous with views out across the village and of their own little orchard to the rear of the garden and of course, that lovely little garden itself. The thatch over the windows appeared to frame the views and from outside the cottage, resembled eyebrows above the bedroom windows.

Neil and Madeline bought Ivy Cottage in a flurry of anticipation and disbelief at their good fortune. There was great excitement to begin with as their family and friends began visiting them, setting the precedent for years to come as indeed they continued to do so throughout the years that followed. They had lived there in harmony for over forty years now, bringing up their two children, David and Sarah, and throwing the house open to guests whenever their busy schedule allowed.

Now the old house seemed a much quieter place as Madeline returned from her visit to the 'Little Manor' Hospital where her husband, Neil, was recovering from a serious bout of pneumonia, which very nearly took his life. This cottage, once so full of fun and laughter, now felt empty and cold as she stepped into the entrance hall, which almost literally 'took her breath away' all those years ago. She told herself that tea was what she needed most right now and so she wandered wearily into the warm, inviting kitchen and placed a well-used kettle on the kitchen range. Madeline slowly looked around her, first at the large kitchen table and chairs and then at the solid oak cupboards, at the original butler's sink beneath the back window and at all the familiar items, accumulated in her kitchen over the years. However, even surrounded by these 'old friends', she was unable to shake off the feeling of melancholy, which descended upon her the day that Neil was taken off to hospital in the ambulance. She meandered into the living room where several logs lay on the fire grate in readiness for a cold day when a fire might be required. It was so typical of Neil to be prepared for all eventualities and this was just such a day of need, so she reached up to find the matches that were always hidden in a little cubby-hole in the brickwork above the fireplace and proceeded to light the fire. Then she quickly returned to the kitchen to brew her much-needed cup of tea, as she could hear the kettle whistling on the range.

The sun was out now and its thin, wintry rays found their way through the back windows of the sitting room where Madeline now sat by the fire to have her tea and biscuits in one of the two sumptuous armchairs which were arranged on either side of the fireplace. The chair opposite looked so empty now, but she told herself that very soon, Neil would be back in it, bringing love and laughter with him. He had the knack of saying the right thing at the right time and was always able to make her laugh, a characteristic of his which she treasured dearly. He was now well on the road to recovery and being the determined man she knew he was, she felt quite sure that it would not be too long before he was back home again. The old clock, which Neil's father made so many years ago, chimed with a rich, deep sound from its lofty position on the gnarled old oak beam that served as a mantelpiece across the fireplace.

Just then, the doorbell rang, waking Madeline from her reverie. It was her daughter, Sarah, who would never miss an opportunity to lend her mother some moral support just when she needed it most. Sarah shivered as she took off her long winter coat and woollen scarf and complained about the biting wind. She hugged her Mother tenderly, squeezing her shoulders reassuringly before they made their way to the sitting room where the fire was now crackling welcomingly in the grate. Sarah was a very caring woman with a cheerful and optimistic disposition, and she loved both of her parents dearly.

"It's a fresh brew," said Madeline, as Sarah rushed off to the kitchen to find another cup.

"Well, Mum?" she asked, "did he say much?"

"No, he mainly complained about being away from home, you know how he hates hospitals, even though he's there for his own good; and you should have heard him moaning at me when I packed a nice brand new pair of pyjamas for him! He hasn't worn pyjamas since he first left home to go to university all those years ago but I have always kept a couple of pairs by for him in case of need. Although this was just such a case, your father quite typically rebelled and flatly refused to wear them until he saw what the hospital provided. He pretty soon changed his mind then, I can tell you."

"Oh Dad," sighed Sarah wistfully, now sitting curled up in her father's favourite chair by the fireside where a weak ray of sunshine slanted across her left shoulder, "I do so love you, you old rascal." Her mother smiled indulgently as Sarah continued. "I've decided to spend a little time with you and Dad when he comes out of hospital, if that's alright with you Mum. I've missed him so much recently and I'm quite sure you could do with a helping hand as well while you're busy looking after him."

Madeline felt uplifted as she always enjoyed her daughter's cheerful presence and positive attitude. She also took great comfort from Sarah's comment "...not *'if'* but *'when'* he comes home." This was just what she needed and as mother and daughter sat quietly staring into the flames as they flickered and crackled,

Madeline began reminiscing about her husband. As she looked up at the old clock, it struck the hour.

"That old clock used to sit on the mantelpiece in the dining room you know dear, but I moved it in here after a dinner party we gave back in the 60's, when you were just a little girl of about five. The old clock kept going for many years until suddenly one day it just stopped working and your father put it away in the loft. Even though it no longer worked, he couldn't bear to part with it because his mother left it to him when she died a few years before. It was your grandfather, of course, who made it in the first place. Well dear, your brother was up in the loft recently, looking for some old book or other that your father asked him to find for him, when he stumbled upon the clock. Without a word to anyone, he took it down to the clockmakers and they cleaned it up and got it working again. David wants it to be a nice surprise for your father when he comes home from hospital."

"Do you know, Mum, I do remember that old clock from when I was a little girl and I actually think I remember something about that party you mentioned as well."

At Neil and Madeline's invitation, a few of their friends gathered for a dinner party late in September some forty years ago……..

Seated at her writing desk one sunny afternoon, Madeline began to review her guest list and to compose a dinner invitation, having previously discussed the outline of her ideas for this reunion with Neil. Each had their own circle of friends, acquired either through college or business, or in her case, whilst carrying out research for her novels. She felt that it was now time to catch up with all those new and exciting events that must have taken place in their lives and of course to enquire into any new goals that some of them may have to impart to their friends. Naturally, the usual place for such gatherings was Neil and Madeline's cottage. She simply could not wait to get started with the planning, which she so loved to do.

They were desperate to meet Ray's new girlfriend who, in his own words, came along and 'turned his world up-side-down'! As Ray was always a very confidant, 'larger than life' type of character, they could hardly imagine what sort of girl might be capable of stopping him in his tracks. However, as Samantha was a well-known fashion model, they were used to seeing her picture in the women's magazines and read a little about her in the newspapers. On the other hand, neither Ray nor Neil could wait for an introduction to Karen's new man, as though they felt she needed their seal of approval. Apparently, Karen described her meeting Mark as 'a whirlwind romance', which drew a predictably mocking response from both Neil and Ray. In their view, Karen did not appear to be the marrying type, preferring to immerse herself in her work, which they always described as 'consuming' her. She rarely took up boyfriends, other than to escort her to parties, dances and other social occasions. In fact, she firmly rebuffed Ray on one memorable occasion when he made a pass at her whilst they were at university together. Both men therefore planned to tease Karen a little, as indeed they always did at every opportunity.

As for Julian, Madeline met him quite frequently, as a business associate of hers and therefore wanted this occasion to be a purely social event of which his wife Caroline could be a part.

CHAPTER II –
The Dinner Party

It was just a week away from their dinner party now and, as usual, Madeline was busy making her preparations well ahead of the occasion. She would peruse the classic cookery books from her large collection, some of which she inherited from her mother, and would then draw on ideas from several of them to dream up a number of different creations in her mind. Madeline would then liaise with Neil for his views before making her final decision. She usually conjured up the most delicious dishes for her guests and the local shopkeepers always knew when she was planning a dinner party. She would ask them to provide a variety of seasonal, and sometimes unusual, fruits and vegetables and various cuts of meat, ordering them in plenty of time for marinating. The local butchers were always ready to provide the best cuts for her, be it the finest beef, new seasons lamb, pheasant, partridge or hare, most of which were plentiful in the countryside. The days of organisation and preparation went as quickly as they came and it seemed that in no time at all the guests were due to arrive. Madeline was an attractive and vivacious young woman, tall and elegant, who thrived on being in the company of interesting people with whom she could enjoy conversation on current affairs, history, politics and almost any other subject that interested her, including some light-hearted banter of course! Neil, on the other hand was relatively quiet and reserved, yet with a sharp wit, always ready with a well-turned phrase and the ability to converse knowledgeably on almost any subject, making him a natural host at Madeline's extravagant dinner parties.

"I think we're just about ready dear!" Madeline called out from the kitchen as the first of their guests played a tattoo on the front-doorbell.

"Oh, hello there, do come in," said Neil, slapping his old friend Ray on the shoulder. "It's good to see you again. It's been far too long; it must be at least a year or more."

"Yes, it must be all of that Neil, but its great to see you again, you old devil," replied Ray, "and this is my darling Samantha." He announced with great pride. Neil had already heard a lot about her, although meeting her now he began to feel that Ray might have deliberately understated her beauty and indeed her rather obvious sex appeal. He was uncharacteristically lost for words for a moment but just then, Madeline appeared in the hallway as if to rescue him.

"I do apologise, I was just finishing things off in the kitchen." She dusted her hands quickly on her apron and greeted Ray with a kiss on both cheeks. Ray reciprocated by hugging her and almost lifting her off the ground.

"Are you well?" he enquired.

"Indeed I am, sweetie-pie," she replied cheekily, "and this must be the lovely Samantha who we have heard so much about. It's so good to meet you at last."

"Oh dear," said Samantha, casting a sideways glance at Ray, "I hope it was all good."

"Well, what do you think? Yes, of course it was." Madeline assured her.

"And by the way, please call me Sam, everyone else does," she added.

"OK. then, Sam it is." Madeline chuckled as Sam struggled to remove her fox fur stole. Then Neil, always the gentleman, quickly came to her rescue, which only encouraged her to wriggle around all the more, as though she was still on the catwalk. She was certainly in the front row when they dished out femininity. Neil felt instantly attracted to Sam and the feeling was clearly quite mutual.

"Oh, thank you Neil,....darling" she purred, flirting wickedly with him as her plunging neckline revealed her cleavage, causing Neil to catch his breath for a moment.

"I love the dress, Sam" Madeline interjected to save her husband's temporary embarrassment. Made of 100% pure silk, Sam's dress fitted her perfectly, displaying her hourglass figure to maximum effect. It was gathered in at the waist, with a waistband about three inches wide, followed by naturally flowing pleats, it hugged her curves beautifully. As Sam was quite accustomed to vast amounts of attention, she fluttered her eyelashes and giggled seductively.

"Why thank you, Madeline, it's an original Dior. A present from Ray for......"

"....being a good girl!" Ray cut in before she could finish the sentence. The pink dress swirled as she spun away from Neil who forgot for the moment that he was supposed to be hanging her stole in the hall.

"Thank you, darling," she mewed as the long slit in her dress revealed a very shapely thigh. Sam wore silk stockings, which glistened on her long slender legs. Her perfume filled the air causing Neil to feel quite giddy whilst Ray just looked on in total admiration.

Ray was a tall man of imposing stature although his dress sense failed to do his frame any justice. How someone with enough money to have the very best was still happy to buy cheap off-the-peg jackets and trousers, somewhat dubious shirts and rather loud, tasteless ties never ceased to amaze Neil. With his booming voice, sometimes gluttonous table manners and often rather crude sense of humour, he was everything Neil was not. Perhaps this was why they got along so well together and, indeed perhaps also why Madeline was always able to overlook Ray's shortcomings, finding him great fun to be with. Ray was the extravagant type with a love of fast cars and the good life, which he tended to live to the full and he frequently proclaimed that the only place to be is in the fast lane. Ray was Neil's roommate at Cambridge and they graduated together but then Ray took over his father's business after the old man suffered a heart attack and his doctor advised him to slow down. The business was broadly speaking import and export, but Ray's father had spent many years in the Far East and become adept at tapping into new markets. One such market was for second-hand spare parts for London taxicabs, which were very popular in that part of the World at that time, and this soon developed into the mainstay of the business. Ray quickly became a natural at salesmanship, travelling frequently to places such as Hong Kong, Singapore and Kuala Lumpur to develop new contacts and service existing clients.

Sam, on the other hand, being a fashion model, was a slim, ultra-feminine young woman with curves in all the right places. She was a natural redhead, with a rather fiery temperament and big brown eyes like deep, limpid pools. Ray often teased her that her 'war cry' was 'Whatever Sam wants, Sam gets!' and this certainly seemed to be an accurate assessment. They first met about a year or so before in a fashionable London nightclub, where Ray was playing the saxophone. He was an accomplished jazz musician, having honed his musical skills whilst at university and he used this talent as a form of relaxation from the manic world of commerce.

Neither Madeline nor Neil could see what could possibly have attracted this stunning beauty to their rather slovenly, yet loveable friend, Ray. However, they say opposites attract and here was a clear case in point. Sam travelled the World on a number of 'no expenses spared' photo shoots in exotic locations where her flamboyant lifestyle often caused something of a stir. Numerous stories about her tempestuous relationships appeared in the tabloid press and there were some spurious reports of her making a nuisance of herself with her antics on long-haul flights when boredom took over from commonsense. On one occasion according to the press, she apparently attempted to seduce an air steward whilst under the influence of alcohol, and then just recently, she was back in the news again for bringing drugs into the country illegally. Naturally, she vehemently denied the charges and they were quickly dropped amid claims that it was all nothing more than a publicity stunt. However, now she was here in his house, Neil could not bring himself to believe a word of those newspaper stories, as she seemed to be so down-to-earth and loving towards his old friend Ray.

"Would anyone care for an aperitif?" Madeline asked as she led the way across the hall to the dining room, through the quaint old rustic door with its black wrought iron latch. Across the dining room was a large natural stone fireplace with a polished oak mantelpiece on which stood an old clock with a rounded, reddish coloured wooden case and a white face with hand painted Roman numerals in black. At either end of the mantelpiece were two large, cut-glass candlestick holders, complete with decorative cream coloured candles, around which Madeline tied little yellow silk bows. In the part of the room to the left of the fireplace, stood a large round mahogany table, the surface of which betrayed the fine patina of age. Neil often quipped that his Dad made it hundreds of years ago for King Arthur and the Knights of Camelot. Madeline laid it out beautifully for eight people, adorning it with her finest silver cutlery, cut glass goblets, silver napkin rings and linen napkins, which she and Neil bought on a visit to Ireland a year or two earlier. The centrepiece was an imposing brass candleholder with five ornate candles, which flickered with the movement of air as Madeline swept into the room. Around the table were eight beautiful reproduction Queen Anne dining room chairs, which Neil was quick to point out were not his father's handiwork but which he felt complemented the table of which he was so rightly proud.

Over to the right of the room and just in front of the window, stood a low coffee table with two armchairs and a couple of pouffes arranged round it. As this was an ideal place to take pre-prandial drinks, Madeline suggested that Neil and Sam might like to sit down and become better acquainted whilst she and Ray fetched some dry sherry. Ray dutifully followed Madeline across the room to the cocktail cabinet, where his hostess quickly delegated the role of waiter to him and hurried back towards the kitchen.

Sniffing the air through the hall, Ray was intrigued about what might be on the menu for tonight. He always loved trying to guess what was cooking, but invariably ended up simply naming all his own favourite dishes in the vain hope that he might guess correctly. Ray used to enjoy making simple pasta and rice concoctions at university, which Neil greatly appreciated, as his own greatest culinary feat was to boil an egg. However, even this was more often than not hard boiled by the time he was ready to eat it, despite his desperate attempts to produce a lovely soft, runny egg.

"Maybe it'll be roast duck a l'orange, or goose with a plum and tarragon stuffing, or perhaps it's going to be partridge in a leek and sour cream sauce? Well, am I right, Maddy?"

"No Ray, you're not, but full marks for trying." At half past six, the doorbell rang again and this time Neil opened the door to welcome Karen and Mark. Karen's face was the picture of happiness as she introduced Mark, who proved to be just as charming as Karen promised Madeline he would be and he seemed delighted to be meeting Karen's old university friends, Neil and Ray, about whom he had heard so much. Karen first met Neil and Ray during her first year at Cambridge and she recalled how they took pity on a poor fresher who looked so lost and alone. Once, Ray invited Karen to join them for a meal, prepared by his own fair hand and, as they were already into their second year, they believed themselves ideally placed to show her the ropes. The friendship and respect became mutual after Ray finally realised that it would take more than a plate of Spaghetti Bolognese to tempt Karen into his bed. Karen always got on extremely well with both Ray and Neil, although she found Ray's overbearing personality a little challenging at times. However, he was a good listener and Karen would often pour her heart out to him over a glass of wine or a cup of coffee when she was having problems with boyfriends, work, or simply suffering from the blues. Karen's respect for Neil's intellectual ability meant that she thoroughly enjoyed the many thought-provoking discussions, which they frequently used to have in those days.

Karen studied archaeology at university, which Neil found an interesting choice although not for him, and Ray described somewhat arbitrarily as 'dead boring'. Her special interest was Ancient Egypt, which resulted in numerous trips to the Middle East over the years since graduation, but it was whilst working at the British Museum that she met Mark. As a schoolteacher, Mark was busily shepherding a group of schoolchildren around the Department for Egyptian studies and was explaining some of the fascinating artefacts to them when he caught sight of Karen. He felt quite overwhelmed by her passion for her subject and by the depth of her knowledge of all things Egyptian. It was love at first sight for them both and Karen certainly did not lose any time in telephoning Madeline to tell her all about the wonderful, charming and handsome man she recently met.

"It's so good to meet you both," he smiled conspiratorially at Neil and Ray, "having heard so much about your wild exploits whilst you were up at Cambridge." Neil and Ray looked at each other and shrugged their shoulders with an assumed lack of comprehension.

"Don't know what you mean, old boy," Ray grinned. At that moment, Madeline appeared in the doorway to greet her visitors.

"Karen, how lovely to see you; you are looking absolutely radiant my dear. I just wonder why." She smiled knowingly, "well, aren't you going to introduce me then?" she added with undisguised excitement.

"Of course I am. This is Mark." She announced proudly.

"I'm so delighted to meet you," Madeline said in a slow, rather enquiring voice, which the others did not appear to have noticed. At this point Mark bowed his head, took her hand and raised it to his lips, kissed it gallantly and said in his most captivating voice, "The pleasure's all mine, I'm sure." Madeline trembled a little and blushed. Caught completely off-guard, she was rather afraid that she might have shown just how beguiled she was with this newcomer. She felt rather uncomfortable and almost overwhelmed by his presence, but was unable to pinpoint the reason for her discomfort. Although she felt confused, she quickly composed herself and showed her guests into the dining room so that they could become acquainted. Again, she excused herself and flew off to her refuge in the kitchen where she would have a few minutes to regain her composure. After all, she was a happily married woman, not some silly teenager, coming face-to-face with the best-looking boy at the dance. She was also the hostess at this gathering of friends and must retain an air of dignity. It was a good thing for her, she thought, that one of her house rules was that nobody was allowed to enter her kitchen during their dinner parties unless she specifically requested their assistance. This suddenly seemed to be especially important now as she was finding it so very hard to regain any self-control at all, in fact really quite the opposite. Madeline was sure that she recognised him although something looked different. 'But it cannot be him', she insisted to herself. 'Is it really such a small world?' 'Oh, my God!' she exclaimed in horror as she imagined what would happen if Neil noticed her reaction and how he, Mark, could remain so perfectly composed. Of course, she could be quite wrong and he might just resemble someone whom she knew from the past, maybe some years ago. She was just thinking how sincerely she hoped that no one else noticed the extent of her reaction to this newcomer, when a large bubble popped in the thick soup, rudely interrupting her thoughts and causing a little splash to catch her hand, "Ouch!" she exclaimed, hoping that nobody could hear her from the other room.

Neil played the perfect host, regularly refreshing glasses and interacting with each guest to ensure everyone became acquainted, whilst Madeline was just about to serve the canapés, the preparation of which occupied her time just prior to her guests' arrival.

Madeline loved cooking for as long as she could remember and would often wander off to the kitchen to create a batch of mouth-watering cakes when she felt the need to ponder the plot of her next novel. She found this recreational time in the kitchen invaluable for working out how each character would act in the particular circumstances that she was considering for the next chapter. Somehow, it seemed as though the time she spent in the kitchen was not only therapeutic but it also stimulated her brain into creating more ideas for her writing. Of course, the children loved it when Madeline was plotting her fictional adventures, as they knew they could expect to enjoy the aroma of peach shortcake, or perhaps a chocolate sponge, but most of all, David and Sarah loved her egg custard tarts.

The doorbell rang again and Neil excused himself to answer it. This time it was Julian and Caroline who he ushered in just as Madeline appeared from the kitchen with a tray of wonderful smelling canapés. The excitement was mounting as Madeline greeted Julian with a kiss and a hug.

"How clever of you to time that so well," he said, reaching out a hand to help himself to a canapé. This met with a disapproving look from his wife, Caroline, a rather upright and meticulous kind of woman whom Madeline had met several times before, either during her visits to Julian's office or occasionally when she dropped by his house to hand him a copy of her latest manuscript.

After graduating from Oxford in 1952, Madeline wrote various articles for magazines and newspapers, which fired her enthusiasm for writing her first novel. Her second followed quite quickly and she was delighted when both of them were subsequently published. It was whilst she was writing her first novel that she came to meet Julian as she needed somebody in the publishing business to read her work and give her some advice and guidance. Julian was very complimentary about her work and agreed to become her agent, as he was in no doubt that her work would sell. Julian was a shrewd and successful businessman with a memory like an elephant and did not suffer fools gladly. However, with his keen eye and roguish sense of humour, he and Madeline soon hit it off both professionally and as friends. Despite his sharp business mind, his manner was usually jovial, gentle and understanding, but Caroline believed him to be the most disorganised man she had ever met. That may well have been due to the fact that Caroline was fussy about everything and kept Julian on a tight rein. Julian, for his part, often quipped that theirs was a marriage made in heaven but fashioned in hell.

"Ah, come on dear, they were offered to me," Julian croaked with more than a touch of embarrassment.

"It's getting rather chilly now, isn't it?" Madeline interjected to save poor Julian's blushes, "and it's supposed to still be summer. Well, late summer... autumn even. How was your journey?"

"Oh," said Caroline, "we caught a little traffic trying to get out of town but once we were out into the country it was all plain sailing really, my dear. What's more, Julian was rather keen to see how his new car handled on the dual carriageways on the way up, so I was forever telling him to slow down. You know what these men are with their new toys".

"I'm sure Julian will get on well with Ray," Madeline laughed, "he loves his cars, especially if they are fast. What is your new car by the way, Julian?"

"Don't start him off, Madeline" Caroline scoffed, "All I hear about at the moment is his wonderful new Triumph 2000. Mind you, it is very comfortable and quiet, and it has this gorgeous little vanity mirror."

"It's a two litre, straight six with automatic gearbox and plenty of oomph when you need it," added Julian, as if his wife's comments were completely irrelevant to Madeline's question.

Madeline laughed. "Come and join our other guests," she said, leading them towards the dining room, where she almost collided with Ray who was already on his way out into the hall, having caught a

glimpse of Julian's initial encounter with the tray of
canapés!

"Alright I was coming your way," Madeline said
as she quickly squeezed past him, raising the tray as
high as she possibly could in the air in the vain hope
of reaching the other guests in the dining room before
Julian and Ray devoured the lot. Ray hurriedly turned
round, following Madeline with long strides in the hope
of overtaking her before the other guests got a look in
at the wonderful-smelling offerings on her tray.

"Ray," Neil called, "have you met Caroline and
Julian?" Ray spun around to meet them with his usual
greeting of a couple of slobbering kisses for the women
and a firm handshake for the men.

"Pleased to meet you, I'm Ray. Sorry if I nearly
knocked you over but Maddy's cooking is well worth
fighting for, as you will no doubt soon discover. That
is if you don't know already, of course."

"Ray and I were up at Cambridge together," said
Neil by way of explanation. He was always a little
apologetic when introducing his uncouth friend. After
all, how could they know on first acquaintance what a
very special person Ray was for Madeline and Neil?

"Yes we did have rather a lot of fun during those
years, didn't we, old boy? You know; work hard, play
hard." Ray boomed in his deep baritone voice as he made
a beeline for the dining room in pursuit of Madeline
and her tray of canapés. He quickly helped himself to a
couple of the caviar and sour cream variety.

"My favourites," he slobbered as he crammed one
into his mouth, whole. "Here, Caroline, Julian, don't
be shy. These are great," he added as Madeline passed

the tray in Mark's direction. Mark took one with a deliberate bow of the head saying, "Mmm, they look absolutely divine." His charm and sophistication still seemed to hypnotise Madeline, who was now quite certain that it really was *him*. What was she to do, she would die if Neil got the slightest wind of this and what if Karen knew? 'Certainly he must remember me,' she thought, feeling a little hurt that he may not have recognised her. 'Was it all for nothing then, am I now no more than a vague memory or just another conquest?' Madeline began to feel quite flustered again and was soon overcome by an urgent need to return as quickly as she could to her place of refuge. She therefore rested the tray on a side table nearby and excused herself as she, once again, disappeared off to the kitchen.

The dining room was now buzzing with lively conversation. Sam was enthralling Caroline and Karen with her exploits on location and with the details of her extravagant lifestyle and extensive wardrobe, especially her beloved Dior and of course the fantastic hairdos. She explained how wonderful it feels to step out onto the catwalk with everyone looking at you, some with envy, but mostly with admiration. She explained, without an ounce of guilt, how she particularly enjoyed the way men would look at her which just made her wiggle and pout all the more as though each move provoked a reaction which she compared to conducting an orchestra. Meanwhile, the subject of Julian's new car spilled over into a debate about the relative merits of the latest models and, of course who would drive what car, given a free choice. Ray was busily explaining how superb his Austin-Healey 3000 was in terms of outright speed, road holding and its ability to attract the female of the species.

"You can't beat hood down motoring, especially at speed," he was saying, "besides, there's no better way of pulling the birds than with a powerful convertible. They just melt into your arms. It's brilliant!"

"He thinks he's James Bond whenever he gets behind the wheel of that car, Julian, on with the sunglasses and the driving gloves and off he goes. Why don't you just go the whole hog and get an Aston, Ray?" Neil teased.

"Because I can't bloody well afford it, that's why, smartass!" retorted Ray jovially.

"Well, I am more than satisfied with the Triumph…" Julian began, but Ray immediately drowned him out again.

"Neil's got a Jag, you know! Mark II model. It goes pretty well for a saloon, too. Still, I reckon the old devil's earning a mint now he's got himself involved with the yanks in their space race."

"Oh do shut up Ray," said Neil "they haven't come here to talk shop. What about you Mark, are you as much of a motoring fanatic as Ray and Julian, here?"

"No," replied Mark, "As a matter of fact, I'm not really. Just as long as the car gets me from A to B in reasonable comfort and safety, I'm quite happy. I don't see the point of having a fast car in this country anyway, where we don't have the roads to do those high speeds."

"Poppycock," bellowed Ray "I got over a ton out of the Healey on the way over here this afternoon, no problem," he went on, "people don't realise how fast you can accelerate and, more importantly, how quickly you can stop when you have the right car."

"What do you drive then, Mark?" enquired Julian calmly in the hope that he might quieten Ray down by moving the conversation on.

"Oh, I've just got a Hillman Minx," replied Mark "that's quite fast enough for me." A sharp intake of breath from Ray made it quite clear what he thought of Mark's choice of vehicle. "However," continued Mark quickly before Ray could intervene again, "I do envy Neil his Jaguar, I've always admired them. Not so much for their undoubted speed but for their refinement, all that wood veneer and lovely, soft leather; absolutely wonderful."

"Well thank you," said Neil, "I'll just have to take you out for a drive, after that. You see Ray, what you never seem to understand, is that there is much more to cars than just speed, road holding and attracting the fair sex. There are also the little creature comforts to consider as well," added Neil "and I bet Sam isn't all that keen on having her hair getting windswept every time you want to blast off down the road at breakneck speed, either."

"Actually, old boy she loves the Healey, but she does always wear a headscarf to protect her gorgeous, curly red locks and, of course, she always wears a pair of classy shades. It goes with the job, you see. Sam has a British Racing Green Mini-Cooper herself. Scares the living daylights out of me the way she screams around the West End in the damn thing."

"Well, well," said Mark "so sometimes the biter gets bitten then, does he?"

"No," argued Ray, "women driving small cars can be an absolute menace at times."

"I should be very careful who you make that kind of comment to if I were you. Some of the ladies here just might make mincemeat of you if they hear that kind of talk." Mark continued, making the most of the feeling that he was gaining the upper hand in this debate.

It was now almost five minutes to seven and Madeline was beginning to get a little anxious because she wanted her guests to take their seats at the dinner table by seven o'clock. Neil therefore ushered the guests to the table in response to Madeline ringing her little porcelain dinner bell, which she loved to use on these occasions. Neil and Madeline enjoyed dispensing with formality, never using those little cardboard nametags or drawing up a table plan, as they preferred the pleasure of watching their guests choose where they wanted to sit. It was often quite interesting to see the final stages.

"We get to choose where we sit do we?" exclaimed Ray. "How very civil of you," said Julian, edging away from Caroline who always watched him like a hawk at the dinner table. She was very particular about using correct etiquette when eating and she felt that Julian was sometimes just a little too relaxed at the table for her taste and she was not above reproaching him. Julian swiftly commandeered the chair next to Sam, which was far enough away to ensure that Caroline's foot would not be able to reach his shins. Ray on the other hand quite fancied the challenge of trying to charm Caroline so, being quick to realise what Julian was up to, he settled himself in beside her. Neil and Madeline stood quietly and watched with amusement, as they knew Ray very well and had already seen Caroline in action over Julian's 'faux pas' with the pre-prandial titbits. As the table was round, there were plenty of opportunities for them to indulge in a little people watching.

Karen and Mark were happy to be sitting close to each other, which met with Madeline's full approval, she felt rather more comfortable that Karen was sitting between her and Mark. In any event, she always made a point of sitting next to Neil on every dinner occasion and, having just reappeared from the kitchen, she made it clear that her seat was the one next to Neil's. It was also nearest the door so that she could get in and out easily without disturbing any of her guests whenever she needed to check on oven temperature or prepare for the next course. Sam was quick off the mark and deliberately sat on the other side of Neil who seemed to fascinate her for some reason that she could not quite fathom. However, as she found the experience fun, she prepared to flirt with him as outrageously as she dared, being so close to his adorable wife. Neil was the strong, silent type who could easily be embarrassed and therefore, as she felt that he might have lowered his defences tonight, she would make the most of the opportunity to have a little fun with him.

"Are you feeling alright?" Mark asked, as Karen appeared to be staring fixedly across the table. "You looked a little distant for a few seconds there."

He wondered whether his face might have given away the fact that he did actually recognise Madeline as soon as he entered the cottage earlier in the evening.

This was the first opportunity for him to be alone with his thoughts since arriving here and to recall the events of the past. After all, it was only a brief, if torrid, affair.

He noticed that, as the clock on the mantelpiece struck seven o'clock, stillness pervaded the room as though some form of ethereal presence was manifesting itself and was commanding everybody's attention.

"Fine darling, it smells quite delicious, doesn't it?" Karen added hesitantly as Madeline made her way to the serving hatch and opened it to reveal a beautiful white china tureen containing the lobster bisque, the smell of which was already wafting by Karen's nose. Madeline placed the tureen in the middle of the table and ladled some of the bisque into the waiting bowls. Karen was particularly partial to shellfish, especially lobster, which made Mark feel all the more curious about her strange behaviour a few moments earlier. It could be that he was feeling guilty about his earlier thoughts but 'what did he have to feel guilty about anyway? That all happened long before he met Karen.' Whether Caroline was winning with Ray as he sat up and waited patiently to be served or whether he was on his best behaviour for his own reasons was not clear, but it was not the normal noisy Ray who peered into his soup bowl with great appreciation. Karen began to look vague again and appeared to be drifting off into a daydream,

...she coughed and spluttered as the smoke and dust drifted towards her and she wondered where on

Earth she was. As she started to move forward through the thick vegetation, she tripped up when her stiletto heel became entangled in the undergrowth. There was a strong smell of oil and some sort of acrid fumes, which she could not identify. As she looked up, after freeing her heel, she thought she could see the tip of an aeroplane wing through the bushes in front of her. Furthermore, she thought she heard a crackling sound, reminiscent of the sound of distant machine gun fire, just a few moments before, but she soon decided that she must have been mistaken.

"Dear God, where am I? What's happened here?" she gasped as she looked around her in total bewilderment. Although all her instincts told her that it could not be true, she appeared to have stumbled upon the site of an aeroplane crash. There were pieces of wood and metal strewn all around and there was thick smoke coming from the trees just ahead of her where she could now see the grey fuselage of an aeroplane at a steep angle to the ground. She could also quite clearly see the oval shaped tail and rudder with red, white and blue stripes running down it. Looking along the fuselage, she then saw the distinctive circular red, white and blue markings of a British combat aircraft. She noticed the double wings with large, polished wooden struts with taut wires holding them in position and realised that this was an old biplane from many years ago. A machine gun hung loosely from the rear seat position and the nose of the plane was firmly wedged against the trunk of a tree, the propeller broken in half. She prayed for signs of life.

Karen then surprised herself. "It's a Bristol Fighter," she exclaimed, "but how on Earth did it get here?" Her recognition of the plane stemmed from a history project she was involved in years ago at school when she was learning about the First World War. Many questions began to swim around inside her head as she advanced cautiously towards the crashed plane, her heart pounding with apprehension. She could see two men wearing goggles and leather helmets. The pilot was slumped forward in the front seat and was not moving at all. The other man was lying on the ground and as he moved slowly, she could hear him calling for help in a rather weak voice. Karen slowly moved forward, her stilettos now getting caught up with almost every step she took. She was not dressed for a walk in the forest, neither was she mentally prepared to take in the sight of this plane, mangled into the trees right in front of her. She tried to think rationally and decided that there must have been a nearby air display featuring veteran aircraft and that this one had unfortunately crashed.

She was sure that she recognised the man calling for help but, although he looked so familiar, she was unable to put a name to the face. When he removed his goggles and helmet and turned towards her, she could see blood covering his shoulder and chest. Karen slowly edged forward, her head still spinning, when she realised that, although she was moving forward, she was actually getting no closer. She thought it must be those damned heels impeding her progress again, but it was not. A strange force seemed to be pulling her away from the scene of the crash. Then she could hear the buzz of conversation, the clatter of cutlery and the gorgeous aroma of lobster bisque...

As she awoke from her daydream, the first thing she heard was Mark's voice, engaged in deep discussion with Caroline about his students and the many books he was obliged to read to keep up with his subject as a history teacher. Ray, who was becoming a little restless by this time, asked if Caroline would excuse him as he headed out towards the hall. She naturally excused him and silently congratulated him on his good manners.

"Is everything alright, Darling?" Mark enquired, seeing Karen looking a little dazed.

"Yes, thanks, I'm fine," she replied "I was just a little lost in my thoughts. I'm sorry, that must have appeared very rude of me."

"No, not at all," Caroline smiled, "I think we all drift off from time to time, don't we?"

"Let me give you a hand, Maddy." Ray boomed out, as he reappeared from the direction of the cloakroom.

"That's very kind of you Ray." Madeline replied, handing him a stack of empty soup bowls, which he then carefully took to the open serving hatch before following her into the kitchen as much in the hope of extracting a sample of the next course from her as to actually be of any real assistance.

"Are you feeling alright Maddy?" he enquired, as he followed closely behind her. "Yes thanks Ray, I'm fine. You know how my adrenaline pumps when I have a dinner party. Don't worry; I'll be able to relax over a coffee, once we've finished dessert". Although Ray knew Madeline pretty well, he wondered if he might be over-reacting a little to her apparent discomfort. However, he was sure that she would be grateful for any help he could give her. Moments later, he returned to the dining room, gently pushing a hostess-trolley piled with hot plates, a steaming gravy boat and a crown roast of lamb on a silver salver. He was busy telling the assembled company that he did actually guess the main course correctly, but nobody really paid any attention to him at the time as the conversation was by now flowing freely. Madeline was fussing anxiously around him in the constant fear that he might collide with some errant piece of furniture and send her beautiful creations flying across the floor. Of course, this was all in her imagination because there was ample room for both the trolley and Ray, despite his apparent ungainliness at times. The diners had all been waiting eagerly for their main course and, as Neil rose to carve the meat, the compliments began to flow as they all savoured the wonderful aromas of the main course.

"It smells absolutely divine," began Sam "but I'm not sure if I'll be able to manage very much." This meal would of course be very different to her usual lettuce leaf and perhaps a crispbread or two, which she deemed essential to maintaining her shape.

"No," added Ray, "you have to look after that hourglass figure of yours, don't you, my sweet?"

"I love your silver salver Madeline," said Caroline, a little enviously and obviously keen to stem the flow of Ray's overt admiration for his girlfriend's many assets.

"Thank you Caroline; yes it really is lovely isn't it? Neil's mother left it to me when she passed away."

"Just keep piling it on the plate, old chap" interrupted Julian, much to Caroline's chagrin.

"Please don't be a pig now, Julian," she muttered behind her hand, although loud enough for Julian to hear. "I'm quite sure there's more than enough for all of us."

"I don't know how you do it, Madeline," Karen broke in, "it's all just so scrumptious."

"Maddy old girl, why do you put these little chef's hats on the lamb's ribs?" Ray guffawed.

"Very funny, old boy," said Neil, carving off a sizeable piece of meat, "how many times have I heard that one before? Is that enough lamb for you Mark?" asked Neil, looking up from the serious job of carving the meat. "Mark, are you alright?" Mark appeared to be looking straight through him as though in a trance, his eyes wide open in a cold stare, causing Caroline to shiver. The clock had just finished chiming eight o'clock and the final ringing was dying away when Mark shook his head. Madeline took the opportunity to gaze in his direction as he swept his fingers through his hair and sighed deeply. She remembered these characteristics well as if it was only yesterday that she witnessed them during their most passionate and intimate moments. She quickly caught her breath as she recalled the time spent together.

...Mark was walking slowly towards an old timber-framed barn and he could hear chickens scratching around for food in the dusty yard. There were several tall trees just beyond the barn and the wind was rustling their leaves in the gentle breeze of early summer. As

he rounded the corner of the barn, Mark could see a young woman carrying a tray slowly back towards the house but he could not see her face as her back was towards him. She wore an old-fashioned smock type of dress with an apron and he wondered idly who she was, but was quickly distracted by the greedy antics of the chickens rushing towards the scraps of food, so recently thrown out for them.

"I really don't understand this." Mark whispered to himself. "I don't know this place and I don't know why I'm here." At first, he found himself walking slowly towards the barn door, but then he felt a strange sensation, as though a sudden gust of wind had lifted him up and propelled him swiftly across the yard and straight in through the door. Once inside, he saw a man of about thirty, standing in front of a heavy, solidly built mahogany workbench. Dressed in a pair of grey flannel trousers and a white collarless shirt, he was planing a length of timber, which was firmly held in a large metal vice with wooden jaws and, although clearly concentrating hard on his work, there was an expression of pure enjoyment on his face. The plane was wooden but with a metal blade secured by a large central adjustable bolt, similar to one that Mark's grandfather used to use.

Mark seemed to have absolutely no control over his movements inside the barn but was being guided around to view various off-cuts of wood, which were piled up in a corner as well as a number of lengths of timber leaning up against the walls. He could also smell the pungent odour of recently heated horse-glue, which was now ready for use. It was all so real to him that he wanted to reach out and touch a smoothly sanded piece of wood that was ready for French polishing. He would have loved to have a discussion with the carpenter, as woodwork fascinated him. However, after trying to start a conversation, it soon became apparent to Mark that the young carpenter could not hear a word of what he was saying. It was as though Mark's voice was in his own head alone and, although he could see and hear what was going on around him, he realised that he could be neither seen nor heard. There came a creaking sound behind him and Mark immediately turned around to see the barn door open and the young woman he saw out in the yard earlier, walked in, her dark raven hair shining in the bright rays of sunshine. She smiled lovingly at her husband, who looked up and smiled back at her saying "Hello Annie, what have you got there?" She was holding a large glass of homemade lemonade and a slice of fruitcake on a small plate, which she put on the bench near to where her husband was working.

"Oh, it's really looking good now, dear" said Annie. "I do love to see the furniture taking shape from those old pieces of wood which you hoard up in here."

"Yes," replied her husband "and I really enjoy the challenge of making each one to fill our new home. It'll not be long now until this table is finished. This mahogany is such a lovely reddish colour once it's polished. As you know, it's my favourite wood."

"And this won't be long now, either," she said patting her stomach gently. Mark noticed that she was heavily pregnant when she first came in.

"Let's see if you can produce a son and heir for me this time, Annie. Not that I wouldn't love a girl just as much," he quickly added. She kissed her husband on the forehead and walked laboriously back towards the open door saying,

"I'll have to see what I can do, Charlie." The dizziness, caused by the unceremonious way in which he was transported into the barn and then whisked around it, made Mark feel quite nauseous and he wanted it to stop, but the buzzing in his head continued until he thought his eardrums would explode…………

He gradually became aware of the conversation going on around him but he still felt quite ill from the experience of being whisked into and around that barn. He thought that this must be how it would feel to be weightless as the Russian astronaut; Yuri Gagarin did, flying around the Earth in that 'Vostok' spacecraft of his. He could not however, seem to tear his mind away from this strange experience and, as he looked across the room, he noticed a photograph in a highly polished mahogany picture frame on the sideboard and thought that the man in the picture looked very familiar. In fact, as he thought about it, he felt quite sure that this was the same man he saw in the barn, albeit a few years younger looking in the picture. He could not understand what was going on in his mind, but decided to give the matter some serious consideration later on, when he could be alone with his thoughts, or perhaps he might discuss it with Karen. He certainly did not wish to appear rude by not joining in the general conversation and that is precisely what would happen if he continued to worry himself about it now. He therefore began to tuck into the tasty dinner, which Madeline worked so hard in the kitchen to prepare, as he felt that this was the least he could do to show his appreciation, no matter how uncomfortable he may be feeling after his rather bizarre recent experience.

The conversation had moved on to the telling of ghost stories and supernatural happenings with everyone trying to surpass each other with their scariest tales of haunted houses, apparitions, poltergeists and other strange manifestations. Ray was trying to scare Caroline by kidding her that Ivy Cottage itself was haunted, but she refused to accept that such a charming family home could possibly have the sort of past which might lead to its housing any sort of ghoulish inhabitants.

"No, no," confided Ray," not the nasty, head-under-the-arm, cackling horrors you see in the films". Then in a low mysterious voice he added, "This is a friendly ghost that makes its presence felt soon after eight o'clock in the evening." Neil and Madeline were quite used to Ray's little jokes and wondered what he planned to do to frighten Caroline into believing him. It did not escape Caroline's notice that it was now just a little after eight.

At that moment there came a sound of hollow creaking outside the door in the hallway, and then another. Madeline and Neil looked at each other, then at Ray, who looked quite shocked himself, and then in the direction of the hallway. Neil, being of a less nervous disposition than his highly imaginative wife, got up from the table to investigate.

"I'll go and take a look. Perhaps someone left a window open," he said quietly, moving slowly towards the door.

"I'll come with you Neil," Ray whispered as he was now quite curious after all the ghostly talk. Caroline was quite convinced that this was a set-up by Ray and Neil to scare her and sat there with a smug look on her face until she caught sight of Madeline looking very apprehensive. Neil slowly opened the door and, looking down, was both surprised and relieved to see his little five year-old daughter, Sarah, standing in the doorway with her teddy bear hanging loosely from her hand, her big brown sleepy eyes looking up at him. He stooped down, swept her up into his arms and cradled her.

"Sarah, darling," he said as he hugged her close, "we wondered who was out here and all the time it was my little Sarah."

"Daddy, I can't sleep," she said in a very tired little voice.

"Never mind my little cherub," he soothed as he laid her head on his shoulder. Ray blew kisses to his little goddaughter, whom he adored, and she seemed to feel assured and comforted as all the grown-ups seated around the table said 'goodnight' to her. Having said a very weary goodnight in return, Sarah snuggled into her Daddy's arms and was happy for him to carry her back upstairs to bed.

After a few minutes, Neil returned to the dining room, smiling with parental satisfaction.

"Has she settled down alright now?" Karen asked.

"Oh yes, no problem. I started to read a story from one of her favourite books and she was sound asleep before I finished the first page."

"Well," said Caroline triumphantly to Ray, "so much for your eight o'clock ghost, eh?" At which point they all joined in the laughter, which helped to cover the fact that they actually all felt a little jittery when they heard the sounds coming from the hall, especially as Ray had just foretold of a ghostly apparition due at any moment.

"Come on then, Ray," Julian asked, "how did you know that little Sarah was about to put in an appearance and scare the living shit out of us all? Does she do this often?"

"Julian! Do mind your language, please," snorted Caroline with embarrassment.

"What? I only said 'shit' didn't I?" argued Julian "What's wrong with that?" He appeared to tease, feeling safe in the knowledge that his shin was some distance from Caroline's foot.

"Perhaps you should have said holy shit rather than living shit." Mark interrupted, "It might have given it a bit more dignity, perhaps."

"That sounds blasphemous to me Mark," said Caroline. "I'm sure you didn't really mean that, did you? You were just trying to get Julian off the hook, weren't you?"

"Yes, alright perhaps I was." Mark admitted, seeing that he would otherwise be digging himself a hole from which he may not be able to extricate himself.

"Do you want to help me clear these dirty crocks away, Julian?" said Madeline, in an attempt to calm the situation. "I expect we're all a little jumpy after all those creepy stories and I wouldn't mind some company in the kitchen, just in case Ray happens to be right for a change." She added cheekily. Ray was quite a thick-skinned individual and, ignoring the jibe, sprang up from his chair as usual to help.

"I do believe you've frightened yourself, Ray" laughed Mark "and now you need Madeline to protect you from the ghouls in your own mind."

"There are plenty of those as well, Mark," said Neil "I have often thought he is as mad as a March hare. Still, Madeline will sort him out; she's used to his funny ways."

"Oh, leave him alone," pouted Sam, gently resting her hand on Neil's, "he's quite a sweetie, really. Love him." Neil quickly cleared his throat with embarrassment, withdrew his hand from Samantha's grasp and excused himself to give Madeline a hand in the kitchen. Sam grinned to herself as she could clearly see that her flirting made Neil feel uncomfortable and this only made him all the more attractive to her. They then quickly cleared the big round table in readiness for cheese, homemade chutneys and some of Madeline's favourite desserts. Neil offered his guests a glass of dessert wine and Ray, who was normally careful not to overindulge with alcohol when he was driving, quickly acquiesced as did Mark, who was now feeling very much better and getting back into the party mood. Sam, who had been steadily shifting glass after glass of claret following her earlier three glasses of dry sherry, blew Neil a big kiss to attract his attention, partly because she wanted some Sauternes but mostly because she wanted to keep up the flirtation. Again she giggled to herself as Neil's discomfort was amusing her but, as the evening wore on, she found herself becoming more attracted to him, perhaps because she was not used to the shy, married, type who would not immediately succumb to her advances.

Meanwhile, Caroline was deeply embroiled in conversation with Ray about his musical abilities, which were of special interest to her as she played the violin at school and was very fond of most forms of music. She was amazed to find how sensitive and intuitive Ray was as a musician and how different his attitude was once onto his favourite subject. She also soon discovered that he was almost a disciple of the late, great Charlie Parker and she left him quite stunned when she told him that she did not only know of the great jazzman, but also that she owned some of his records. Her father was a great 'be-bop' fan, which influenced her musical appreciation at an early age and now she loved modern jazz, especially the saxophone pieces. Caroline had never been to a nightclub and therefore found some of Ray's anecdotes both amusing and intriguing. Of course, Ray loved to embellish his stories for any willing listener and Caroline received the full treatment. As she became more entranced by his recollections, her gaze hardly left him and she clung to his every word. The rich tones of the clock rang out again…7…8…9.

…...Caroline slowly realised that the man she was now looking at was not Ray, although like Ray, he was tall and heavily built. However, this man was

much older with greasy, grey hair and a hairy chest showing through his dirty, unbuttoned shirt. He wore thick braces and grubby trousers and what appeared to be rather scruffy ex-army boots. Not only did she not recognise the man standing in front of her, but she was also completely ignorant as to where she was, or how she came to be there. A number of questions began to form in her mind and she felt totally disorientated and more than a little concerned about the fact that she seemed to be no longer in control of her own destiny. Caroline was the sort of person who always felt the need to be in control of whatever situation she found herself in and this just would not do at all. However, the plain fact was that she was no longer in control of her own actions and therefore, being unable to move where she wanted to go, she resigned herself to the fact that she was being ushered along by some unseen force. She thought she could hear the sound of wind chimes coming and going softly on the gentle breeze; now it was there, now all was silent. Soft zephyrs brushed her hair like tiny fingers passing through it and she found the sensation most pleasurable. The delicate sound came again. She loved that sound so very much and, as she strained to hear it again, she thought that it reminded her more of panpipes in the distance than of wind chimes. Her inability to control her own movements left her feeling quite dizzy and she was unable to figure out what was happening to her. The only clue was the strong smell of wood and the sawdust all over the ground. That strong aroma of freshly cut wood pervaded her senses and, although the light was poor, she now realised that she was walking, slowly and quietly through a timber merchant's outbuilding. The man she saw before had walked out into the yard and was now engaged in conversation with a younger man. They appeared to be involved in some sort of negotiation and so, being of an inquisitive nature, Caroline listened intently to their conversation.

"I'm making a few items of furniture for the house and I've used up rather more wood than I expected to on the table for the dining room," said the young carpenter, "and I still have a couple of small pieces of furniture yet to make." he continued. "I was wondering if you might be able to do me a good deal on some mahogany."

"Well, let me see now," replied the timber merchant, stroking his grey, stubbly chin with a huge, hairy hand. "I've got some very nice pieces over here." he said, limping heavily across to a small pile of timber in a shady corner of the yard that was covered by a makeshift corrugated iron roof. "This ought to do you nicely. Take the lot and I'll let you have it for half price, seeing as how I've only got these few bits left over from the original load. What do you think, eh?"

Although the wood was the typical rich, reddish colour of mahogany, its appearance seemed enhanced by some unusual flecks of deep cherry red. Caroline became so completely absorbed by these negotiations that she forgot her concern about where she was and how she got there.

"Why am I here, eavesdropping on these two men and their discussion about these bits of wood?" she whispered to herself, when suddenly she was overcome by the feeling that she recognised this young man,

although she could not remember where she might have seen him. Being of a forthright nature, Caroline called out to him straight away, but no answer came. She assumed that they were so engrossed in their conversation that they did not hear her and so decided that she must try again. She tried again but to her surprise, she could not even hear her own voice clearly. In fact, she thought that her voice sounded as though she was under water and it soon became apparent that there was no further point in resisting whatever power had taken her over. The two men shook hands and it appeared to Caroline that they had struck a deal as the timber merchant's offer must have been too good to miss. Certainly, the young man seemed well pleased with the outcome. Caroline followed the two men outside to witness them loading the pieces of timber into the back of an old truck and she watched as the young man slowly drove off. To her surprise, Caroline seemed to be drifting along behind the truck as it made its way along the winding, dusty road until it eventually disappeared around a bend. She looked aimlessly down at the road as the dust cleared and saw what appeared to be fresh drops of blood on the ground where the truck was standing a short while before.........

As the chimes of the clock slowly died away, Caroline felt herself drawn back by the hubbub of conversation and Ray noisily imitating the sound of a car.

"Poor old Sam's foot was down hard on the accelerator, but that E-Type was gone - whoosh." Ray continued.

"Well if they're so fast Ray, why don't you get one and join us Jaguar boys?" Neil teased his old friend.

"No, I'm not going to buy one just to please you. Anyway, I told you if I do decide to sell the Healey, I'd rather replace it with an Aston, didn't I?" he added quickly.

"I thought you said a little while ago that you reckon you couldn't afford an Aston." Neil reminded him.

"Well then darling," Sam joined in "I'll just have buy him one myself, won't I?" Julian turned to Caroline to ask her if she would care to buy him an Aston Martin similar to James Bond's when he noticed her looking uncharacteristically vague. Ray also noticed that she looked somewhat bewildered and he thought that perhaps he might have confused her with all the talk of fast cars. Surely though, Caroline would have just stopped him and questioned him if there was anything she did not understand. She was too confident a woman to sit there quietly, not understanding and not asking.

Caroline was trying to make some sense of what had just happened to her a few moments before, but there were no obvious answers to the questions spinning around in her head. She smiled at them both and assured them that she was fine and that she was just thinking of something else. She watched almost vacantly as Ray sipped his port and savoured a mouthful of Stilton, his favourite cheese, with the appreciation of the connoisseur.

Mark, on the other hand, appeared to prefer a glass of Sauternes while he partook of some Coeur à la crème, drizzled with raspberry sauce. This gave Mark yet another opportunity to reiterate how much he admired Madeline's culinary expertise and how he appreciated the time she must have put in to prepare such a feast.

Alone with his thoughts for a moment, Mark took advantage of the situation to reminisce as he peeled back the years in his mind to the three nights they spent together whilst he was at training college and Madeline had just graduated. A keen interest in literature was common to them both and so they both travelled to New York to join the many others from the literary world at The Pullitzer Prize awards that year. They struck up a conversation in a bar, having discovered that they were both English and for each of them the attraction was instantaneous. Three nights of deep discussions, followed by hot and passionate hours between the sheets, then ensued. Mark remembered well the dash through the streets of New York by cab, arriving at the airport just in time to catch his flight back to England!

As he sipped his Sauternes, he felt confident that nobody was likely to guess his thoughts other than, of course Madeline, who had sought his mental attention since he arrived at her house earlier in the evening. Mark just turned up 'out of the blue' and sent her mind into turmoil.

Ray leapt from his chair, rushed over to the record player and put on the Beatles' latest hit, 'A Hard Day's Night'. He thought this was rather appropriate under the circumstances and so he turned up the volume, as the Frank Sinatra record, which was playing beforehand, was turned down quite low to provide quiet background music. Mark got the message and, not being a pop music fan, suggested that the volume be reduced again. Neil quietly got up and switched the record player off, saying that perhaps it was time to dispense with the background music now that the meal was finished and coffee was on the way.

Madeline was captivated by board games and she loved to inveigle her guests into playing them whenever she got the chance. Although 'Monopoly' was always a firm favourite she enjoyed ringing the changes if possible and, on this occasion, suggested that they play a new detective game called 'Cluedo', which had become very popular in recent years. However, try as she might, she could not seem to whip up any enthusiasm for it. Ray suggested they play 'strip poker' but all the women present jeered at his idea, except that is, for Sam who was usually game for anything. Neil, trying hard to find a consensus, suggested they play another, more acceptable card game such as 'pontoon', but this too failed to gain the approval of the assembled company, bringing forth groans from Ray and Julian. It was Mark who suggested playing charades, but without leaving the table as this would mean that the players would have no time to plan what they were going to do and this would make for some very funny moments. Karen offered to go first, at which point Ray immediately began trying to guess even before she started.

"Oh, shut up, you!" she shouted happily at her old friend's typically raucous interruptions, when suddénly, ...whoosh; a swirling gust of icy cold wind swept through the room.

It was as if the front door and the door leading from the hall to the dining room were both blown open simultaneously; and on a cold winter's day at that! However, both doors were still quite firmly closed. The candle flames danced about crazily in the draft and very nearly went out as everyone looked around questioningly at each other. Madeline looked at Neil who just stared back at her without any sign of explanation, although she could not help feeling that Neil knew something and was keeping his own counsel. Ray looked straight at a rather amazed Karen and grinned,

"I know, Karen, you're the Snow Queen!" Although this lessened the tension and brought a few smiles, nobody could explain that gust of cold wind and everyone looked very apprehensive. Ray was no stranger to Ivy Cottage, having been Neil's Best Man at his wedding, helped them move into the house and been a frequent visitor, especially after becoming Godfather to the children. He knew that it could be a little draughty at times and tried to lighten the mood by telling them all that he did try to warn Madeline and Neil against coming to live in a three hundred year-old cottage, but they would never listen to him. He told them how he teased his friends about wanting to live in this old barn of a place because they thought it looked so cute with its thatched roof, lots of pretty roses and ivy and a lovely 'English country garden'. Neil suggested that perhaps the telling of too many ghost stories might be the real reason for everyone feeling nervous and suggested that they continue with their after dinner games.

Ray however, was in absolutely no doubt as to the cause of the icy wind because it was he who experienced, at that precise moment, something about which the others could not possibly have any idea whatsoever. At the instant that the candles flickered and almost blew out, Ray saw a face rushing towards him, as though in a dream. As the vision passed over him, he gained the impression of a middle-aged woman with a kindly face, olive complexion and greying hair, although still with some of its original jet-black colour, and she was dressed in white linen. As the apparition passed, he felt a kind of serenity, as though he had been empowered in some way. It was obviously due to this feeling that he found himself able to become the calming influence in the room. Although he did not understand the cause of, or reason for, what just happened to him, he instinctively knew that this was not an isolated incident. Instead, he was quite certain that this was actually the start of something, but he knew not what.

At that moment, the door opened and a very tired looking seven year-old boy rolled around the door and staggered across to his mummy, quietly sobbing. Madeline hugged him tightly.

"What's wrong, David, can't you sleep either?" she asked. Once the warmth of his mother's caress and her soothing voice had calmed him down a little, David began to tell her in a very low and tired voice about the nightmare that woke him up. "There, there," she said, "come along and tell Mummy all about it while she gets you a nice drop of warm milk. That'll help you sleep, won't it my precious little boy?" As Madeline excused herself, Neil repeated his suggestion that Karen should continue with her charade, as he was quite sure that

Ray's guess about the 'Snow Queen' was completely wrong.

"As I've had my guess and got it wrong, old chap, perhaps you will excuse me while I go and help Madeline with little David." said Ray, slowly and thoughtfully rising from his chair. On reaching the kitchen, Ray offered to sit David on his lap so that Madeline could prepare the hot milk for him.

"It was really horrible, Uncle Ray." David began and, as he recalled his nightmare he started sobbing again, Ray took a clean handkerchief from his pocket and instructed his little godson to blow good and hard.

"Now, tell us what happened in that nasty old nightmare of yours. It'll be much better if you can get it off your chest." Ray told him.

"There were these horrible long faces, white with black markings on their faces and their eyes were black and they were all dancing about in front of me," he sobbed.

"Here you are darling," said his mother, holding a mug of warm milk up to his mouth, "that'll make you feel better and soon you'll be able to go back to sleep. He loves his hot milk, Ray, don't you David?" she added. David started to sip his milk but the vision of those faces came back again.

"They were really scary Mummy and they just wouldn't leave me alone. I ran as fast as I could but they just kept following me and shouting out horrible, strange words that I didn't understand. Then one of them came right at me and I fell over backwards. Then I woke up and found that I'd fallen out of bed and it was ever so cold, Mummy, really freezing!"

"There, there my darling, it's alright now."

"I could hear you all downstairs but I was too frightened to come down at first. I was so scared that they would come and get me again but then I felt braver, so I came down but it was still cold until I got into the dining room. I love you, Mummy," he said, his wide eyes looking up at Madeline. She carefully lifted him from Ray's lap and cuddled him close.

"And I love you too my little treasure," she replied tenderly.

"Let me take him back upstairs and give his face a wash, Maddy. You look as though you could do with a brandy or something. David will be just fine with me now, won't you my little man?" Ray said as he took the sleepy boy from his mother's arms.

"Goodnight darling," Madeline said, giving David a kiss, "sleep tight."

"And don't let the bedbugs bite." David rejoined with a conspiratorial grin. This was his father's favourite phrase when he was saying goodnight to his children and they both enjoyed chorusing it together. As Ray and David ascended the stairs to the boy's bedroom, Madeline returned to the dining room to rejoin her guests.

Ray gently washed David's face and patted it dry with a soft towel, ruffled his hair and said in his most soothing voice, "Come on now young David, we'll soon have you sound asleep again. Let's have no more bad dreams otherwise you'll start to frighten your Uncle Ray as well, and that won't do now, will it?" He then tucked David up in his warm bed and pulled up the beautiful handmade patchwork quilt, which

David's Grandma Annie made for him when he first moved from the cot in the nursery to his own proper bed. Annie died a year ago after suffering from cancer for several years and young David missed her very much. He especially missed the stories she used to tell him about his Grandad, who he never really knew as he died when David was just a baby. Ray pulled up the colourful quilt and joked that when it was right up under David's chin, it made him look like Joseph with his coat of many colours. He sat on the end of the bed and began crooning to his little Godson and it was whilst he was humming the tune 'Call me Irresponsible,' that David finally fell asleep again. Ray quietly stood up and tiptoed out of David's room. It was when he reached the bottom of the stairs, it became apparent to him that for reasons unbeknown to him, that David's nightmare began to disturb and trouble him. Could it be that he felt sorry for the little chap when he saw him crying, as it was unusual for David to cry, because he was normally quite a happy and tough little lad, or was there something more to it than that? He wondered whether there might be a connection between David's nightmare and the vision, which he saw at about the same time. Whilst still pondering these possibilities, he slipped quietly back into the dining room to find that everyone was now chatting away happily again, apparently having forgotten all about the cold draught, the effects of which was troubling them at the time he left.

"Great, Ray is back," Madeline enthused "how's little David, bless him? Sleeping peacefully right now, no doubt," she asked.

"Oh yes, no problem. As I didn't have the sax with me, I hummed a little tune for him." Ray replied rather thoughtfully.

"That was an unusually understated entrance for you, Ray," Neil enquired "are you alright?" Ray appeared to ponder the question for a moment, as though he was unsure how to answer but then confirmed that he was fine.

"Well what are we playing now?" asked Ray "Are we still doing charades?"

"Yes, sweetie and, seeing as you have been out of the room for far too long, it must be your turn now." Sam scolded him.

"Right then, now let me see." Ray was trying to think of something clever and then with a smile started to tap on Caroline's back with the tips of his fingers and with a quizzical expression appeared to be listening to something through a pretend gadget in his ears.

"Easy," cried Sam in a raucous voice. "You're a doctor but you don't have the balls to listen to Caroline's chest, although I bet she wouldn't mind you fondling her tits." There was a stunned silence for a moment, which was amazingly broken by Caroline herself, who made it quite clear that, whilst she was not about to invite Ray to touch her breasts, she was not at all shocked by Sam's comment. Furthermore, she actually applauded her attempt to liven up the party and said that she could not wait to see Sam's charade.

"Well," said Ray in response to Sam's guess, "You are partly right. I am a doctor but there's more to it than that." Neil spotted the deliberately quizzical look on Ray's face during his charade and began to think through Kipling's faithful servants, what, where, when, why, which, how, who! That was it, he thought, who.

"Doctor Who!" he blurted out before anybody else could guess it and beat him to it.

"Correct, old man!" Ray confirmed. "Spot on."

"Well done, Neil" Caroline enthused "that was a good one, wasn't it, Julian?"

However, Julian had lost concentration and was not even aware that Neil guessed Ray's charade correctly, neither was he aware that his wife was speaking to him. The clock began to chime eleven o'clock.

...the smell of wood filled Julian's nostrils and he could feel the softness of sawdust under his feet but he felt quite bemused by his sudden change of surroundings. He was not at all sure if he was dreaming or whether this was actually happening to him and the dinner party, which he had so recently left, was soon gone from his mind. He could definitely feel a floating sensation and was somewhat alarmed that he seemed to have no control over his feet. Looking around him, he could clearly see that this was an old timber yard with lengths of wood strewn about in what seemed to Julian to be a disorderly manner. He could see a heavily built man with grey hair and scruffy clothes sitting beside a large wooden crate on which he could see two mugs containing what he took to be tea and another man was looking for a box to sit on. It was late afternoon and the sun was beginning to fall towards the horizon with the promise of a glorious sunset. The two men appeared to be friends and from Julian's vantage point, he could hear their conversation quite clearly.

The timber merchant was saying that he must get rid of something as soon as he could, but Julian had no idea what the subject of their conversation was, as he joined them half way through their discussion .

"*There was a heavy sort of atmosphere in the yard ever since I bought that damned wood, it just didn't feel right. One day I was working away, sawing up some lengths of timber for that builder fellow down in the town, when suddenly the yard doors starts to open, but there was nobody there. Then again, they opened and then they closed again, repeatedly, like. Opening and closing they was, opening and closing, even though there weren't even a breath of wind, like.*"

"*It sounds right creepy, does that,*" *replied the timber merchant's friend.*

"*But how do you know it was to do with those bits of mahogany?*"

"*Because none of this ever happened before them there bits of mahogany arrived here, that's how.*"

"*But where did it come from in the first place?*" *asked the friend.*

"*Somewhere tropical, weren't it? Mahogany comes from tropical places like the Caribbean and the Far East, Burma an' that. Well I was told that this lot was shipped in from the West Indies a few months back. The shippers said I could have it cheap as there was only a small amount and I thought I would be able to shift it easy like. Well, mahogany usually sells quite well. Not this lot though, nobody so much as looked at it for months.*"

"*Haunted then, was it?*" *his friend enquired, warming to his theme,*" *You never know what goes on in some of them places what they calls Paradise. All that dancing and chanting and stuff they do to keep the so-called evil spirits away."*

"You don't believe in all that stuff, do you?" asked the grey-haired man.

"What? Devil Worshipping and all that sort of business. People disappearing without trace an' all that? Nah, course not!" replied the friend, churning it over in his mind."Well, I dunno, really."

"Like young girls, virgins an' all, being sacrificed and all that business" continued the timber merchant.

"My uncle went to the West Indies on business some time ago," began the friend "well, when he returned, I heard him telling my aunt about some strange goings-on that took place there at night. It was always late at night, in the dark, away from the villages and always deep in the woods." Julian felt very uncomfortable and rather frustrated, as he could not figure out what force brought him here, or why, just to listen to these two idiots talking about a subject about which they clearly knew nothing. However, he kept very still because he was acutely aware that they did not know that anyone was eavesdropping on their conversation. Little did he know at that point that even if he wanted to move and walk away he would not have been able to do so, as his movements were under the total control of some unseen force.

"I feel quite privileged to be in the presence of such experts in Black Magic," he whispered to himself sarcastically. However, although some of their remarks were clearly nonsense, he could not dismiss everything

they said, there being more than a grain of truth in one or two of their comments. Even though the conversation of these two uneducated men was going nowhere, he felt compelled to keep listening. The only concrete fact in their discussion was that there had been some very strange happenings in this timber yard since the arrival of the wood of which they were speaking. In his publishing work, Julian read a wide variety of novels, some of which dealt with the subject of magic and witchcraft and he found it quite interesting. As he listened to the two men droning on, Julian wondered why he had travelled back in time to what appeared to be the 1920s, judging by the men's clothing and the vintage of lorry parked in the yard. Julian felt himself drifting over to where the two men were now standing and just then, he thought he could hear the faint sound of drumbeats and chanting in the distance. He lifted his head to hear the sounds more clearly but was unable to ascertain the direction.

The timber merchant was pointing his podgy finger towards an area in the corner of the yard, under a rusting section of corrugated iron roofing, where the offending lengths of mahogany were stored before the young carpenter bought them. He clearly had something interesting to show his friend.

"What do you make of that?" he asked, pointing at the rough concrete floor in the shaded corner of the yard.

"It looks like some kind of art work to me," said his friend. "So what is it, then?"

"This one's kind of snake-like, ain't it? And all done in red and white, too." The timber merchant continued. "And here, this one looks like one of them signs of the Zodiac, the twins or something and here's a drawing of an animal, a goat or something with big curly horns." He shivered slightly, even though the air was warm and added nervously. "And another thing, no matter how warm the weather, ever since that wood arrived, and even now it's gone, it always feels cold in this corner of the yard. But here's the strangest thing of all, no matter how hard I tries to scrub it, just when I thinks it's gone, it always reappears, as though soap and water never touched it."

Julian found himself becoming increasingly interested as he recalled seeing something similar when one of his young author friends was doing some research into black magic and the occult. He felt that the men were really onto something sinister here and he too felt cold, especially now that he could hear the drums and the chanting louder and clearer than ever. Could the two men hear this too, or were these sounds only inside his own head, Julian wondered. The noise was getting louder and louder and the wind was whistling around his head. It seemed to be repeating a message over, and over again in a language he did not recognise. Then suddenly it became clearer and he heard a light, haunting voice whispering 'Free me, free me from the dark prison of the undead'………

The whispering slowly resolved into the laughter of well-fed diners and the beating drums and chanting voices faded away, for which Julian felt extremely grateful, if somewhat confused. As he regained his equilibrium, he saw Ray banging his hands on the table whilst making ludicrous chicken sounds and everyone was laughing too loud to hear Karen trying to guess his charade. As the laughter died away, Karen tried yet again,

"Bangkok!" she yelled triumphantly to the amusement of the assembled company.

"Yes, yes!" Roared Ray with tears running down his cheeks. "It was so easy really, wasn't it?" he laughed uncontrollably.

"Yes," cried Madeline, "it was but your antics were so funny that no-one could speak for laughing, could they?" Nobody seemed to have noticed Julian sitting there so deep in thought. He was now beginning to wish that he could have stayed to find out more about those peculiar markings and that chanting and drumbeats. Even though at one stage he thought the men were talking utter rubbish, he would have been interested to find out more. The laughter and conversation around the table began to demand more of his attention and he felt obliged to leave his thoughts behind for a while and rejoin the group. He was, of course, completely oblivious to the fact that some of the other guests had also been through similar experiences during the past four hours and that even his own wife, Caroline, was transported back in time to that same timber yard.

The game of charades appeared to have completely broken down in the general mirth led mainly by Ray and Karen, both of whom had entered into the spirit of the evening in rather raucous fashion, doing more turns than some of their less gregarious compatriots. Sam was quieter than one might have expected, being the only one present with anything approaching celebrity status, but then she had been over-indulging on the alcohol front. Julian, who could normally be relied upon to be the life and soul of any party if one were needed, realised that in Ray he had met his match. He was therefore quite content to play 'second fiddle' to the natural clown who was even now, guffawing at Neil's satirical humour. Neil was one of those quiet, comfortable people in whose company everyone felt both safe and at ease and Julian warmed to him at their first meeting. Neil's wit was razor-sharp, which made the repartee with Ray all the more enjoyable for those not quick enough to join in. However, those who did venture to cross swords with Neil verbally soon found themselves out-manoeuvred by his agile mind. He was never rude or sarcastic in such situations, except with Ray, and always somehow managed to charm his victims into admiration for his, often satirical, comments. The friendship between Neil and Ray had already stood the test of time but it was equally clear that they would stand by each other through thick and thin, as though they were brothers. Caroline was usually a rather sober and precise person, but she seemed to have enjoyed the opportunity to let her hair down a little and was joining in the general fun, egged on by Madeline who knew her well enough to know just how far to go. Madeline was one of the few of her husband's clients who Caroline felt relaxed with as she felt that most of them came into the category which she described as 'arty farty' people. Madeline, on the other hand, was down-to-earth but with a coquettish sense of humour and an inner radiance which well suited her regal looks and tall, elegant figure. Added to that, Madeline was, of course, an exceptionally fine cook and often gave Caroline tips for her own dinner parties when she was stuck for an original idea. Mark was, by nature, a quiet man who was happy to provide whatever support his lovely, bubbly Karen might need. He taught history at a Grammar School, was especially interested in Ancient Egypt, and therefore often related the story of how he met Karen at the British Museum. One of his pupils was apparently causing some merriment, laughing at a statue of a black cat, which appeared to be wearing earrings. The noise of youngsters having fun caught her attention and Karen therefore intervened to explain the background to this particular artefact. She told the youngsters that the cat was a sacred representation of the goddess Bastet, a daughter of the great sun god, Ra and that cats had long been associated with Ancient Egypt, when she came face to face with Mark, whose knees went to jelly as soon as he saw her. He immediately compared himself with Mark Anthony meeting Cleopatra for the first time, which was the cause for great hilarity between them during their ensuing courtship.

It was fast approaching midnight and it had not escaped Neil's attention that some of their guests appeared to have become drowsy each time the clock struck the hour. He was also wondering what could have caused that sudden, cold draught at ten o'clock, just before David came down complaining that he was having a nightmare. He hoped that Madeline had not noticed their guests' unusual hourly behaviour, although he knew perfectly well that she was worried when that draught blew through the dining room. He was always rather over-protective of Madeline but he felt very uneasy about the situation and hoped that there would be no more odd occurrences before the end of the evening. He was soon rudely awoken from his reverie when, once again, Julian and Karen led the chorus of laughter at another of Ray's risqué jokes.

As the clock struck midnight, Karen pointed straight at Sam and laughed that it was now the witching hour and it was her turn to do a charade. Almost immediately, Sam's head slumped forward and hung apparently lifeless, causing Julian and Mark to enquire whether that was it, or would there be more of her charade to follow. No movement came and Ray began to look anxious. Neil, who was sitting next to Sam, gently put his hand on hers to enquire what was wrong but, just as he did so, there was another strong gust of wind, which this time blew the candles out completely, leaving smoke swirling away from them and dancing about franticly in its wake. There was silence as everyone looked around at each other as if gauging their reaction to the sudden extinguishing of the candles by this freak icy current of air. They all instinctively knew that this was more than just a cold draught, but no-one seemed ready to offer an explanation, which only added to the tension that now hung palpably in the room. Sam suddenly sat bolt upright as if every muscle in her body had become rigid. The burden on whatever force was causing these manifestations was obviously heavy, as previously it only transported one mind to reveal the hidden secrets of something dark and mysterious from the past, but this time it had captured two minds. Neil's head also lolled forward as he gripped the slender hand of the young model. Ray and Madeline were the only ones to look concerned because the others thought that Neil and Sam were performing a joint charade and were eagerly awaiting whatever was to come next...

...Sam could feel water between her toes. It was not cold, just comfortable, in fact. Now she felt as though she was gliding under water, but she did not have to struggle for breath. She wondered idly whether someone had spiked her drink, as she felt drugged and she knew from previous experience how that felt. There were sounds of clinking glasses, vague laughter and the buzz of conversation slowly fading. It was soon gone and the air now blowing over her face was cool and pleasant. She was floating and holding tightly to someone's hand and she knew somehow that she dared not let go, so she kept her eyes closed tightly and clung even tighter to the hand that was gripping hers.

She could not feel her feet beneath her, only the floating sensation and the cool breeze playing with her hair and caressing her face. Then she felt a tickling sensation around her legs. Sam had to open her eyes now, slowly at first and, feeling quite nauseous from the floating sensation, she discovered that she was now sitting in a thicket of long grassy leaves. The sweet scent of jasmine hung heavily in the air and she was still clinging to the hand that was in turn still holding hers just as tightly. Still in a daze, she looked around her and realised that the hand belonged to Neil. The buzzing of a mosquito around his ears caused Neil to raise his other hand and brush it away. Opening his eyes, he turned to find Sam gazing at him in a daze.

"What on Earth happened?" She asked in a frightened voice.

"I have no idea," he replied "Where have the others all gone and where are we?" Sam was too bewildered to let go of Neil's hand and decided, in view of what just took place, she had better keep hanging on. They seemed to be in a tropical country judging by the palm trees swaying overhead in the gentle breeze and the warm dusty ground that surrounded them. Judging by the sequestering sun and their long shadows, they deduced that it must by early evening. Across the dusty road, they could see a little house that was crudely made of timber, the roof equally fashioned out of corrugated iron and there were about four or five wooden, 'open tread' steps leading up to the door, which stood ajar. The exterior was obviously once a reddish-brown colour, but the paint was now mostly peeled off, leaving it looking rather forlorn. The wooden shutters were wide open and appeared to have also suffered from the heat of the tropical sun over the years. A few goats foraged at the side of the road where there was barely enough vegetation to feed even their scrawny bodies and two thin, mangy looking cows were staring at them from a nearby field. In a small makeshift pen made of odd pieces of wood and wire beside this ramshackle little

house, a couple of pigs were laying in the dust bowl, which their bodies had created.

"Neil, I don't understand," said Sam as she realised that they were now hovering about two feet or so above the ground, slowly gliding over a few undulations in the area between the thicket and the little house itself. As they drifted slowly across the dusty road through the hot, sticky air, they could see in through one of the open shutters. A woman, dressed in white with her arms folded across her chest was lying on a bed with an open book laid upon her and she appeared to be at peace with the World. There were people standing around her, the elderly were sitting with what appeared to be prayer books on their laps. All were silent, their heads bowed as if in prayer. Neil and Sam slowly ascended higher into sky over the top of the house. Sam asked Neil what he made of the little house and its occupants but, apart from the obvious conclusion that the woman in white had just died, he could offer no further explanation.

Slowly they drifted through the air over the house and then away across open country, guided by a force, against which they were powerless to exert any kind of control or influence, whilst behind them the warm orange glow of the early evening sun told them that night was fast approaching, as it always seems to in the tropics. Their lazy drifting began to gather pace until quite suddenly it became a rush and now they felt as though the wind would take their breath away as they rolled over, and over in midair, still franticly clinging to each other as they fell through a vortex of time and space. They were falling backwards now and could see faces and scenes passing their eyes too quickly for them to recognise anything, as though they were watching a newsreel rewinding at great speed. The wind seemed to be in complete control of their destiny but then, just as they thought their time was up, all became calm again just as suddenly and they found themselves dropping serenely down through wispy clouds towards an area of dense woodland. Although the experience took but a few moments, it felt as though they had been flying through the air for a long time.

"I think I can hear them singing now," Sam said.

"No, I don't think we're anywhere near that house anymore, Sam," Neil replied. "I feel as though we have travelled a long way backwards in time, although forwards in distance, but actually in a very short space of time. I really don't understand what's going on here at all." Sam agreed, although she still thought she could hear singing in the distance. They were losing altitude quickly now and were approaching the dark, dense area of woodland, which they saw from their lofty vantage point just a short while ago. As they dropped below the canopy of the trees, fireflies darted around them in every direction and the noise of crickets and tree frogs grew ever louder.

"We'll need to find somewhere to shelter for the night," Neil began, "the crickets are already in full song."

"Yes, I just love that sound." Sam replied.

"Look out!" cried Neil. "Grab hold of your dress!" Sam quickly complied, using her free hand as she was determined not to let go of Neil under any circumstances.

She was only just in time as they narrowly missed a low branch of one of the trees. In that instant, they dropped the last few feet to the ground.

"Neil! What's going on over there?" Sam whispered. They were at the edge of a small clearing and could clearly see about a dozen or so people wearing black hoods, adorned with the skulls of small animals and, what looked from this distance to be black loincloths, fashioned from animal skins. A few of them carried small drums, which they were now beginning to beat with the tips of their fingers and the palms of their hands. Neil whispered to Sam that their drums looked similar to the bongo drums that Ray used to mess about with at university. Sam was too concerned at what was taking place in front of her to pay much attention to Neil's comments about Ray. In fact, Ray seemed to her to be a million miles away, just when she needed him most. Typical, she thought, to be nowhere in sight when you need him most; still Neil was here and that gave her a warm, safe feeling. They stayed crouching low behind a few bushes, fearful that those in the clearing might detect their presence. However, unbeknown to them, they could be neither seen nor heard by the hooded figures in front of them. As these strange figures began to move slowly round in a circle in the fast fading light, they started chanting in a tongue which neither Sam nor Neil had ever heard before, nor could they understand it. The chanting became louder and more intense as the drumbeats quickened and their dark skinned bodies began to glisten with sweat as their dancing became more and more feverish. The whole area was now lit by hand-made torches, which appeared to be nothing

more than large bottles containing some form of liquid, stuffed with rags and set alight. Neil presumed that they contained paraffin or oil but Sam's thoughts were less scientific than those of her calm companion, in fact she was now almost rigid with fear! The beating of the drums grew louder and faster. Her fingernails dug deep into Neil's knuckles until they bled and she was still clinging on to her lovely pink Dior dress with the other hand.

"Ouch Sam, your fingernails are sharp!" Neil exclaimed in pain.

"Well I'm bloody terrified Neil!" she almost shouted. "What's happening over there? What the hell is going on, Neil? I'm scared stiff, aren't you?"

"It looks as though they are waiting for someone, or something." Neil did not want Sam to know that he was also getting more nervous by the minute and was very concerned about what the people in the clearing might actually be about to do. He had read several books about devil worshippers and witchcraft in his earlier years as a student, when he used to soak up fiction like a sponge and this bore all the hallmarks of a satanic ritual unfolding before their eyes. Now he too, was scared but he knew he must not show it in case her fear caused her to do something sudden and give away their hiding place. He dare not let her know what he was thinking either as that might just scare her to death. In that instant, Sam let out a blood-curdling shriek! Neil clamped his hand firmly over her mouth and kept it there until he was sure that she would not give a repeat performance and give away their position.

A heavily built man with shiny, rippling muscles and a large snake entwined around his shoulders, burst into the clearing and was now moving forwards with an unearthly kind of grace, his face was painted white with black markings. Large black rings around his eyes gave the appearance of huge black eyes. His head was clean-shaven and painted white to match his face. He danced rhythmically to the beat of the drums as he held the snake within inches of his face and appeared to go into a frenzied trance; he was surely possessed. As he gyrated around the clearing with the snake's head always in front of his face, his dark skin started to glow with perspiration from his exertions. Neil was amazed when the figures in front of them showed no reaction to Sam's scream, whilst the force which guided them here, was moving them slowly closer to the dancers. They tried to fight against whatever it was that had taken hold of them, but they were helpless against it and continued to drift slowly closer. Neil felt sure that these devil worshippers, or whatever they were, must have seen them by now. Beads of sweat seeped from his forehead and a wave of panic struck when he thought that they could be the intended victims for sacrifice. Sam, however just kept trying feverishly to free herself from this damned force and run back to the bushes for cover.

"They'll see us," Sam whimpered "and I hate snakes!" She finally let go of her dress and flung both arms around Neil, clinging to him with all her might. Although he felt very apprehensive, Neil realised that for some inexplicable reason the dancers could not see

either him or Sam. He wanted to get a little closer to the action anyway out of sheer curiosity, even though they should now be within full view of everyone in the clearing. Their presence did not seem to affect the ritual that was now building up to a climax and suddenly it came to Neil that the force, which was controlling their movements, was also ensuring that they could be neither seen, nor heard. The dancers' movements became more frenzied, the drumbeats became more urgent and the chanting louder, more harsh and so devilish that it sounded as though it would wake the dead. Being closer to all this action, they could clearly see the exertion on their faces, the sweat glistening on the dancers' bodies and running down their chests. Neil could not help noticing that some of the dancers were women and that they were bare from the waist up with their breasts bouncing and heaving with the rhythm. Then two more figures seemed to glide out of the bushes. One was very tall, wearing a long white robe with bizarre black markings on it. His shoulders were draped with the dried skin of a goat and its skull, with two large, curled horns adorned his head. His face also appeared to be that of a goat with cold, staring eyes, which lent him an utterly evil appearance. By his side was a shorter figure, similarly attired, but her hair was plaited in two, each plait stretching down to her ankles. A goatskin covered her shoulders as well and the skull of a goat adorned her head, whilst her goat-like face looked even more wicked and bizarre, framed as it was by long, feminine plaits. Neil assumed that they must be some kind of high priest and priestess, although he did not care to guess what kind of religion theirs might be. He knew that the goat's horns were associated with the devil and he feared the worst. For her part, Sam did not know whether these two evil looking creatures were man or beast, although she was quite ready to believe them to be demons.

Neil and Sam could now feel the ground beneath their feet, but were still unable to control their movements and furthermore, it was now evident they could not be seen either. The dancing slowed and the black-clad figures were now swaying to the rhythmic beating of the drums. Abruptly the beats came to a halt! There was silence and all movement ceased as though someone had thrown a switch, it became quite dark and the night was still. The flames from the torches flickered in the light breeze. Just then, they heard a faint whimpering sound that seemed to be getting closer and closer until it became apparent that it was the pitiful sobbing of a child.

"I'm sure I can hear a child crying, Neil." Sam whispered just as two people also dressed in long white robes and headdresses emerged from the bushes carrying a young girl wrapped in a white sheet so that only her head was showing. Neil noticed for the first time that there was a thick, flat, reddish piece of wood, about the size of a tabletop, wedged between two tree trunks just in front of the high priest and priestess. At each corner was a short, thick black candle, which the snake carrier now lit from one of the dancer's torches. The young girl, who looked as though she was in her early teens, was laid on the makeshift altar on her back, her hands and feet bound, and her dark hair neatly tied

behind the back of her head. Her face glowed in the eerie light of the torches and her eyes glistened with the moisture of her tears as they darted back and forth in abject terror.

Sam was now absolutely frozen with fear, unclear about what was actually taking place before her eyes, but at the same time, fearing what might happen next, even though she somehow just could not believe what she was witnessing, or why.

"Neil, we have to help her!" Sam almost squeaked at him. She had just about reached breaking point when the man with the snake reappeared and the drums resumed their sensual rhythm. The snake-man began to sway slowly back and forth, drawing closer to the altar, moving in gradually closer and closer to the terrified girl. Suddenly she opened her eyes wide with anticipation as, with a faint glimmer of hope, she thought she saw a familiar face and uttered the name she knew so well. She tried again to struggle free, but seeing the look in the snake-man's eyes, realised to her horror that all hope was now gone. She wriggled, as he poked the snake's head tantalisingly within inches of her face until she could take no more, let loose a piercing scream, and then fainted. The high priest and priestess slowly approached the altar and the others all knelt and bowed their heads, continuing to sway to the rhythm of the drums. The high priest drew a long, sharp, S-shaped dagger from beneath his cloak and, grasping it in both hands, held it high above the young girl's body and began murmuring an incantation in a low voice. Sam knew that he must be aiming the knife

straight at the girl's heart and screamed at the top of her voice. "Noooooo..." she cried, as she looked on in horror and disbelief. "Neil, come on." She was trying to drag him across the clearing towards the altar, but she was unable to move. The torches were beginning to gutter in the strong wind, which whipped up suddenly. Neil pointed in the opposite direction to those taking part in the ritual.

"Sam, listen." She stopped struggling and listened as Neil thought he could hear noises in the bushes behind them, the breaking of twigs beneath someone's feet. "Somebody's coming, Sam" he said, spinning round to see who it could be. Sam called out, hopelessly. "Help, help over here!" No sooner were the two of them distracted from the scene at the altar, than the deed was done. The blood drenched body of the young girl lay lifeless on the altar before them, that gruesome knife now dripping with the blood of an innocent child, held high again. Sam buried her head in Neil's chest as the tears, which she could no longer hold back, flowed down her cheeks. She was frightened, confused and far away from home. She longed to wake from this terrible dream, this dreadful nightmare and to be back where she came from in her own time, for she was sure they had gone back many years in time to visit this horrible place. However, most of all, she realised now that she missed Ray more than he would ever know and she just wanted to tell him so. She silently thanked God that Neil was with her and she knew that she would not have been able to cope with this terrifying ordeal on her own.

As Neil spun round, two men came crashing through the bushes carrying torches and as they came out into the clearing, followed by several more men, Sam and Neil turned to see that the high priest and priestess, the snake man, the dancers and their unfortunate victim had all vanished. All the men could find were, the wooden altar with its four sinister black candles still flickering in the disturbed air and a stream of blood flowing down over the roots of the tree to the ground. The evil ritual was over and the participants were quick to remove their victim's body, they simply melted back into the depths of the woods. The men fanned out into the forest in hot pursuit carrying torches and cudgels, intent on overtaking the evil doers. One, however, stayed near to the makeshift altar and appeared to be examining the candles and the blood as it dripped down from the altar.

"Oh my God," Sam sobbed, "please take me back to civilisation and sanity." ………

As Neil heard Sam's voice, he also began to hear other voices. He opened his eyes and looked up to see the familiar surroundings of his own dining room. His guests were still trying to guess Sam's charade and as he looked at her, she too was opening her eyes and looking around her with the sheer relief of being back.

"But why do you need to hold hands with Sam?" Julian enquired of Neil as the clock rang the last note of midnight. "And another thing, why couldn't you wait your turn along with the rest of us, instead of doing a double act with Sam? That sounds like cheating to me." Neil turned and looked deep into Sam's eyes. He could see they were a little puffy and slightly red.

"Are you alright?" he whispered softly to Sam, with a firm squeeze of her hand. Neil glanced at the clock sitting on the mantelpiece and noticed that it was only a few seconds after midnight. He felt as though they were gone for hours, so much had happened. Was it just a dream he thought to himself as the images of their experience swirled around in his head or was it something else, something he did not wish to contemplate.

"So what were you supposed to be then, Sam?" inquired Mark, "I don't get it."

"Neither do I!" agreed Madeline, who was not convinced that Sam was actually playing charades at all. Ray looked on very thoughtfully.

"It's alright really" Sam confessed, "I was intending to be a witch as it was the witching hour after all, but as I threw my head back I sort of blacked out. Must have taken one too many drinks."

"I thought something was wrong," Neil added quickly, "that's why I held your hand. Just to see if you were OK, I mean." There was an awkward silence as nobody was quite sure what to believe.

"Oh, look it's getting rather late. We'd better be going," said Caroline diplomatically. Julian stretched and followed it up with a yawn, which he did not even try to stifle. After all, hadn't his own dear wife made the first move? Madeline was quick to agree with Julian.

"Yes, some of you have quite long journeys home, haven't you? Neil darling, will you get their coats for them?" Madeline added.

"Yes, of course darling." Neil responded, still rather deep in thought.

"I'll give you a hand Neil," said Karen "as we need to get going too."

As Karen and Neil left the room, Mark quickly turned to Madeline, but as he opened his mouth to speak, Madeline whispered furtively so that the others would not hear. "I couldn't believe it was you!" "No," he replied, "I had no idea that it was *your* house we were invited to."

"Mark, we have to be discreet about this. They must not find out."

"Yes I totally agree, Shh, I think they're coming."

"It's been a really super evening, Madeline," Mark began graciously as Karen and Neil returned with the coats, "and I have really enjoyed meeting everyone so much. I think Karen had a lot of fun too."

"You're more than welcome," Madeline replied, "and do feel free to visit us any time you're in the area. We'd love to see you, wouldn't we, Neil?" Madeline replied. "Absolutely! Any time." Neil agreed.

"It's been a truly spiritual evening." Karen ventured with a twinkle in her eye.

"Wonderful food, as ever, Madeline and such entertaining company, too." Caroline commented, dragging Julian towards the hall before he embarrassed her with another almighty yawn.

"The food was sublime." Julian added, feeling the need to top his wife's comment. Ray was sitting, looking rather pensive, in an armchair near the coffee table as Sam had rushed out to the toilet to ensure that nobody else could beat her to it.

"Goodbye, Karen. Goodbye Mark, it was lovely meeting you. Goodbye Caroline, have a safe journey home. Oh, Julian I must talk to you next week about that article. Bye." Madeline waved as her guests walked to their cars, calling back their goodbyes to their hosts. Madeline rushed back indoors, commenting that it was getting quite cold outside and went to find Ray. As Neil closed the front door, Sam emerged from the cloakroom.

"Neil" she began, a little apprehensively. "Were you, um, there too? You know what I mean, don't you?" Unfortunately, before Neil could answer, Ray appeared in the hall with her fox fur stole, ready for the journey home.

"Come on Sam, it's time we hit the road, too." Ray helped Sam with her stole and remarked how pale she was looking. "I think you could do with a good lie in tomorrow morning; and I'll bring you a rather late breakfast in bed when you finally decide to wake up!" he added. She felt quite agreeable to this excellent suggestion, especially as she felt quite jaded after her evening's exertions.

Ray hugged Madeline and reaffirmed his faith in her culinary skills.

"Nobody can cook as well as you can, Maddy. You're the best."

"And you are the World's greatest flatterer. I suppose you get this from him all the time, Sam. He'll never change though, bless him."

"Amen to that." Said Sam, with rather more sincerity than usual. "Come on, big man, let's go home."

"We must meet up again soon, Ray," Neil said, putting his arm around his friend's broad shoulders, "there's something I need to discuss with you. And you make sure you look after Sam as well, she's a lovely girl."

Ray waved as he lowered his bulk into the low-slung Austin-Healey and grinned at Neil as the engine roared into life with a throaty growl. The car slowly moved off down the gravel drive and Neil and Madeline waved from the cottage door. Ray stuck his hand out through the side-screen as far as he could and waved wildly as the car rolled out through the gates and turned down the lane towards the village.

It had been an enjoyable evening, but it was now getting quite late so Neil locked up and agreed with Madeline that they would clear away the mess from the dinner party in the morning. They made their way upstairs to bed, checking on both David and Sarah, who were now sound asleep, before settling into bed.

"That was quite an eventful evening, darling." Madeline said as she turned to Neil. He did not appear to want to give too much away, and he was glad that the lights were out so she could not read his expression.

"You were brilliant," he replied, "they all loved you."

"Well you were the perfect host, as ever my darling." She responded. "I thought Sam looked very pale and tired towards the end of the evening. Do you think she might have been a little bit tipsy?"

"Yes, probably darling. Although I am quite sure these young 'jet-setters' can take it. I expect she has been working too hard. Anyway, I'm sure Ray will look after her and she'll be as right as rain in a day or so."

"I'm sure you're right. As a matter of fact, I feel pretty tired myself after all the preparations today and staying up late, so if you don't mind, I'll just say goodnight now."

"Goodnight darling, sweet dreams."

CHAPTER III –
The Initiation

Ray was concentrating on driving as smoothly as possible along the winding country lanes, whilst also trying to keep up a reasonable speed, despite there being no street lighting in these rural areas. Sam sat cocooned in the comfort of a thick tartan car blanket, which they bought from a little craft shop on a recent visit to the Isle of Skye. She really cherished the memory of that short break and her mind began to drift back to the joy they shared walking in the heather, watching otters playing on the seashore and seeing seals basking on the rocks. They took several photographs of each other with the Cuillin Hills in the background and then enjoyed eating wonderful local seafood in a charming little restaurant as they watched the sun setting over the Outer Isles. With these happy thoughts in her mind, she drifted off to sleep.

"Sam." Ray whispered, but there was no reply. He was not surprised that she had already nodded off as it was now in the early hours of the morning, and the car's engine usually had a soporific effect on her when it was late at night and furthermore, she did have quite a lot to drink. He could not possibly know, of course, that she had endured a frightening experience earlier in the evening, which she desperately wanted to forget. For her part, she felt that if she mentioned it to him, he might think her foolish and suggest that her overindulgence in alcohol was the cause of what he would have seen as hallucinations. Sleep was the only answer and it came to her soon enough. The journey seemed shorter than usual and soon they were back, safe in Ray's London flat, but there was very little conversation as Sam did not feel very talkative and Ray was also deep in thought.

A little while later as she lay in bed, Sam's mind kept replaying the incredible adventure with Neil, which she remembered so vividly, and she began to wish that she could have spoken to him about it before leaving Ivy Cottage. She was so close to getting the chance when she came out of the cloakroom and Neil was standing there alone in the hall, but then Ray had come striding out of the dining room in a hurry to make a move for home and her opportunity was gone. Although she knew that Ray could have no way of knowing what she had just gone through, she felt sure that Neil would have understood. Nonetheless, she felt uncharacteristically self-conscious and wondered what would be the best way of approaching the subject with Neil the next time she got the chance. As she was absorbed in her own thoughts, Sam did not notice that Ray was lying there still awake with something on his mind too. She was completely unaware that Ray also felt troubled by something that happened during the dinner party that night and she finally drifted off into a troubled sleep. Each time Ray closed his eyes there she was again, the woman whose face came to him when that cold gust of wind whistled through the room at the dinner party. Her skin was olive in colour, her hair was obviously once black but was now greying and her eyes the deepest shade of jade green. He hoped that in a few hours, when he would awaken from his sleep, this haunting vision would seem like a distant dream. He would call Neil about mid-morning and arrange the meeting, which his friend mentioned, as it was some time since the two of them had enjoyed a lunch together. Neil rarely seemed to find the time to visit the City these days since taking on a lot of new research work in connection with the American space mission, and he really wanted to find out more about what his old friend was doing. However, he was well aware that getting information from Neil was akin to getting blood out of a stone but, with these happy thoughts, Ray drifted off to sleep.

A few hours later, he awoke from a restless sleep, quietly slipped out of bed without disturbing Sam, and tiptoed out to the kitchen to get a glass of water. Slowly drinking the water, he peered out of the window and idly watched two starlings squabbling over a scrap of food on the adjacent roof and envied their apparently simple life. But even as he watched these two amusing figures in their titanic tussle for what seemed to him to be a worthless piece of rotting bacon rind, the vision of that face came back to haunt him once more. What the hell is going on, he thought to himself. Who on Earth is this woman? I'm sure I've never seen her before, so why should her face keep appearing in my mind? It's so real that I feel I could reach out and touch her. Am I going mad? I must call Neil; no, it's far too early, he and Madeline will still be asleep at this hour. What will I tell Sam?

At her home in the middle of leafy Hertfordshire, Caroline was also awake early that morning and immediately felt the need for a cup of refreshing tea. She felt as though she had spent the night next to a whale, who seemed to time it just right to blow every time she began to drift off to sleep. His snoring was a bone of contention between them at the best of times, but this felt to Caroline more like the worst of times and, by God, was she going to let him know what a lousy night she had just suffered when he finally decided to wake up. However, as she got downstairs to the kitchen she realised that it was much earlier than she thought and Julian would probably not surface for at least another hour. That was the last straw she thought, so why not take him up a cup of tea and wake him up to drink it, after all it was his fault that she did not slept a wink all night.

"Come along, Julian now, wake up. I've got a lovely cup of tea for you, dear," called Caroline as she walked back into the bedroom to interrupt Julian's one-man nasal orchestra.

"Oh, thank you Caroline, my angel," he began in a groggy voice, having been woken up rather abruptly by Caroline's stentorian announcement of early morning refreshments. "My saviour. That's just what I need. I've had a bitch of a night."

"*You've* had a bitch of a night?" yelled Caroline, "Excuse me but I haven't slept a wink, what with you tossing and turning and snoring like a damned foghorn!"

"Oh, come on now, Caroline. Give me a break, will you? I don't recall getting any sleep at all." Julian countered. "As a matter of fact, I experienced something very odd last night at the dinner party and it kept playing on my mind and I couldn't talk to you about it because you were fast asleep all night."

"Fat chance!" snorted Caroline. "So what was this bad experience then, Julian. Do tell."

"Come to think of it, I doubt if you would understand anyway. I don't know why I mentioned it." Julian retorted angrily.

"Try me." She taunted, "Mr. Grumpy!" This made him soften a little and he thought how lucky he was to have a wife who was able to make him laugh, even when he was tired, angry, and in this case, a little confused.

"Well," Julian began, "I think it was when the clock started to strike eleven last night at the dinner party. I felt as though I was going into some kind of a trance or daydream or something. Neil's father must have been a real master of his craft to produce such a timepiece;

I mean the workmanship was quite exquisite and the chime so rich and clear. Anyway, as I was saying, I went off into a kind of trance."

"No change there then, my dear." Caroline teased, trying to make light of what he was saying, although she was now beginning to feel slightly uneasy about her own experience of the previous evening.

"Yes, very amusing," Julian continued, "but this really isn't funny because I couldn't get the bloody dream out of my head all night."

"Julian, you're not going to believe this, but a similar thing happened to me last night and that's why your snoring was annoying me so much. I desperately needed to sleep to get that awful memory out of my head." Caroline confided.

"Well I'll be damned," he replied, "so what happened to you, then?"

"I seemed to be floating about in a sort of timber merchant's place but I wasn't able to go where I wanted to." She said, trying to remember just what did happen.

"I was in a timber yard as well," said Julian, "but I didn't see you there. I wonder if it was the same one. All I saw was those two idiots jabbering on about witchcraft, or voodoo or something, the clowns. But the thing that really concerned me was those weird markings on the ground over in the corner."

"I didn't see any markings, Julian. Unless you mean those drops of blood in the road after that young carpenter went off with the wood. That really worried me because I couldn't tell where it came from and

I just went cold all over for some reason." Caroline interrupted.

"What blood, Caroline, that wasn't blood. They were some kind of primitive paintings on the ground and what's more, they looked vaguely familiar, but I just can't remember where I have seen them before. I think it was in a television series I used to watch and there was this episode where someone gets murdered in Hawaii and the police suspected......."

"Julian, never mind the damn television series, that blood scared me for some reason and I'm still a bit frightened now actually, because how did you have the same dream as me or, at least, go to the same place. What is going on, Julian?" Caroline was now beginning to feel rather unnerved by the whole business.

"What carpenter, Caroline? There wasn't any carpenter there. That other bloke was a friend of the timber merchant's and a damned stupid one at that. Oh, and what did you make of that distant chanting and drumming?"

"Julian, that wasn't chanting, they were panpipes and I didn't hear any drums either. Surely, you can tell the difference between panpipes and drums and chanting, or whatever it was you think you heard. They were panpipes or wind chimes or some such thing, coming and going on the breeze."

"Well, I can't make head or tail of it Caroline," Julian confessed, "but I'll tell you something. I don't think you and I were in that yard at the same time. It's as though we were meant to see the same place but at a different time so that we would witness separate things, but why?"

"Julian, do you think any of the others had similar dreams?"

"I don't know, but I think we should keep this to ourselves for now. At least until we've thought a bit more about it. It's all too bizarre for my liking and I can't imagine anyone there would have spiked our drinks or done any such thing, do you?" Julian wondered.

"Don't be absurd," Caroline replied angrily, "none of them would do that!"

Although Karen always got on extremely well with her parents, she was strongly independent and therefore bought her first flat as soon as she had saved up enough money to put down the necessary deposit from her first year's earnings as an archaeologist. However, since moving into the flat, her parents soon became her most frequent visitors, her father helping with the decorating and those little maintenance tasks that are forever cropping up when you have no time to spare. Her work meant that she was often away from home for long spells at a time but she could always rely on her parents to keep an eye on the flat. However, since meeting Mark, her parents became more discreet, telephoning before visiting and making sure that it was convenient for them to come around. Karen was thinking how lucky she was to have such strong parental support, as she brewed up an early morning coffee for Mark and herself. Then Mark, who stayed the night as they were late getting back from Madeline and Neil's dinner party, wandered into the kitchen yawning and trying to rub the sleep from his eyes.

"That was a super party last night, wasn't it?" he said, stifling a second yawn. "That Ray really is a bit of a character though, isn't he?"

"He's lovely, always ready with a smile and a supportive word when you need it. Did you notice how he was always jumping up to help Madeline in the kitchen, clearing the dishes away and so on, as though he was one of the family? Well, in a way I suppose he is just that. He is godfather to both of their children, you know."

"Yes, I saw how he was straight there when the kids came down. He obviously idolises them both." Mark sipped his coffee appreciatively. "You do make a good cup of coffee I must say, Karen. That's really lovely, just what I needed."

"I'm so glad you're enjoying it, my darling." she purred.

"By the way," said Mark, as if trying to find his way with a difficult subject, "what did you make of that cold rush of air blowing the candles out at the party last night? I mean, although I have never really given much credence to ghost stories as such, I have always tried to keep an open mind about the spirit world, if you follow me."

"Yes, Mark, I do know what you mean and, as you know, there is little doubt in my mind that the human spirit, or soul, outlives the flesh. I couldn't help feeling last night that someone, or something, apart from the eight of us at the table, was there amongst us."

"Tell me more, Karen," Mark asked attentively, "what else did you feel, or experience?" Karen regarded her tousle-haired boyfriend, who looked a mess at this hour of the morning having just crawled out of bed, with a mixture of love and growing comprehension. In that instant she realised that he too must have felt some sort of paranormal experience. She was now feeling really excited because she knew that he would not ridicule any talk of odd happenings in that lovely old cottage but instead would be willing to share his own experiences with her.

"We'd only just sat down to dinner and I remember the gorgeous smell of that lobster bisque which Madeline was about to serve up when I suddenly felt quite faint," she began, "and you asked me if I felt alright."

"Yes, I do remember that Karen. I remember that very clearly. You were staring across the room and then there came that beautiful rich sound of their clock striking the hour and I felt as though everything went still for a moment. It reminded me of when I was a little boy sitting down to a meal, and the conversation stopped and it all went eerily quiet and my auntie used to say 'it's alright, it's just the angel passing over.' Do you know, that always seemed to me to be at either twenty past the hour or twenty to the hour. Last night though, it was bang on the hour and I remember thinking to myself that my dear old auntie definitely got that one wrong this time." Karen was looking at him indulgently as it was, after all, she who was supposed to be recounting her memories of the previous night.

"I'm sorry, I interrupted your train of thought there, darling" he apologised.

"That's OK, but as I was saying," she continued, "I then had a very vivid dream about a plane crash and as

I was trying to get a closer look, my damned heels kept getting caught up in the grass. I knew it was during the First World War as the plane was a Bristol Fighter, which I remembered from a project I did at school about the truth behind the Red Baron and the Blue Max stories. Anyway, one of the crew had been thrown out as the plane crashed and he was hurt but, try as I might, I could not get to him because some invisible force was holding me back."

"And don't tell me, he couldn't hear you or see you either." Mark said with certainty.

"How did you know that?" cried Karen.

"Because I had a similar out-of-body experience or dream, or time travel sequence, or whatever it was, in my subconscious mind." Karen looked flabbergasted.

"My God," she whispered "not you too. So what was your scenario, then?"

"I saw this chap doing some joinery in a really quaint old country barn," Mark began "and he was making furniture and then his rather pregnant, but very pretty looking wife, brought him some refreshments. Oh, and I remember her feeding the hens when I first arrived on the scene as well. However, my over-riding impression was of being moved around against my will as though someone, or something, was trying to show me what it wanted me to see, rather than letting me see what I wanted to see. I felt as though it was showing me some wood piled in the corner, then the carpenter, then the furniture he was making and finally, his pregnant wife."

"Trust you to be analytical about it. I bet you remember the whole thing in detail too, don't you?" Karen smiled with admiration.

"I don't know about that, my love," Mark said almost shyly, "and I don't know what caused it, but I think I know what the trigger was. You know how dreams often seem to feature people you met or things that happened to you during the day and then somehow get all scrambled up? Well, when I looked across the room, whilst trying to readjust to being back with the rest of you, I noticed a photograph of a First World War pilot set in a beautiful, reddish mahogany frame and, guess what?, it was the same man who I saw in my dream. Mind you, he was younger in the photo. So I think I must have been absent-mindedly looking at that picture when I just sort of dozed off and so when I came to, that was the first thing I saw." said Mark, feeling rather pleased that he had solved the mystery.

"Of course," agreed Karen, "I wondered why that face looked so familiar. He was the man I saw at the crash site where that plane ploughed into the tree and came to rest with the tail right up in the air. It's no wonder the poor man fell out from that angle. It must have hit that tree with quite a force. But Mark, if the picture was the reason for us having those rather odd sort of daydreams, or whatever you want to call them, how do you explain the force which seemed to be directing our movements against our will?"

"Good point Karen. You've got me there. I can't."

Ray decided that he could wait no longer and picked up the telephone to call Neil as it was getting on for mid-morning now.

Neil had just gone downstairs to collect the Sunday newspaper from the letterbox when the telephone rang, so he was able to pick it up quickly to avoid its waking the whole household, especially Madeline, who was having a well-earned lie-in.

"Neil, I'm glad it was you who answered the phone," Ray blurted out.

"Hi Ray, is everything OK?" came Neil's measured response.

"Yes, fine thanks Neil. Look, I need to speak to you soon. You said last night that you wanted to meet up shortly. Can we meet in the City, soon? Can you manage something mid-week perhaps?" Neil immediately picked up the sense of urgency and anxiety in Ray's voice, and it was also clear that he was trying to keep his voice down and keep his telephone conversation discreet.

"Yes, actually I have a meeting in London on Tuesday so I could see you then."

"Brilliant. How about that old wine bar that we used to frequent, you remember, the one in Martin Lane, just off Cannon Street?"

"Yes of course I remember old man. I haven't been there for years. I look forward to that. Shall we say one o'clock?"

"Yes, that's fine Neil. Excellent, in fact, I'll be there." Ray sounded extremely relieved.

"Oh, and by the way, how's Sam this morning?" Neil asked, "She looked worn out when she left here last night."

"To tell you the truth, old boy, she's still asleep, but I'm sure she'll be fine after a decent rest. Give my love to Madeline and the kids, Neil."

"Of course I will. You look after yourself and give our love to Sam. Bye now."

Ray felt comforted that he would soon have the opportunity to share his secret with Neil, although he wondered what Neil would make of it all as he was not given to flights of fancy, always pointing out in his logical, scientific way that there is usually a rational explanation for everything. Neil would probably tease him about his visions and the strange feeling he got when he first saw the woman's face in Neil's dining room last night. But on recollection, Neil did look a little shocked himself when that cold rush of air blew the candles out and he did not come forward with an explanation then, so perhaps on this occasion he would be ready to listen rather than dismiss the matter as mere whimsy. It was time to take Sam some breakfast so Ray busied himself preparing scrambled eggs and coffee, which he felt sure she would appreciate.

Sam was already awake when Ray entered the bedroom but she seemed to be staring into space.

"Good morning, Sam. Did you have a good night's rest?" He enquired as he rested the tray on her bedside table and kissed her on the forehead.

"Not bad thanks, Ray. What about you, did you sleep well?"

"No, not really, I woke pretty early so I crept out to the kitchen so as not to wake you."

"Thanks for the breakfast, Ray...but I'm sorry I'm not really feeling hungry this morning. I'll just have the coffee."

"Oh, that's a shame. I prepared it all specially." Ray said, feeling a little disheartened by her lack of appetite.

"Well I don't want it, Ray!" she retorted. Her behaviour took him off guard as he really needed to talk to her about the events of the previous evening and was intending to take the opportunity to broach the subject with her while she ate her breakfast.

"Come on now Sam, what's bothering you?"

"I'm sorry, darling," she said quietly, "I'm feeling extremely edgy this morning. To tell you the truth I had a dreadful night's sleep and I feel terrible this morning. It was wrong of me to take it out on you Ray, I'm sorry."

"That's OK, darling. That's what I'm here for."

Sam could not bring herself to tell Ray what was troubling her because she doubted if he would take it seriously and she felt very vulnerable. Knowing that she would tell him when she was ready, Ray smiled wanly and slipped out of the room. As much as he loved Sam, she was not easy to live with and could be easily provoked and at times, he just needed to give her the space to sort herself out. Sam flopped back onto the bed tearfully as Ray left the room because she felt unable to tell the man she loved what was wrong, but she was equally unable to call Neil to discuss the matter without arousing suspicion with Madeline. She was sure that at least one of the other guests took her flirting with him last night a little too seriously and now she did not know what to do.

Shortly after Ray arrived at his office on the Monday morning, the telephone rang and, assuming it was a business call, he put on his executive voice to answer it. However, he hardly began to speak before a familiar voice interrupted him.

"Is that really you, Ray?" Karen's voice teased, "It sounds far too posh. I must have got the wrong number. Sorry!"

"No Karen, it *is* me, don't hang up. I'm so pleased to hear from you." Ray exclaimed.

"And I'm glad to hear you too Ray," Karen giggled, "what's wrong?"

"Look Karen, I haven't slept a wink since Madeline and Neil's dinner party and things have become a little strained between Sam and me as well."

"Ray, something rather bizarre happened at Ivy Cottage, didn't it?"

"Yes Karen, it did. Sometimes I think I'm going crazy, but I keep getting a recurrence of a sort of vision I had at the cottage, but I don't know how to tell Sam. She has come over very awkward and picky in the last day or so. I just don't know what's wrong with her." Ray sounded uncharacteristically worried.

"Perhaps it's just her time of the month, Ray? I'm sure there's nothing to worry about, she'll be fine, you'll see. Now, tell me about this vision of yours," Karen encouraged.

Ray described how he saw the woman's face rushing at him when the candles blew out and how he felt strangely strengthened by the experience. He also told her how the visions keep returning and that they seemed to be getting more and more vivid each time. "It's as though I'm expected to do something Karen, but I have no idea what it is that she wants from me."

"Well Ray, if it helps at all, you may be interested to know that Mark and I also experienced something quite odd that evening as well." She recounted her conversation with Mark and mentioned how their experiences appeared to have some sort of connection with the photograph of Neil's father in the dining room. Ray was amazed, and also more than a little relieved, to hear that he was not the only one to have experienced something unusual that evening. He therefore speedily agreed to visit Karen's flat that evening to discuss it further, especially as Mark would also be there. The three of them would be able to talk freely together about the events at Ivy Cottage during Madeline and Neil's dinner party and Ray hoped that it would prove to be therapeutic for him.

Madeline opened the backdoor carefully and quietly because it was still early in the morning and she did not want to rouse the children who were still fast asleep in bed. She carried her basket of washing to the clothesline and delved deeply into her pockets for some clothes pegs. It was a cool morning with a gentle breeze and the sun's rays were not yet strong enough to burn off the early morning mist that had gathered amongst the apple trees. Madeline's chief concern was to get her laundry aired, especially as the forecast was for a nice dry day and she wanted to make the most of it. Absorbed in her thoughts and plans for the coming week, Madeline gradually became aware of the muffled sound of laughter borne on the light breeze. She stopped and listened carefully but there was no mistake about it. Hearing it again, she spun around and, in so doing, felt a sudden draught, as though someone had just whisked past her.

"Who's there?" she demanded in a firm voice, but there was no reply. Then, within a split second, there came the crunching sound of a footstep on the pile of dried leaves, which Neil had recently swept up on the path nearby. She stood quite still and listened carefully again, straining her ears and tilting her head as the laughter became more apparent. Madeline walked slowly towards the orchard, where she perceived the sound to be coming from, but the laughter appeared to come from behind her now. A little confused, she stopped in her tracks,

"Sarah? Sarah! David?" she called out, but there was no reply. She started to move stealthily towards the orchard again, although she could not imagine who might be there at this time of the morning.

"Who's there?" she called. The sound became much clearer and Madeline now realised that it was not laughter as she first thought, but the sobbing of a child, which now grew louder and more desperate. Although she felt a little foolish, wandering around the garden in the early hours of the morning in search of someone whom she could hear but not see, Madeline felt sure that all she needed to do was to walk in the direction of the sound and she would find the child. She continued her search for a short while, but it proved to be in vain. There was no one else in the garden; at least, no one who she could see.

The evening could not come quickly enough for Ray and on the stroke of five he packed up and left the office for the night and rushed off to the Underground station in order to get home as soon as possible to collect his car. He was soon hustling the Austin-Healey through the rush-hour traffic out of London and, despite the usual queues, managed to reach Karen's flat within the hour.

"Well, am I glad to see you, young Raymond?" Karen smiled as she embraced him. "I don't know when I've heard you sounding so ruffled. Are you sure you're OK?"

"To be honest, Karen, I don't know what the hell is happening to me, this woman's face is driving me to distraction. I have never been through anything like this before in my life and, to be perfectly honest, it's beginning to scare me."

As they reached the top of the stairs, Mark was waiting for them.

"Hello again, Ray. Come on in and sit down. Can I get you a beer? You look as though the devil himself has been after you!" Mark was genuinely concerned for Karen's old friend.

"Yes thanks Mark, I could use a beer and, yes I do feel as though I've had 'Old Nick' on my tail, but I think it was only the cops." He said with a grin, lightening a little at Mark's kindly manner and hospitality, "I did put my foot down a bit on the way over here, after getting out of London that is. I was that desperate to get here. You don't know what it means to me to have someone to confide in about all this."

As Ray began explaining to Karen and Mark how he felt, he soon realised that he had their full attention, which made him feel much better. Mark said that he had heard about this type of manifestation before and suggested that they get together with Madeline, Neil and all the others as soon as possible.

"Well I do hope to find out some more when I meet Neil for lunch." Ray replied hopefully. Karen leant over Ray, kissed his forehead and squeezed his shoulder reassuringly.

"It'll be alright Ray. I'm sure of that, but there may be a little way to go before this business is brought to a conclusion."

"With her interest in Egyptology, Karen is no stranger to the afterlife and all its mysteries," added Mark. "We are right with you on this one Ray and together we can sort it out. Just try not to let it worry you too much in the meantime."

"I do hope you're right," replied Ray, "I don't know how much more of this I can take, especially if it gets any worse."

It seemed an age to Ray before his lunch with Neil finally came around, as he was so eager to meet him again and to tell him how his life had changed since his recent visit to Ivy Cottage. The morning seemed to drag, but soon enough it was one o'clock and he was back in the oldest wine bar in town. With its

Dickensian atmosphere, wood-panelled walls, well-worn heavy wooden tables bearing the patina of age, high-backed seats and bare floorboards, it always felt as though this place could not really have changed too much in the three hundred years of its existence. In fact, the manager once told Ray that back in the 17th Century, the merchants would do their deals here whilst smoking their clay churchwarden pipes, to which the yellow-brown colour of the ceiling bore witness. As he sat and recalled the many happy times he and Neil had spent here in the past, he idly watched figures drifting past the obscure glass of the bow-fronted window and wondered whether his friend would be much longer. He had already ordered lunch, remembering that Neil had a passion for the poached salmon and watercress sandwiches, which was their speciality, whilst his own favourite was their lamb and mint sauce sandwiches, or 'lambwiches' as he used to call them.

Just then, a familiar figure passed the window, the door swung open and Neil walked in. He was dressed in a smart pinstripe suit, white shirt and dark blue paisley patterned tie.

"It must have been an important meeting Neil," Ray began, getting up out of his chair, "you look a million dollars in that suit. Savile Row job, is it?" Neil could not help laughing at Ray's light-hearted teasing.

"It's good to see you Ray, and you're sounding a lot more like your old self than you did on the phone the other day. How are you feeling now?"

"All the better for seeing you old pal, and it's so good to be back in this place. It's really great here, isn't it? It's as good as a tonic just being here."

"And you remembered my favourite salmon sandwiches too, you old bugger. I think they use crème fraiche you know, that's what makes them so special." He sipped the glass of red wine that Ray had placed in front of him. "And this is a remarkably good Claret, Ray. I have to ask what all this is leading up to." Having asked after Madeline and the children and explaining to Neil that Sam seemed to have become a little withdrawn lately, Ray wasted no further time on pleasantries.

"Neil, I am well aware that you can get a little frustrated on the subject of the paranormal, and the two of us have had some laughs scaring the girls with ghost stories in the past, because we always saw such things as a lot of nonsense anyway. Now, suppose I told you that I underwent a psychic experience at your house on Saturday evening. What would you say to that?" Ray asked in a very serious tone, which made Neil feel a little uncomfortable after the good humour of their meeting up to this point.

"Carry on Ray, I'm listening." Neil replied, with rather more interest than his companion was expecting. It immediately occurred to Ray that perhaps this conversation would be less difficult than he expected. He therefore began to warm to his theme now that he was sure that Neil would not ridicule his experiences, but actually be interested in what he had to say.

"You remember when that cold draught nearly blew the candles out and young David came downstairs crying because he was having a nightmare?" Ray continued. "Well, at the precise moment the draught came through the room, I saw a vision. There was an olive-skinned woman, middle-aged with greying hair and green eyes. And she was dressed all in white." Neil took a gulp of his wine and looked very thoughtful. "Don't say anything yet, Neil. Just listen to this first." Ray instructed.

"OK," said Neil calmly, "the floor is all yours. Tell me when I can join in," he smiled warmly at his old friend, "no I mean it, Ray. I really am interested."

"Neil, this vision has plagued me ever since. I keep seeing this woman's face when I least expect it and it's getting stronger and more frequent now. What's more, there's something deeply disturbing about it. It's as though…." He paused, trying to gauge Neil's reaction before continuing, "…it's as though she's trying to tell me something."

"How do you know that this vision, as you call it, wasn't the result of having a few glasses of wine combined with the tales of the supernatural we were telling earlier?" Neil ventured.

"No Neil, this was real!" Ray cut in.

"But Ray, how can you be so sure about this? You have always been just as sceptical as I have in the past, so why the sudden change of heart? Are you sure you haven't been overworking and perhaps taking too many trips to the Far East recently."

"Neil, you have to help me with this. I haven't even been able to mention this to Sam yet. We had a bit of a disagreement and she has been rather distant ever since. I don't know what's wrong with her." He sounded more worried now than Neil could ever remember. Ray was always the one with his feet planted firmly on the ground, nothing ever ruffled him.

"Look Ray, I don't know if this helps at all, but something odd happened to me on Saturday night as well and I am still trying to come to terms with it. It isn't quite the same as what you're describing, but still a little worrying and I really do feel that I need to give it some more thought before talking about it to anybody else. Do you mind, old son? Perhaps we can meet up again soon. Why don't you bring Sam over for lunch on Sunday when we'll have more time to talk?"

"Thanks Neil, I would appreciate that. I'll speak to Sam and give you a call." Ray felt reassured that Neil was at least listening to him and wondered what Neil had been subjected to himself, although he knew better than to push his friend on the subject if he was not yet ready to talk.

"Now then, I think we could manage another bottle of Claret, don't you?" Neil suggested on a more definite note. "I think we both deserve it."

When Ray mentioned visiting Madeline and Neil again to Sam, he was surprised how quickly she jumped at the idea. She even asked whether they could go sooner but he explained that they would have to wait until the weekend, as Neil was very busy on a new project, following the meeting that took him to London on the day they met up for lunch. It was only then that Ray realised that he completely forgot to ask Neil about his new project. He would make a mental note to take an interest in his friend's work and to find out more about it on Sunday.

Neil made his way quietly downstairs, having just read the children their bedtime stories. He wandered into his study, sat down at the desk, pushed his back into the chair and stretched. It had been a long day at the office and now he needed to sort through the pile of letters on his desk in order to keep abreast of the latest developments. He had recently agreed to manage a new project and this was putting him under some pressure, as there was a very tight deadline to meet. Although the meeting with the NASA officials in Florida was two months away, he knew that the main deliverables would not be achievable without some extra resource and he therefore began to formulate a plan to ensure that he would get what he needed in enough time for it to make the difference between success and failure. He would present the plan at next week's Executive Management meeting and underline the necessity for more resources if the company really wanted to keep this high profile project alive. He knew deep down that this contract was so important to them that they would provide him with whatever he required, but he also knew that they always made him work hard to get what he needed from them. He was deep in thought and did not notice when Madeline entered the study.

"Can I get you anything darling?" she said wandering over to him. She stood behind his chair and wrapped her arms around his shoulders.

"Oh, a small gin and tonic would be great, thanks. Why don't you join me in one?"

"It certainly sounds appealing. I'm sure I could be tempted." Madeline went off to the dining room to prepare the drinks. Moments later, carefully balancing two glasses, she was on her way back to the study when she stopped in her tracks and cocked her ear towards the stairs. She was not imagining the cries of a child, this time it was actually coming from upstairs. Madeline carried on into the study and placed the two glasses on the desk.

"I won't be a minute, just a quick check on the children. I though I heard Sarah stirring."

"OK, shout if you need a hand" said Neil as he reached for his drink.

Madeline climbed the stairs slowly and carefully, she knew exactly where the old stairs creaked and avoided putting any pressure there. When she got closer to the top of the stairs, she could clearly hear a low sniffling sound coming from Sarah's room. The children went to bed about an hour before, so Madeline wondered whether Sarah might have a tummy ache or perhaps need a drink. She carefully pushed the door open and quietly tiptoed into the room, lit only by a small night-light. In the half-light that it produced she noticed that Sarah's blankets were lying on the floor and, thinking that she must be feeling cold, picked them up and threw them over her daughter and prepared to tuck her in snugly.

"Sarah?" Madeline jumped back in horror. "Oh my God, Sarah!" she yelled. "What's happened to...?" As Madeline backed away in fear, she looked at the young girl lying on the bed, her dark hair neatly tied behind her head, her body enrobed in a long white gown and her eyes staring in terror as tears rolled down her cheeks. "Why are you here? What have you done to my Sarah?" Madeline yelled hysterically at the unfamiliar figure lying on Sarah's bed. As she stepped backwards in confusion, a pair of arms engulfed her tightly from behind, but as she struggled and screamed, they spun her around. Tears blurred her sight, she felt confused, but soon realised that it was Neil. She buried her head deep in his chest and sobbed.

"What's happening, Neil, where's Sarah?"

"It's alright Madeline, Sarah's fine," Neil reassured her as he coaxed her to turn back to the bed with him. "Look." Sarah was lying there fast asleep. She only needed her blankets tucked in to keep her snug and warm. Madeline's hands trembled as she gently stroked a few wisps of hair on her daughter's forehead; she then leant over and kissed Sarah's brow.

Sunday morning dawned bright and sunny, enabling Ray and Sam to enjoy an invigorating drive northwards through the Essex countryside with the convertible's hood folded down, which they did at every opportunity. At Sam's request, they stopped briefly at the beautiful little village of Finchingfield to enjoy the well-known view of the village green and the river and to feed the ever-hungry ducks by the roadside. They each had their own reasons for wanting to go back to Madeline and Neil's cottage so soon after their last visit, although neither was aware of the other's burning need to do so.

As the Austin-Healey turned in through the open gates of Ivy Cottage and the gravel crunched under the car's tyres, Ray could already see the invitingly open front door. He never tired of the beauty of this perfect little hideaway in one of the most picturesque corners of North Essex. As the car swung round to the right of the porch, Sam's spirits lifted as she saw Neil leathering off his car. He waved Ray on to park next to him now that he was finished brandishing the hose. Sam felt a mixture of emotions welling up inside her and she told herself that Neil would be kind and understanding. She also hoped that this meeting would provide her with the means to tell Ray what she so desperately needed to tell him. Until now, she felt unable to broach the subject, as she could not be sure if Neil had shared in her terrifying adventure. Neither did she know whether she was alone in having experienced a strange occurrence in this very house a week ago. As they got out of the car, Madeline called to them from the front door, having come straight from the kitchen where she had been preparing the Sunday roast. She dried her hands and called out to them.

"How lovely to see you again so soon Sam," she exclaimed, throwing her arms around the young model and giving her a warm hug. "Oh, do excuse the tea towel, I was just preparing lunch."

"As ever, Maddy, busy in the kitchen; and long may it be that way, eh Neil?" Ray laughed. It felt good to be back again so soon. He hugged Madeline and gave her a big squelchy kiss and a bear hug, as was his custom.

"Come on inside folks," said Neil, leading the way towards the front door, "the kids were out in the orchard, but I daresay they will have heard your car turning up, Ray."

"How are my little angels"? Ray enquired.

"Oh they are just fine." Madeline replied. "I'm sure they'll be in soon."

"No more bad nights or re-occurring dreams for young David then"?

"No, he appears to have forgotten all about his nightmare. You know how it is with kids. They seem to have so much to occupy their minds at that age. They are far more resilient than us adults."

Neil ushered his guests into the living room, which always seemed so bright and airy with its lovely view across the back lawn towards the orchard, whilst Madeline prepared some coffee. Ray could see the children playing in the orchard and asked Madeline not to call them in yet as they were obviously having far more fun out there than they were likely to have with a group of stuffy old adults. Besides, he had something important to say which was not for the children's ears.

Ray took a sip of his coffee and nodded appreciatively at Madeline who smiled back indulgently. "Well," he began, "I am assuming that I was not the only one to have had some sort of spiritual experience last Saturday at dinner in this very house. In fact I already know that Karen and Mark did." Madeline quickly confirmed that Julian had intimated to her that he and Caroline shared almost identical experiences that evening too.

"Yes, the very same thing happened to Neil and me." Sam piped up turning to look at Neil for confirmation, but Neil simply stared at the ground and nodded thoughtfully. Ray looked shocked for a moment but then the realisation hit him that Sam's recent moodiness must have been a direct result of her having to harbour this secret. She too had an experience that she could neither understand nor discuss with him. Ray felt a little uneasy, glancing first at Sam and then at Madeline, because he knew that Sam would not readily understand why Neil was holding back. Knowing her as well as he did however, he was well aware that this would simply strengthen her resolve to orchestrate a situation in which they *would* discuss it on their own. At that moment, Sam took the opportunity to excuse herself and go to 'powder her nose'.

"Will she be alright, Ray?" asked Madeline solicitously.

"Yes, I'm sure she will, Maddy. I think we have both just realised that we are actually in the same boat, so to speak, and I for one feel a bit stupid for not realising it before. It was selfish of me to be so concerned with my own troubles that I didn't pay enough attention to what might be worrying Sam." Madeline put a consoling hand on Ray's arm.

"Poor old Ray, you do seem to be going through it at the moment don't you, but I'm sure everything will work out alright."

"Excuse me folks," said Neil, clearing his throat to gain their attention, "I just need to pop outside for a moment for some fresh air. Besides, Sam hasn't seen the garden or the orchard yet, so she might want to join me."

Sam felt better for having freshened up and, in the time it took her to do so, she formulated a plan to corner Neil and get some answers from him. She also felt compassion for Ray now that she knew that he was carrying a similar burden. As she closed the cloakroom door behind her to make her way back to the living room, a calm, familiar voice behind her interrupted her thoughts, causing her to spin round.

"Neil! You made me jump."

"I'm sorry Sam; I didn't mean to startle you. Do you fancy a chat somewhere, in the garden perhaps?"

"Yes please Neil, I would love that." Whether he realised it or not Neil had just made things considerably easier for her.

"What did you tell the others?" she asked him.

"Oh, I said I needed some air and would perhaps show you around the garden. Would you care for a stroll in the garden, Sam?" Neil ventured.

"Indeed I would!" Sam replied enthusiastically.

"Come on then. If we go through the front door and round the side of the cottage, you will be able to see more of the garden and perhaps we'll catch the kids on their way in. They must be very hungry by now. They've been playing out in the orchard for ages."

"That sounds great, Neil. I would love to see David and Sarah. They were in bed the last time I came, except when they wandered downstairs rather sleepily one after the other."

Ray poured another cup of coffee for Madeline, whilst telling her that he was now quite sure that Neil and Sam had actually shared a common experience.

"After all, Maddy," he began, "her comment to Neil just now suggests that they did share an experience, and he did nod, didn't he? Why else would she not want to talk about it before coming back here?"

"From what I can make out from Julian, he and Caroline visited the same place but at different times but, as you say, Sam and Neil seem to have been to, wherever it was they went, together. It's all very odd, isn't it?" As they gazed out through the wide, leaded-light rear window and watched Sam and Neil wandering across the garden towards the orchard, they agreed that it would be good for Neil if Sam could manage to break down his defences and perhaps open up his mind a little. Neil was sometimes a bit too rational in his approach to things and Madeline, being the more creative of the two, sometimes felt frustrated that he seemed unable to join in her flights of fancy. She sometimes felt quite exasperated by his assurances that there is a logical explanation for everything. Well, how would he explain this away when all eight of them were inextricably involved in this paranormal web? He would have some serious thinking to do.

"I'm sure Neil has told you about the visions I've been having, Maddy and, to tell you the truth, they are getting more frequent." Ray continued. "I don't want to go to the doctor about it in case he wants to send me to a shrink and I don't think I'm going mad."

"Of course you're not Ray, but we do need to try and sort this out as soon as we can. I know I would if it happened to me" she confided.

"Although I know about Karen and Mark's story, and you've told me what Julian said Maddy, I still can't get a clear picture in my head about all this or where it might be leading." Ray seemed troubled that it made no real sense to him. "I don't think I told you that Karen called me, did I?" he continued. "She invited me to her flat and took the opportunity to tell me about her experience and so did Mark as he was there too. Karen had a close encounter with a Bristol Fighter. Now they really were magnificent machines, Maddy. I once saw one in an aircraft museum in Bedfordshire and the mechanic there reckoned it was his favourite exhibit, so beautifully made, and by very skilled craftsmen. It was powered by an advanced V-12 engine; can you believe that, back in 1917 or so?"

"But Ray," said Madeline, interrupting him to draw him back to the serious point of their discussion, "you've had such a rough time since that evening. How are things going with you now?"

"Well, although the images I get are very vivid, I don't really feel frightened or threatened by them at all. As I was saying to Neil, it is as though this woman is trying to tell me something or wants me to do something, but I just don't know what." Ray explained.

"You know," Madeline began "in a perverse sort of way I felt rather left out when you all started talking about these paranormal happenings. I wondered if there was a reason for my exclusion and I was unsure whether I should feel disappointed or glad. Now I realise that I should have been content with things being the way they were because I have now been through two very disturbing incidents myself and, to tell you the truth, I wish I hadn't."

"I'm sorry Maddy, I didn't realise that...please share them with me?"

"Well, first I heard what I thought was laughter out in the orchard early one morning, it turned out to be someone sobbing...a child I think but I couldn't find anyone. Then on another occasion, I heard sobbing, coming from Sarah's room and when I went in, her blankets were all over the floor. I picked them up to throw them back over her and got the fright of my life."

"What happened, Maddy?"

"It wasn't Sarah in her bed but another girl. She stared back at me, tears rolling down her cheeks and terror in her eyes. She was dressed in a long white gown and she was sobbing...oh Ray, it was really horrible!"

"Who was she, Maddy – did you know her?"

"No Ray, I don't think so, but I do know I was terrified for a moment. Then Neil came in to see what all the fuss was about and folded his arms around me and then I seemed to wake up from that ghastly nightmare! He said Sarah was fine and pointed to the bed where she was still fast asleep – there was no more sign of the unknown girl at all."

"Does Neil have any idea who the girl might have been?"

"I am sure he was just as surprised as I was, although to be honest, I'm not sure if he actually saw what I did? He was too involved in trying to calm me down. He seemed anxious, but appeared quick to dismiss the whole affair when I tried to raise the subject later. I am quite sure now that there is some connection with what he and Sam saw."

"I must ask Sam if she recognises anyone with that description," said Ray thoughtfully. He was quite sure that Madeline was right about the young girl but why should she be disturbing Madeline?

A crashing and banging at the back door heralded the entrance of two small, dirty children who had been busily collecting windfall apples and arguing who collected the most. "Hi Uncle Ray" they chorused as they ran into the living room, "Hi to you too! What have you been up to, scrumping your Dad's apples, I'll bet."

"Yes, and we saw your girlfriend in the garden with Daddy" David gabbled excitedly. "She's really lovely, Uncle Ray" enthused Sarah, "I hope I grow up to be as beautiful as her."

"I am quite sure you will, my little princess." Ray assured her.

"Now go upstairs and get washed the pair of you or you won't be getting any lunch." Madeline threatened and out they ran, pushing and shoving to be first through the door. "Such high spirits" Ray laughed, "I bet there's never a dull moment with those two around."

Madeline was amused to see Sam obviously warming to her subject, waving her arms about and gesticulating to make her point. Neil had only mentioned his experience to Madeline very briefly but now, after talking to Ray, she realised that Neil needed to speak to Sam first as it appeared that the two of them somehow shared their experience. It was also clear to her that the time the two of them spent together in the garden would be extremely valuable to them both, especially as she felt quite confident that nothing was going on between them. Madeline felt sorry for her husband now having to stand his ground against this tempestuous and determined young redhead. His defence of logic would cut no ice with her!

The soft green grass beneath her feet reminded Sam of the evening their spirits wandered off together from the dining room to the tropics. She was making some headway with Neil and he was now speaking more openly about what they had been through together as they compared notes.

"I'm sorry I scratched you," she said "I was so scared I didn't know what I was doing. Did you show your wounds to Madeline?"

"No, and she hasn't mentioned it either. She probably didn't even notice. It was only a scratch anyway and it soon healed." Neil seemed dismissive of his wounds.

"Neil, I haven't been able to talk to Ray because I was so scared that it was all in my mind and that you might say you didn't know what I as talking about. Have you spoken to Madeline about it at all?"

"No, we haven't really spoken about it very much because, to tell you the truth, I have also been trying to come to terms with what happened. I no longer seem to know what's true and what isn't." They stopped walking for a moment for Sam to enjoy the scent of a large red rose whilst she gathered her thoughts, then she suddenly turned to Neil and asked with a note of desperation in her voice,

"Neil, do you think it will happen again? I don't know if I could survive another such harrowing experience. I'm glad you were there." she added softly, taking Neil's hand in hers. "What do we do now?"

"I believe that's why Ray has got us all together. Shall we go in and join the others?" he replied, carefully freeing his hand before they came back into view of the cottage windows.

Neil was pleased to rejoin Madeline and Ray and still held out some hope that there might be a simple and rational explanation for all that had happened to them. Madeline had just percolated some more coffee. Ray poured another cup for Sam and one for Neil, who was now looking a little calmer.

"Maddy and I were just discussing how we might resolve this situation and I believe she's got an idea worth trying. She thinks we should call a Medium in to try to make contact with the woman who keeps plaguing me and perhaps we might also gain some understanding of these dreams."

"No Ray!" Neil firmly rebuked his friend. "That sort of thing is for novels and films, not real life. There is no place for Spiritualism in modern life and besides, it has been disproved and disgraced repeatedly. These people are charlatans. I'm sorry, Madeline, I know it was your idea but you know my views on the subject." Madeline slowly sipped her drink and considered her husband's words for a moment.

"I don't think this is a case of who is right and who is wrong, Neil. We have a situation here that is beyond our understanding and it doesn't seem as though it will just go away. I think we should act now while it's still as fresh in our minds as if it were yesterday."

"Yes, I agree we should act my dear but, a *medium*?"

"Why not, do you have a better idea, Neil?"

"Perhaps we all just need to go and see a psychiatrist and have done with it." Neil countered with a mixture of sarcasm and real concern, which Madeline immediately registered.

"I am sure none of us needs that kind of help Neil, but I do suggest we get professional help of some kind." Madeline replied calmly.

"Do you mean a priest?" asked Ray, "to perform some kind of exorcism?"

"But there is nothing wrong with the cottage!" Neil interrupted. "We've never experienced anything strange like this before and we've given plenty of dinner parties, as you well know because you were present at most of them."

"That's the very reason why we need to establish how this particular evening was different," Madeline stressed "and I'm not suggesting that we need a priest to exorcise Ray's ghost or to perform any sort of blessing of the house to cleanse it of evil spirits or anything of that sort. Perhaps we should arrange for a Medium to be present, invite the same people to attend and have them all sitting exactly where they sat on the evening when it all happened."

"Please Neil." Sam pleaded. Neil felt cornered by their enthusiasm and looked first at Madeline and then at Ray, as though he needed their approbation, even though it was their idea in the first place. He could see that there was much more to Sam than just a pretty face. He was beginning to see that she had hidden depths and now realised why his old friend was so attracted to her. She was a most resourceful girl and knew how to get her own way and he recalled Ray telling him 'what Sam wants, Sam gets'. Madeline and Ray were both looking at him and gently nodding as if almost willing him to agree.

"It seems as though I'm outvoted and you are all so keen on this idea, I suppose we should give it a go. But don't get upset if I laugh at the ridiculous nature of the proceedings."

"We won't!" They all agreed, not quite believing their ears.

"But one condition" Neil continued, "the children must not be in the house when this *person* comes."

"I totally agree, darling." Madeline said quickly seizing on Neil's acquiescence. "That sounds brilliant Maddy." Ray trumpeted, in a tone that he hadn't used since the manifestation.

"Thank you so much Neil." Sam was almost purring again.

Ray was quick to ask everyone present to consult his or her diaries so that Madeline could come up with a date for the Medium to attend as quickly as possible.

"What astonishes me though Neil, and I'll have to get to the bottom of this one," Ray continued "is that Maddy had nothing to report along the same lines as you or any of the others. But then I suppose you wouldn't have either if you hadn't held Sam's hand at that precise moment." Ray said excitedly.

"I really have no idea." Neil replied, still deep in thought. With each new revelation, Ray became more animated. It was as though he could see things more clearly since returning to Ivy Cottage and some parts of the jigsaw were beginning to fit into place. If Neil's adventure with Sam only happened because he had taken hold of her hand, why was it that he and Madeline were not supposed to have been included in these occurrences? Why was the apparition for his eyes only? He wondered if there was any pattern or sense to it all, or whether it was just meant to happen that way for some reason that was simply not yet apparent. His mind started racing as he considered the variables, when it occurred to him that he was perhaps being a little scientific in his approach to this problem. After all, was he not a party to the request that Neil should broaden his mind? He instinctively knew that the answer to this matter would not be scientific, logical or at all what he expected. However, he did not know what to expect, but he was now beginning to find it all very exciting since returning to the scene of the manifestation. Perhaps there was something still in the air here, but what?

Whatever it was, Ray would not allow this new thread of mystery to interfere with lunch. The aroma of roast beef was already commanding his attention and he began to feel very hungry.

"By the way Neil," Ray began, "I've been meaning to ask you how you are getting on with that project of yours but I got so wrapped up in this damn mystery that I keep forgetting."

"OK then Ray, I'll tell you about it over lunch."

Having compared diaries, Madeline confirmed that she would get in touch with a colleague who knew of a reputable Medium and would then call Ray within a couple of days to firm up on a date. Madeline always believed in doing things properly and therefore did exactly as she promised later that Sunday afternoon after Sam and Ray left. She therefore called Ray a couple of days later to agree the date that she had tentatively arranged with the Medium who had pointed out that they should proceed as soon as possible, that is to say, while the trail was still hot. She also told Ray that she would get in touch with the others to tell them the arrangements for the following Friday, suggesting 7.30pm for an 8.00pm start.

"That's excellent, Maddy," Ray boomed "but unfortunately Sam won't be able to make it. She has a long-standing arrangement with one of the fashion catalogues to do some modelling for them in Madrid. She is going to be over there for several days and, to be honest; she was a little apprehensive about what might happen, as she has never been to a séance before. Do you think it will matter if she's not there?"

"No Ray, that's fine. I have already asked the Medium, 'Madame Rosina', if it would be a problem if we couldn't all make it and she said it's more important to have the séance as soon as possible, than to have everyone present. She also mentioned that we should have no more than eight people at the séance and that is exactly the number that was at the dinner party. So, although Sam can't make it, with Madame Rosina we'll still have eight people, so it will work out just right."

"Thank God for that." Ray sounded relieved. He was a little surprised at his own initial reaction and wondered why he felt as though his life depended on it. "Great, that's settled then. I look forward to seeing you again on Friday. Oh, and Maddy, thanks for all your help in organising this and keeping Neil sweet."

"No problem Ray. For you, my dear - anything! I think it's all rather exciting and I can't wait to see what happens. Anyway, I look forward to seeing you on Friday at seven-thirty then, and give my love to Sam," said Madeline "bye now."

Madeline went upstairs to give Neil a hand with the nightly ritual of putting the children to bed. Earlier on Neil had been doing battle with his son using David's new toy soldiers, but it had now moved on to battleships and Madeline could hear lots of splashes in the bathroom as she passed by on her way to Sarah's bedroom. 'Boys will be boys' she mused as she listened idly to the guttural sounds of war emanating from the throats of father and son.

Sarah was sitting up in bed waiting for her bedtime story and, as Madeline came into the room, she cuddled her teddy and asked if he could choose the story for tonight?

"Of course darling." said Madeline, settling herself at the head of Sarah's bed. Sarah put her lips to her mother's ear, whispered teddy's choice, settled herself down and made sure teddy was comfortable too. Then Madeline began to read. About half an hour later, as she slowly closed Sarah's door behind her she guessed that Neil would already have David tucked up in bed, so she went in to see him. Neil was about halfway through the story selected for this evening's reading, but as David was still wide-awake, Madeline took the opportunity to tell him that Uncle Ray's sister Dorothy had invited Sarah and him to spend the weekend on her farm near Hertford. He was very excited when she told him that they would be able to help with milking the cows, feeding the animals and perhaps even have a ride on a pony. Auntie Dorothy would collect them both on Friday morning.

Caroline was quick to confirm her attendance at the séance and amused Madeline with her dithering about what she should wear and how Julian said she was being absurd and then threatened to turn up dressed like a gypsy with a gold earring and brightly coloured silk shirt and headscarf. Although Julian did not share Neil's very rational view of life, he did share his views about clairvoyance and could not help seeing the funny side of what they were planning. Caroline had made him swear to behave but she felt bound to admit that she felt herself unable to guarantee his behaviour, and Madeline knew exactly what she meant by that.

Karen and Mark also wasted no time in confirming that they would be free on the Friday and could therefore also attend. Karen could scarcely wait to experience her first séance and told Madeline that the days could not pass quickly enough for her. Mark was always keen to experience something different but admitted to being a little apprehensive on this occasion because, not only was it to be for a pre-determined reason, but also as it was one that followed on from some pretty strange happenings in the very room where they were due to hold the séance. Furthermore, his unexpected meeting with Madeline had stirred some very sweet memories and felt unable to quell the desire to see her again.

CHAPTER IV –
The Séance

Madeline and Neil were amazed how quickly the next five days went by and Madame Rosina's visit was already upon them. As agreed in her preliminary discussions with Madeline, she needed to be at Ivy Cottage about an hour before the séance was due to begin in order to *'feel the atmosphere'*, so Madeline spent much of the day engaged in her usual preparations. Ray's sister, Dorothy arrived in the morning to collect the children, who were by this time almost uncontrollable at the prospect of spending some time with the ponies and were fascinated at the possibility of being allowed to milk the cows. The children finally departed amidst great excitement with much hugging and kissing and then frantic waves from the back window of Dorothy's Land Rover as it pulled out through the gates. Now that the children were gone, some semblance of peace descended upon Ivy Cottage once more, allowing Madeline to get on with the serious business of preparing for visitors.

As the séance was to take place around the table in the dining room, she decided to spread the refreshments out in the sitting room where there would be sufficient chairs for her guests. This would also enable Madame Rosina to be on her own for a little while before the séance began, as she requested. Madeline therefore busied herself laying out a light 'finger' buffet on the sideboard. With the large coffee table in front of the ingle-nook fireplace and the little nest of tables, which she always kept near the back window, there would be ample places for them to rest their plates, cups and glasses.

At precisely seven o'clock, an old pre-war Daimler glided up the drive and came to a halt directly in front of the porch. Neil heard the car's tyres on the gravel and, as he glanced out from an upstairs window, he noticed that the driver had carefully positioned the rear passenger door of the car as close to the porch as possible. A tall, thin, balding man, dressed in black, alighted from the driver's door and walked with a slow and deliberate gait around the back of the car to the passenger door nearest to the porch. He opened the door slowly and precisely and assisted a rather large, rotund woman to ease herself out of the car. As she stepped clear, the release of her weight from the car's suspension on that side caused the car to rock back and forth until it found its equilibrium.

By this time, a broad grin was spreading across Neil's face as the thought struck him that the man resembled a cross between a butler and a stork with his slow deliberate movements and the woman fleetingly reminded him of a pantomime dame. The woman rested her hand on the thin man's arm and wobbled along as he guided her around to the boot. He proceeded to open the boot in an imperious manner to reveal a large black leather bag and a crooked walking stick. He handed the latter to the fat woman who then began to hobble towards the front door of the cottage whilst he deposited the bag on the doorstep. Without further ado or any word to the woman, he then walked back to the car, climbed in and slowly moved off. This reminded Neil of a scene from one of those black and white 'whodunit' films and just kept on grinning from ear to ear.

He rushed downstairs to find Madeline, who was still so busy with last-minute details that she was quite unaware of the scene unfolding outside her own front door.

"She's here!" he called out and Madeline, on hearing this, made her way swiftly into the hallway, where she met her husband who was hurrying downstairs.

"Great. She's on time." Madeline said as she stood by the front door, ready to greet Madame Rosina. Neil stood behind her, trying hard to stifle the grin, which the paradox of the thin man and the fat woman had planted firmly on his face when he witnessed the amusing spectacle outside the front door just a few moments before.

Madeline opened the front door and watched with a mixture of surprise and amusement as Madame Rosina hobbled and wobbled up the step and across the threshold into the hall. She was carrying a great deal of weight and most certainly needed her stick to help with the weight distribution at every breathless step. Having finally made the treacherous ascent of the front step, she stopped, huffing and puffing with the exertion and then smiled at her hosts for the evening. Madeline's immediate impression was that, despite her obesity, Madame Rosina had a lovely, warm smile and would probably be quite attractive if she could only shed a few stones. Greeting her guest with a warm handshake, Madeline introduced Neil, who shook her hand firmly and enquired as to her journey. She smiled and confirmed that her journey was without incident.

It struck Neil that, for a woman of her enormous size, their guest's voice was quite soft and velvety, although there was an air of confidence about her. The pleasant aroma of lavender wafted in as she entered the house and Neil could not help thinking that this must be to counter any odour of sweat, which he assumed might be a problem for someone of her portly build. The few steps from the car to the front door rendered her breathless and there were tiny beads of sweat on her forehead from the exertion.

Even on this quite chilly October evening, she was dressed in light flowery cottons with plenty of frills and laces and Madeline noticed that she had tiny ankles, which probably explained the need for the walking stick. She wore her hair in a bun directly on top of her head and it bobbed up and down comically as she walked across the hall.

"Come this way Madame Rosina, we're so glad you could make it," said Madeline, leading the way to the dining room, "this is where we had our dinner party."

"Yes, I know." replied Madame Rosina in a soft, knowing and almost musical voice. Madeline was just about to show her to one of the comfortable chairs when she made her way straight for the dining table and placed her large black bag on the floor next to it in complete silence. She closed her eyes, took several deep breaths, rested both hands on her walking stick just in front of her and began swaying slightly. Neither Madeline nor Neil moved, they glanced questioningly at each other and waited for her next move, which seemed to take an eternity. Neil thought to himself 'Oh my God, please don't faint. I would need to send for help to get you back on your feet again.' Madeline recalled that Madame Rosina had specified that she would need some time *'to prepare'* before the others arrived. Moments later, she opened her eyes and slowly wandered over to the sideboard near to the front window, hobbled slowly along its length and paused at the wooden picture frame that held the photograph of Neil's father in his Royal Flying Corps uniform, taken during the First World War. Neil and Madeline were intrigued as she then moved directly to the fireplace and stood by the clock.

It was just after five past seven and the others were not due for at least another twenty-five minutes.

"Is there anything we can help you with?" asked Neil, but still there was silence for a moment or two before she finally spoke.

"I detected strong and positive energy when I entered the house. It's very odd though, I am receiving mixed vibrations now; but only in this room."

"What do you mean?" Neil questioned as Madeline listened with interest.

"Well, the positive energy is strongest in the surrounding atmosphere until I move anywhere near the picture frame or the clock," she said touching the smooth, highly polished contours of the mahogany clock with the tips of her fingers. Then she suddenly jumped back as though stunned by an electric shock. However, she quickly regained her composure and continued.

"What craftsmanship…it's quite exquisite…how did you come by it?" She enquired; her face quite close to it now as she scrutinised it further.

"My father made it over thirty years ago and it always took pride of place on the mantelpiece in my parents' house until just before my mother died last year, when she gave it to me. It has stood on this mantelpiece ever since." Madame Rosina summed up her initial preparations by intimating to Madeline and Neil that she detected negative vibrations from the clock, the dining table and the picture frame and if all went well she hoped to get some explanations for them very soon. Following these pre-séance discussions, she established that Neil's father Charles, was the carpenter who made all the furniture for his family home many years ago and when he died, Neil's mother Annie having given her son a few of his favourite pieces, including those to which she had so quickly gravitated.

It was just a little after a quarter to eight when Karen and Mark arrived and pulled up next to Ray, who was already on his way to the front door, having arrived literally a few moments before.

"Hi there Ray," Karen called out "wait for us, we'll be right with you." Ray stopped to wait for them and they greeted each other warmly before ringing the doorbell.

"I wonder if she has arrived yet." Ray said apprehensively.

"I certainly hope so. Madeline told me that this Madame Rosina wanted some time to prepare before we arrived, and we are due to start at eight o'clock." Although Mark was quite clearly a little uneasy about what lie ahead, Karen was always hugely excited at the prospect of dabbling with the supernatural and this was no exception.

"The sooner we get through this evening the better and hopefully we will all be more enlightened by then." Mark exclaimed.

"Absolutely!" agreed Ray as Neil opened the front door to welcome the trio of friends. They stepped into the hall, took off their coats and exchanged pleasantries before he ushered them all into the sitting room where Madeline waited to introduce them to Madame Rosina, who was happy to chat to them over a cup of tea. Mark, whose unease made him feel the need for a small snack before the séance, edged discreetly towards the buffet and Madeline wasted no time in appearing by his side to assist him with a run-down of what was on the menu. He still felt the chemistry between them when her hand brushed his arm and she was only making matters worse by being so close to him. Her seductive perfume rekindled memories of the nights they spent together in New York and he wondered if she was deliberately teasing him, or whether she was unaware of the effect that she was having on him, now that she seemed to be so happily married and settled. Karen was already deep in conversation with Ray and her excitement was obvious as she tried to keep him calm before what he was convinced would be an important night in his life.

Julian and Caroline arrived a little later, explaining that there were a few problems with the traffic as usual, but were pleased not to be late for their appointment with the Medium. They joined the others for drinks and some of Madeline's delicious buffet offerings but it was, not surprisingly, Julian who was first to comment on Madame Rosina's size.

"Do you think she hides any conjuring tricks in her underskirts?" he whispered to Caroline.

"This is serious Julian!" came the harsh response from Caroline, albeit under her breath.

"I've been told she has a good reputation. In fact, she is so clairvoyant that she probably picked up every word you just said. So I would just say kind, sweet things from now on if I were you Julian, dear!" She hissed sarcastically.

"Oh, aren't we supposed to tell the truth at these gatherings then, and why are we whispering?" he whispered.

"Because you can't behave yourself, that's why! You're nothing more than a naughty little boy sometimes, Julian! Please try to exercise some control tonight, at least for our friends' sake." Caroline's tone was now somewhat more solicitous as she did not want him to be outrageous simply to wind her up, as she knew he very well could.

"Can you smell lavender, Caroline? Do you suppose she sprinkles that all over us as part of the ritual?"

"Julian, will you shut up?" She snapped. "I don't know what's going to happen any more than you do, so we will just have to wait and see, won't we? And please don't embarrass me in front of our friends any more."

"OK, OK, I'll be a good boy, honest."

Madeline heard the whispering and glimpsed the angry look on Caroline's face.

"Is everything alright, Caroline?" she enquired.

"Yes, fine thanks Madeline, we were just saying how delicious your vol-au-vents are, my dear. Weren't we, Julian?"

"Yes, that's right, we were. They're superb, as ever." Julian quickly agreed, catching on to his wife's little deception.

Madeline, realising that it was fast approaching eight o'clock, indicated that everyone should now move through to the dining room and take their seats at the table. Madame Rosina had already slipped away and was making her way to the chair at the dining table, which was opposite the door and close to the clock. Although he tried very hard not to even think it, Julian wondered how she was ever going to fit on the chair, furthermore, the legs could give way! As if by magic, she descended gracefully onto her chosen chair. Her skirts puffed up with air and then slowly deflated, causing the aroma of lavender to permeate the room once more. Julian and the others could breathe again. Ray sat on Madame Rosina's left with his back to the fireplace, thinking how much he would have preferred to be sitting next to Sam, had she been there. He was missing her very much and already looked forward to telling her about the events of the evening, despite the fact that it had hardly begun yet.

With everyone seated, Madame Rosina asked if she could have the lights lowered, she rested her hands on the table in front of her and began to speak slowly in a low voice.

"I feel a presence…someone entered this house about ten minutes ago…" Julian thought to himself, yes, yes, that's pretty obvious and we're all here, so tell us something we don't already know. Caroline saw the look on his face and from years of practice found his foot immediately with hers and pressed on it discreetly yet firmly with her sharp heel. She knew her husband only too well and realised that he might need some help in taking this matter seriously. Madame Rosina paused and then continued.

"This person is not known to us, but needs our help…" She stopped and bent down to rummage around in her black leather bag and pulled out a large bottle, which she placed on the table, the label read, 'Lavender Water". However, she then swiftly exchanged the bottle for a battered old silver tablespoon, which she placed in the middle of the table. She now spoke with a deep, strong and commanding voice, which made everyone sit up to attention. This voice could not have been more different to the soft, gentle tone she used before.

"Now then, you all have a part to play if we are
to achieve success this evening. Your full co-operation
is required...and I *warn* you, there may be serious
consequences if this ring is broken. I sense we have
a disbeliever amongst us, we are not all in tune...we
will need to get in tune and someone in this room...
someone around this table, does not believe!" At this
point Madeline squeezed Neil's hand tightly and Julian
could not escape Caroline's glare.

"Please take a moment to examine your minds...
and get in tune, we must be as one if we are to get
results. She waited for a few moments and then, raising
her hands above the table, asked them all to join hands.
As they did so, she reverted once more to that deep and
commanding voice.

"Let *not* this ring be broken...whatever you see or
feel, *do not*...break the ring!" Neil glanced at Madeline
who was sitting to his right, where Sam was on the
night of the dinner party, and he nervously cleared his
throat. Madame Rosina was seated on Neil's left and
she held his hand firmly as if she were aware of his
scepticism. Julian sat on the other side of Madeline next
to Caroline, then Mark and Karen. Finally, completing
the ring, Ray sat between Karen and Madame Rosina.

The Medium bowed her head, then without lifting it
again, raised her eyes to examine everyone once more
around the table. She looked from right to left, then to
her right again. Caroline shivered as she could almost
hear Julian saying 'it's safe to cross now'. 'Yes' came a
mutter from Madame Rosina, next she gave them all a
knowing smile and said in her softest voice.

"It's time to begin."

There was silence, the air was still and then a low murmur came from her slightly parted lips. Although it was none too clear, some of the words were easier to pick out than others and she seemed to be saying:

> *"With her head upon ......breast*
> *I..... her..... I...... not rest*
> *...... her spirit,... set free*
> *To join .... in Eternity..."*

The round table began to vibrate gently for a few moments, and then it stopped. All was calm for a few moments and then suddenly the table shook so violently that Neil almost lost his balance as he rocked backwards with surprise. His chair almost toppled over but Madame Rosina was gripping his hand very tightly and so was Madeline on the other side of him. Then the vibrations slowed down and stopped as quickly as they had begun. Madame Rosina spoke again and repeated the same verse as before, but this time they could hear the words far more clearly.

> *"With her head upon my breast*
> *I promised her I should not rest*
> *Until her spirit, we set free*
> *To join me in Eternity"*

Perspiration glistened on her forehead but they remembered her warning and held hands very tightly as they waited with baited breath for whatever might happen next. Ray expected to have endured another vision by now, but nothing came to him. Instead, he found himself thinking about the words that Madame Rosina had uttered. They seemed to be haunting him as though they were familiar to him, but he could not remember where from. However, his thoughts were abruptly interrupted as Madame Rosina started to rock back and forth, back and forth, until he thought his arm would break. Then her body writhed, first in his direction, then in Neil's and she uttered the verse again, but this time louder and clearer than before and her face winced as though she was in great pain. Madeline's grasp tightened on Julian's hand when she noticed that the surface of the table appeared wet and slippery. She looked down at the table and, in horror, saw that it *was* wet, but not with water,…it was *blood!* Small blisters were appearing all over the top of the table and were oozing slowly, soaking her sleeves in blood. Julian looked down at the table, then at Caroline who was trying hard not to retch, whispering to Julian that she was feeling extremely sick. Caroline appeared to have braced herself against the movement, but she was actually stiffening with fear. Mark's eyes grew wide and his face paled, especially when he caught sight of the picture frame on the sideboard because a few drops of blood were oozing from that as well. Karen's expression was a mixture of fear and fascination as she, along with the others, became transfixed by the spectacle unfolding before their eyes.

Ray froze, his mouth wide open with horror, as he stared at the closed door leading to the hall. There she was, approaching from the shadows in the doorway. The woman of his nightmares made her entrance gliding straight through the door and slowly approaching the table right behind Mark. This apparition now fully revealed herself to him and he could see the full length of her body robed in white linen. There it was, that same face with those beautiful deep jade green eyes, long shiny hair and glowing olive skin that he could never forget, because she had haunted him so many, many times. In his agitation, he knew that he must warn Mark that she was right behind him, but he could not find his voice.

She was carrying something in her hands. He could see it now…*it was the clock*! Something was dripping from it….*blood*! He could clearly see now that her robes were blood stained and her lips were moving, miming the verse that Madame Rosina had recited, and she kept on reciting it. Madame Rosina fell into a deep trance, her eyes rolled back, so that only the whites were visible in the dimly lit room, her head flopped, her mouth opened and she recited the same verse again:

> *"With her head upon my breast*
> *I promised her I should not rest*
> *Until her spirit, we set free*
> *To join me in Eternity………….."*

The hands of the clock were turning, moving very fast anti-clockwise and occasionally Ray could hear a deep, sonorous chime as the clock hands spun around wildly. The table shook again; the woman carried the clock with the blood dripping from it towards Ray. The table and the picture frame were bleeding and shaking too. Ray felt her unblinking green eyes burning into him and they did not flicker even once as she approached him. He prayed hard for her to turn around and go back wherever she came from but she just kept on coming towards him.

"What do you want of me?" he muttered, shaking with fear, sweat now streaming down his temples. Tears were beginning to cloud his vision and he desperately wanted to wake up from this nightmare, but to no avail. Madame Rosina's warning rang through his head 'Let *not* this ring be broken, whatever you see or feel, *do… not*…break the ring!' Panic welled up in his chest and he thought he was going to die as she came closer and closer to him.

"I *must* stop her," he wailed, trying desperately to get his hand away from Madame Rosina's tight grip, but in the struggle, he managed to free his other hand from Karen's grasp and thrust it out in front of him to push the apparition aside. His effort was utterly pointless. She just walked straight through him, still carrying the clock. Then she was gone. She seemed to have simply melted through the wall above the fireplace and, as Ray turned round, he was amazed to see that the clock was still standing on the mantelpiece in its usual place, as though nothing had happened.

He could hardly believe that nobody tried to help him, not even looked in his direction, although Karen did instantly grab his hand again and held on firmly. He assumed that they were themselves so frightened by what was going on that they were unable to help him. He was quite unaware that his companions could not see the vision, which terrified him so, and that they were only able to hear the message through Madame Rosina. Ray felt hot and sweaty and longed to wipe his brow with his handkerchief, but he knew he must wait. He dare not risk breaking the ring again. Eventually, Madame Rosina spoke once more,

"I see great seas, a wide ocean…I see a long journey ahead," she said now in a quieter and more restrained voice. Despite all the shaking and vibrating from the table underneath it, the silver spoon, now spotted with blood, remained exactly where Madame Rosina had originally placed it. Then it began to spin, slowly at first, then faster and faster until it gathered great speed. It continued to spin for another three or four seconds and then gradually slowed down until it finally stopped.

"Take heed, there is grave danger ahead," Madame Rosina warned again in her deep commanding voice. Then in a higher pitched voice, "Free me...Free my spirit", then again came the deeper, more strident tone. "You will know what to do when the time comes...then you must act! If ever you need help, just ask and I will guide you."

Madame Rosina exhaled and slowly lifted her head and straightened up, she opened her eyes and then closed them again. Julian looked at Neil who was thinking that the proceedings must surely now be drawing to a close and that the séance must soon be over. Yet Madame Rosina did not relax her grip of Neil and Ray's hands and so the others, guided by her, remained locked in the ring, but more importantly, she had not yet given the command. They sat still and silent as they watched her every move.

Finally, she opened her eyes and looked down at the spoon. Then she spoke again. "Prepare to travel to a distant land where you will meet both friend and foe." She had now come to the end of the séance and held both Neil's and Ray's hands in full view of everyone around the table. She gave them all her knowing look again followed by that captivating smile, just as she did at the beginning of the séance. She then released her grip on Neil and Ray's hands but nobody moved for a moment, except Madame Rosina herself, who rummaged through her black leather bag again. Seconds later, she produced her large bottle of 'Lavender Water' and a handkerchief. As everyone watched, entranced, she dabbed a little on her forehead and some on her wrists and informed Mark, as he was nearest to the door, that she no longer needed the lights to remain dimmed.

Caroline looked at Madeline and then at the table and was amazed to see that there was no longer any trace of the blood which gave her such a shock a little earlier on. Madeline looked first at her sleeves, and then at the surface of the table and was quite confused when she saw that there was no sign of the blood which she knew was there just a short while ago. Her sleeves were clean and the surface of the table was the usual smooth, beautifully polished reddish mahogany that it had always been.

Madame Rosina rested her hands on the arms of her chair, and with a supreme effort managed to rise up from the table. Neil stood up too, but was still in quite a daze.

"Would you care for a glass of water?" he asked Madame Rosina quietly.

"Yes, indeed I would, thank you." she replied with a nod. Neil crossed hesitantly to the sideboard, stared at the photograph of his father and its highly polished picture frame and then poured the glass of water. As he walked back to the table and handed it to her, he could not help noticing how exhausted she looked. He instinctively poured another glass for Madeline who took it from him silently and with a wan smile. She could see that her husband was just as shaken by the experience, as she was herself. Karen rose from the table and crouched down next to Mark's chair. He slowly put his arm around her shoulder and stroked her hair lovingly. Neither spoke. Julian was standing behind Caroline's chair now with his hands resting gently on her shoulders. For once in his life, he was lost for words. Ray felt the overwhelming need to go and wash the perspiration from his face and then get himself a stiff drink.

CHAPTER V –
The Mysterious Woman

The shrill ringing of the telephone stirred Neil from the newspaper that he was reading in the quiet solitude of his study, whilst Madeline was busy tidying up the children's rooms in readiness for their return from Hertfordshire. Something told him it would be Ray and his hunch proved correct.

"Hello Neil, I'm glad I caught you at home. Is it convenient to talk now? I'll only take up a few minutes of your time."

"Of course Ray. The kids aren't due back until tomorrow so we were just enjoying a little bit of peace and quiet for a change."

"I don't blame you. I know Dorothy was really looking forward to having them around the place. In fact, come to think of it, so would the ponies. They love plenty of attention and they will have been getting lots of extra fussing and grooming with the kids there."

"I'm sure you're right and I bet the kids soon forgot all about us for the time being." Neil laughed. "But Ray, on a more serious note, how are you feeling? After the events of last night, I mean. You did seem to have a pretty rough time of it."

"I'm not too bad, thanks Neil, all things considered. But how are you and Maddy though, are you OK? It was pretty scary stuff wasn't it?"

"We're fine thanks, but yes it certainly gave us plenty to think about. By the way, have you heard from Sam yet?"

"Yes, she called me a little while ago. I do miss her, you know. Still, she'll be back some time tomorrow evening, so it's not too long to have to wait."

"Did you tell her about what happened at the séance, Ray?"

"No I didn't, well not really. I didn't want to worry her while she's away from home. I'll update her on the details tomorrow"

"Good idea. That would be one hell of a message to receive over the phone, wouldn't it?"

"Look, I'm trying to make some sense of all this, Neil and I need your help."

"No problem. Why not come over and then we can compare notes."

"Yes, I would appreciate that very much, if you really don't mind."

"Right, we'll see you later on then."

"Thanks Neil. I'll be on my way soon."

Madeline was standing by the porch with a pair of secateurs, dead heading the last of the roses when Ray arrived.

"Am I in time for elevenses, Maddy?" he enquired, giving her his customary bear hug.

"Yes, I should think so Ray, but you'll have to put me down first, you great soft thing" she laughed. Ray complied and followed her into the hall.

"Neil told me that you said you were alright after last night, but are you *really* alright, Ray?"

"I'm more than just a bit shaken actually, Maddy. In fact, I hardly slept a wink last night. Somehow I have to get to the bottom of this and then, maybe, I'll be able to get back to a normal life again."

"Yes, I do know what you mean. Neil is in the dining room. Why don't you go on in while I get some coffee?"

"That would be marvellous," Ray smiled "thanks Maddy." He wandered into the dining room to find Neil sitting at the table. He was carefully running his hand along the grain of the wood as though he had never really seen it before and was now admiring its natural beauty for the first time.

"Hello Ray" said Neil rather pensively, "you know, this is actually quite an unusual piece of mahogany. But I still don't understand how…"

"I know how you feel. This is all just a bit too much to take in, isn't it? One day you're happily mooching along through life and the next you're up to you neck in something supernatural and mysterious like this."

"Yes, quite. I was just remembering how much Mum used to love this table. She often commented on these little dark flecks here. Can you see them?" Neil said, pointing out several small marks in the grain.

"Yes I can, now you come to mention it, Neil."

"I dread to think what she would have done if she had been here last night for the séance, though. Poor old Mum."

"Or your Dad if it comes to that, especially as he made it" Ray stroked his chin thoughtfully for a moment, as though something had suddenly occurred to him.

"Neil, that picture on the sideboard, that is your Dad, isn't it?"

"Yes it is, Ray. I must have showed it to you before. He had it taken during the First World War when he was in the RFC. It became the RAF later on but in those early days, it was known as the Royal Flying Corps. He flew in a Bristol Fighter, you know. I've got a picture of him standing next to it, somewhere."

"Did he get shot down, Neil?" Ray asked with mounting interest.

"Yes he did as a matter of fact. What made you ask that?"

"Didn't Karen tell you about what happened to her on the night of the dinner party?"

"No, to tell you the truth, I haven't had much of a chance to talk to her about it. She did tell Madeline something about having stumbled on the site of a plane crash in her dream, but I don't know any more than that. Madeline didn't get any of the details from Karen."

"Neil, she went back to the First World War and witnessed a plane crashing into the trees. It was a Bristol Fighter!"

"Good God, do you mean she thinks she saw my Dad's crash?"

"It is beginning to look that way. Was your Dad the pilot?"

"No. He sat in the rear seat doing all the hard work such as navigating and shooting at the enemy with a Lewis gun."

"Well that clinches it then, Neil. Karen saw the pilot slumped forward in the cockpit and the man from the rear seat was lying on the ground, wounded. What's more, she said that she thought she recognised the man on the ground from this picture of your father."

"Well I'll be damned. Of course, she could have seen his picture on the sideboard here before she drifted off and that's why she thought she recognised him." Neil offered a little weakly, but Ray was warming to his theme now.

"So how did she know that he crashed in a Bristol Fighter? And before you ask how she knew what the plane was, she recognised it from a project she did at school."

The scene that greeted Madeline, as she brought the coffee into the dining room, was enough to bring her up with a start. Both men were staring fixedly at the photograph of Neil's father on the sideboard.

"What's wrong with you two then…has the cat got your tongues?" she laughed. Neil proceeded to outline what Ray had revealed and he looked quite astounded by it all.

"Well I knew about Karen's dream, as you call it, but I just didn't connect it with your Dad, Neil. But then I wouldn't know a Bristol Fighter if I saw one, anyway," Madeline replied, "I'm not that well up on aeroplanes."

"My Dad salvaged some wood from that plane and started making picture frames, clock cases and all sorts from the wood. That was how he first became involved in furniture making. Then, when he married Mum, he decided to make all the furniture for the house."

"And this rather grand round table was one of those pieces." Ray added.

"Yes," Madeline broke in "and also the picture frame which you two were so busily admiring when I came in. Oh, and of course he made the clock."

"So when Caroline said she saw a young man buying wood from a timber merchant, that was probably your Dad too, wasn't it, Neil?" Madeline said, trying to coax her husband into telling more of his father's story.

"Yes and it seems to tie in with Mark saying how he saw a young carpenter making a table in an old barn out in the country and how his pregnant wife came out to see him while Mark was there. And he recognised the man from this photograph, as if we need any more evidence." Ray said emphatically.

"Do you suppose that she was expecting you then, Neil?" Madeline added with mounting excitement.

"I really don't know. I have no idea what year this was supposed to be. But it is possible I suppose." Neil sounded rattled.

"You don't need to be so tetchy Neil." Madeline reproached.

"I don't mean to sound annoyed Madeline, but I am a little upset that other people have been experiencing fragments of my parents' lives at a time before I was born. If anyone should be shown these things then surely it should be me?"

"I do understand, darling. It must be hard for you to accept, especially as this whole thing seems to hinge on your parents but surely, it's better to try to understand why it has happened. I'm sure it will all make sense in the end." Madeline tried to reassure her husband.

"OK then, I suppose you're right. I'm sorry but I really can't see why Karen, Mark and Caroline should have dreamt about something that happened to my parents?" Neil replied. Ray seemed eager to speak again.

"So what have we got then, Neil? There appears to be a link between your father salvaging wood from the crash, buying wood from a timber merchant and making furniture with it," said Ray, trying to see the connection with what happened to Sam and Neil. "Then you and Sam are whisked off to some tropical island and witness the ritual slaughter of an innocent girl. What's the connection?"

"I don't know," said Madeline, "but its Julian's account that concerns me most because it suggests that there was something sinister going on in the timber yard where your Dad bought his wood, Neil."

"And this woman who I keep seeing," added Ray, "where does she fit in to the story?"

"Well Ray, from your description it can't be my mother and I can't think of anyone, who my parents knew, to fit that description. I'm afraid I'm stumped on that one." Madeline was deep in thought.

"Neil, what did you deduce from Julian's description of the markings on the ground in the timber yard?"

"I need to talk to Julian about that Madeline, because Caroline disagreed with what he was saying and he just gave up on it in the end. I think she thought they were there at the same time and that his memory was failing him, but he maintains that they visited the timber yard at different times and saw different aspects of the yard."

"Madeline, I hate to mention this," Ray began hesitantly "but…has David suffered any more nightmares recently?"

"No he hasn't, I'm relieved to say. Why do you ask?" she replied inquisitively.

"His description of the faces suggested painted masks to me. Do you remember him saying they were white with black markings and they kept coming at him, right in his face?" Ray enquired.

"I think I know where this is leading, Madeline." Neil interrupted. "You think that David saw the same faces that Sam and I saw in the clearing, don't you, Ray?"

"It did occur to me Neil."

"Even if he did, how is any of this connected to what happened last night at the séance? We watched a rather eccentric woman go off into a trance and emit voices, which were supposed to be those of the dead and we know that you experienced an apparition which was more prolonged than before and which caused you a lot of distress."

"Her clothing was bloodstained and she was carrying your clock until she passed right through me and then through the wall!" Ray interrupted, almost hysterically now as though re-living the event.

"It's alright Ray," Madeline soothed "we'll sort this all out, you'll see."

"And then," continued Neil, raising his voice "we all saw the blood oozing out of the table top, the picture frame and the clock. But what's the damned connection with what Sam and I saw?"

"Don't get annoyed Neil. You can see that Ray is already upset. We will unravel this mystery, but let's all try to be rational about it. I'm going to get some more coffee; does anybody else want a cup?" Both men readily accepted the offer as they realised they needed a break. They felt as though their lives were turned upside down and they did not have any idea why, nor what they could do about it.

Neil's nerves were a little raw. He never gave any credence to the supernatural but was now having to face the unpalatable fact that something happened in his own home, for which he could find no logical explanation. Added to that, some of his friends saw brief cameos of his parents' early, married life and he felt excluded. He felt betrayed and cheated. Why had he been involved in such a bizarre adventure with Ray's girlfriend and what was the meaning of that revolting ritual which they were forced to witness? He had also been questioning himself about his feelings for Sam. Whilst he found her attractive, his love for Madeline was as strong as ever. He felt confused. Who is the woman who Ray keeps seeing in his head and, furthermore, what is happening to solid, dependable old Ray? Neil excused himself and wandered out to the kitchen because just then he felt the need to give his wife a big hug.

"What's all this about then, Neil?" Madeline teased, feeling at the same time both surprised and pleased by the sudden unexpected attention.

"I just love you, that's all." Neil replied.

"Sorry, have I turned up at the wrong moment?" Ray asked from the kitchen doorway.

"No, don't be daft." Madeline laughed as she slipped free from Neil's grasp. "He just wanted to be a bit friendly. Didn't you darling?"

"Neil, are you quite sure you don't recall this woman from your childhood? I'm sorry to be going on about it but there has to be some sort of link with your parents." Ray pressed.

"Neil...." Madeline began, "didn't you tell me once that your sister had a friend some time ago from the Far East somewhere, wasn't it Singapore? Perhaps she would fit Ray's description?"

"Oh yes, I know who you mean. What was her name now? Her father was Portuguese, a merchant seaman who my Dad knew from way back. He apparently married a Malaysian woman and settled down out there. Then Dad heard from him 'out of the blue' when his daughter wanted to take up nursing. Yes, I remember now, her name was Stella. As Rebecca was a nurse, he asked Dad to help Stella to get into a teaching hospital in England and Rebecca took her under her wing as a student nurse. For some reason, I remember that Mum felt unable to warm to that girl. I think she was rather a strong-minded individual and therefore probably clashed with Mum at times. Mum was a bit domineering herself, as you know. Stella was half-Portuguese, half-Singaporean and quite attractive as I recall. Mind you, I hardly ever saw her because all this was going on when I was at university."

"How well do you remember her though Neil, apart from her being attractive I mean? Can you describe her to us, did she have olive skin and green eyes, for example?" Neil stared silently at Ray for a moment.

"It depends what you mean by olive skin, Ray. To me, the term olive skin typifies the Mediterranean look. This girl's skin was a sort of golden brown, but I imagine she must have taken after her mother in appearance. More of an Eastern look, if you know what I mean, but what I do remember now is her eyes. They were a brilliant, sparkling green." Ray's jaw literally dropped at this revelation.

"But if it is her," Madeline gasped, "why would she manifest herself to Ray as a ghostly apparition? You don't think she's dead, do you Neil?"

"I have no idea. She would be about the same age as me, so if she is dead it must have been sudden; an accident or something."

"Neil," Ray interrupted urgently, "your description of her eyes is just as I see them in these visions - sparkling jade green!"

"It could of course be her mother." Neil mused. "I'll give Rebecca a call to see if she has heard from Stella recently."

"Oh my god, Neil," Madeline looked shocked as she spoke, "we haven't mentioned the spoon to Ray yet, have we? This is all beginning to add up now. Remember what Madame Rosina said about the spoon? Don't you see, Neil?"

"No Madeline, I don't see." Neil answered.

"What about the bloody spoon." Ray was beginning to feel frustrated that he had no idea what anyone else was talking about.

"Well Ray, I telephoned Madame Rosina because Neil assumed that when she said someone should prepare to travel, she meant whoever the handle of the spoon was pointing at. But the handle was pointing in the general direction of Julian, but I would have thought that it would have been Neil who was going to travel as this all seems to be about his parents."

"So what did Madame Rosina say then, Maddy?" Ray sounded even more frustrated that Madeline seemed to be beating around the bush.

"She said that the bowl of the spoon was pointing at the person who would be travelling overseas to do whatever needs to be done. Ray, it was pointing at you."

"But Madeline, Ray is always travelling overseas. That's his job. Madame Rosina was hardly telling us anything we didn't already know there, now was she?" Neil retorted.

"But if Ray's vision is of Stella or her mother, then perhaps he has to go to Singapore to unravel this mystery."

"You could be right there Maddy. After all, I do have business contacts in Singapore and I know the place quite well. It does fit, doesn't it?"

"But why you, Ray? Why not me, after all, I did meet Stella and if there is a connection here with the visions the others had about my parents, it would make sense for me to go, wouldn't it?"

"Then why was the spoon pointing at Ray? If we are going to accept what Madame Rosina told us then we have to assume it is Ray who will go."

"Do you have a trip to Singapore planned, Ray?" Neil enquired.

"No, but I can easily arrange one if necessary."

"Let me speak to Rebecca first, otherwise this could easily turn out to be a wild goose chase. God knows, I want this business resolved as much as you do but let's not over-react."

Standing on the balcony of his London flat the following night, Ray looked up at the starry sky and reflected on his good fortune at having such staunch friends as Neil and Madeline. He doubted whether he could have handled this situation without their tremendous support, after all it was easily the most frightening experience of his life. He also knew that he had to overcome it and do whatever was necessary to resume control of his life, but he would not have to face it alone. The cold air on his face was refreshing and the great vault of the sky made him feel very humble and a little lonely. It reminded him just how much he missed Sam and how much he was looking forward to seeing her again. Still, he knew he would not have long to wait now as she had telephoned him from the airport for a few words before boarding the plane. She sounded very tired but quite cheerful and could hardly wait to get home. It was good to know that she missed him as much as he was missing her.

The familiar sound of Sam's Mini-Cooper brought Ray sharply back down to Earth and he looked down to see the car come to a screeching halt on the road immediately below him. His heart leapt for joy as he watched her swing those lovely legs out of the car. She looked up, waved at him and blew him a kiss, which he happily returned. Ray ran inside, closed the doors behind him and, before he knew it, Sam was in his arms in a tight embrace. He then held her at arm's length to look at her and admire her sun-kissed skin. As a model, she was always dressed in the latest fashions and the new mini-skirt she was wearing almost took his breath away.

"Sam, I have missed you so much. Thank God you're back."

"Ray, are you alright? You look dreadful, what have you been doing with yourself? Oh, and how was the séance?"

Although she could sometimes cope with him having stubble on his chin, he had obviously not bothered to shave or spruce himself up for her return, which was unusual for Ray. His eyes were a little bloodshot and strained-looking, and she was unsure whether it was from drinking or lack of sleep. He was clearly in need of help and she was going to be the one to provide it.

"Look Ray, why don't I go and freshen up and then you can tell me all about the séance and what you've been up to while I've been away?" Sam persuaded him.

"Good idea," he agreed, "I do have a hell of a lot to tell you, my love. I'll just go and fetch your luggage and then I'll fix us a drink." He soon returned to the sound of running water and splashing from the bathroom. As he popped his head around the door, he could clearly hear Sam humming the Flower Song from Bizet's opera, Carmen.

"That's a bit highbrow isn't it darling?" he asked in a rather surprised tone, Sam being a confirmed Beatles fan.

"They were playing it a lot on the shoot and now I can't get it out of my head." She called back to him. "Da dum dum dum, de dum dum dum, da da da dudda dudda dum dum dum...."

"Oh, I see. Look, I just popped out quickly to get your luggage from the car" he said, holding up a small white vanity case and matching suitcase. She was still humming and he could see her silhouette through the opaque glass of the shower cubicle. She opened the door to blow him a kiss, but Ray was already there. Fully clothed or not, he was not concerned about getting soaked, their lips met and it was then he remembered how sweet they tasted. He stroked the warm soapy water over the soft skin of her back with a foamy sponge, then washed and stroked her with his large hands. Sam loved the feeling of his skin against hers as he ran his hand over her buttocks. The water ran down from her head, over her breasts and around her nipples.

His lips soon found her nipples and his tongue flashed eagerly over them, as she arched her body and purred with delight. Ray was now completely drenched but happy as he worked his way further down. She thought she would explode as he teased her with his warm tongue and she gently ran her fingers through his hair. Ray slowly stood up and Sam seized the opportunity to unbutton his shirt and, as they looked lustfully into each other's eyes, she unzipped his trousers and pulled them down for him to step out. She shampooed his hair, worked up the lather on his hairy chest, and then began to make her way slowly downwards. Ray knew very well what was coming and trembled in anticipation. He groaned with pleasure as he gently cupped her head in his hands...

Taking a large bath sheet, he wrapped Sam and carefully carried her to the bedroom whilst she giggled and wriggled her feet as she enacted her special fantasy of being the damsel in distress, rescued by a gentle giant who was taking her to his secret hideaway! Ray lowered her gently onto the bed, kissed her toes, then her ankles, then her knees, and then stroked and ran his tongue over the inside of her thighs. She felt helpless and totally within his power. She had waited long enough for this moment and kissed him hard as her tongue darted passionately around his. He gently lowered his body onto hers, entered her and began thrusting mercilessly, she moaned in ecstasy, and hung on tightly to his muscular arms.

Lounging together on a low, soft leather sofa and enjoying a glass of wine by candlelight later that night, they were finally ready to bring each other up to date on what had been going on in their lives. Ray had cooked up a snack of Welsh Rabbit to replenish their energy levels and, as he sprinkled the cheese on the thick, freshly sliced bread, spread with plenty of butter, he felt comfortable and relaxed after the last couple of hours he had enjoyed with Sam. It certainly helped him to escape the horrors of the last couple of days, although he wondered for how long, especially as Sam wanted to hear all the detail of the events that had taken place since she left for Spain on Friday morning. He did not want to re-live it all, but he knew that she had a right to know, especially as her own experience on the night was so harrowing. Besides, she had already told him about the rain on Saturday morning, just as they landed in Spain, which delayed their schedule a little. Regardless of that, they worked on and still managed to complete the shoot early this morning.

Although he would have preferred not to relive the horror of the séance, Ray knew that he must tell Sam everything if she was to help him through this nightmare. He therefore left no stone unturned in his description and was greatly encouraged to see that she was hanging on to his every word. She could hardly believe that a normal dinner party could have turned into something as frightening as this. However, she was pleased to hear that Neil was more forthcoming when Ray called at Ivy Cottage the previous day to discuss a few things that were still nagging away at his mind. He also told her that he learnt a little more about Neil's father and his furniture making.

"And you know Sam, with everything appearing to be so normal again; it makes it hard to accept that all those curious things really happened there."

"Does it feel in anyway sinister going back to the cottage now Ray?"

"Not at all," Ray assured her, "although, I do get a strange feeling in the dining room. It's difficult to describe. It's almost a feeling of sorrow, although I can't say I ever felt it there before. Well, not before the dinner party that I can recall."

"Ray, it seems to me as though this is all one big puzzle and I can't say I really understand any of it, but we must try to put all the pieces together."

"That's exactly what I said to Neil yesterday morning, when we were trying to rationalise this whole business and figure why I'm having this repetitive vision; and why no-one else can see her."

"Darling, we will resolve this, you'll see. Just tell me what I need to do, and when. We must start though, by discussing everything, no matter how silly it may sound. I only wish that I had been brave enough to speak to you straight after the dinner party. I know now that I should have told you then. It was very embarrassing for both of us over at Ivy Cottage when we amazed each other with our revelations. We really do need to get some answers." Sam's confidence and determination to find the underlying cause of all this gave Ray the reassurance he needed.

He was thinking hard about the one thing he had not mentioned to Sam or anyone else for that matter. He was certainly keeping it from Madeline and Neil for fear that they might think he was going out of his mind. In fact, he had questioned himself as to whether this might be evidence that he was losing his grip on reality, but since Sam's return he felt reassured that he was still sane. He could just imagine what Neil's reaction would be if he were to tell him how he found some tangible evidence immediately after the séance. Neil would have given him one of those looks, put a fatherly arm around him and encouraged him to seek professional help whilst intimating to Madeline that poor old Ray has lost his mind.

Sam watched him over the rim of her wineglass and she could clearly see that he was becoming a little nervous and agitated about something, did he have something to tell her, but could not find the words? How right she was about that. Ray jumped up from the sofa, went to where his black leather jacket was hanging on a hook and took something out of the pocket and rushed back to take his place beside her again.

"Sam," he began, "I've got something to show you. Nobody else knows about this yet, not even Maddy and Neil."

"Yes?" she replied a little apprehensively.

"I feel a little awkward about this, and a bit stupid as well I suppose, but in view of the conversation we've just had, I felt I ought to share this with you. You see, I sweated so much during the séance that I rushed out to the cloakroom immediately afterwards to wash my face and hands. Sam, I just could not believe it. When I got into the cloakroom, there in the palm of my hand was a torn piece of *white linen, stained with blood!*" Sam gasped and shook her head in disbelief as he unclenched his hand to reveal his tiny piece of evidence.

"But how, Ray? You can't take a real piece of material from a…a ghost!" she stammered.

"If only I had the answer to that one Sam, I think our problems would be over. Now please, tell me honestly, you do believe me, don't you?"

"Of course I do, Ray. After the terrifying ordeal I went through, I have no doubt that something is going on which I dread to unveil, but somehow I know we must."

"And you don't think I'm going mad?" he almost pleaded.

"No Ray, you're not. I'm really glad you told me about it."

"Sam, I would prefer it if you don't breathe a word of this to any of the others for the time being." Sam took both his hands in hers, looked him in the eye and promised him that she would not say anything about this to anyone. Ray was absolutely convinced that he must have torn this scrap of cloth from the woman's robes when she passed through him and he fell backwards off his chair. He no longer felt alone now that Sam had seen the evidence and believed his explanation as to how it came to be in his possession.

Sam was now between assignments and had a couple of weeks to assume the role of 'the housewife', which amused her as she so rarely got the chance to do so. She particularly enjoyed going out occasionally to do a little shopping for a few of their favourite things, especially items that Ray had specifically requested. On returning, she would neatly arrange on the kitchen table any ingredients that Ray needed to make up a dish for their evening meal, as she was hopeless at cooking. However, she completely refused to do any housework such as dusting and polishing, partly for fear of ruining her nails but also because she did not want to fall out with their cleaner. Lilly, Ray's cleaner from his bachelor days, had agreed to stay on after Sam moved in and keep the flat shipshape for them. She was extremely discreet and trustworthy and took a great deal of pride in her work, which was once the cause of unfortunate consequences for Ray, when he came home early one afternoon and interrupted her precise schedule. Ray gave Sam a graphic description of Lilly's rage, telling her how Lilly had yelled at him for walking on the wet floor and putting sticky fingerprints on the freshly polished woodwork. He caused great hilarity when he acted out the highlights in a very theatrical manner. He told her that he thought that he must have come through the wrong door when he was met by an apparently raving lunatic who ordered him out of his own house and told him not to come back for at least another two hours.

On arriving home from her shopping spree, Sam lowered her shopping bags in the entrance hall and heaved a sigh of relief to be home. She was indeed very pleased with herself for noting it was cleaning day and that it was important to keep out of Lilly's way. Everywhere was dust free and gleaming and the fresh smell of beeswax wafted through each room. Ray appeared much brighter that evening when he returned from the City, not only because the flat was clean and tidy, but also because Sam was there to welcome him home and help to give him the feeling of stability that he desperately needed at present.

"I really can't see how it can take you so long just to choose a shed, Julian." Caroline scoffed, thumbing through the brochure that he had just handed her to look through. "There, that one looks nice, with its little windows at the front. It's just what you want, Julian. See, you have been looking through that brochure for hours and I've found you one in less than a minute, Men!"

"Thank you so much Caroline. What would I do without you? Now please hand me back the brochure so that I can continue my evaluation. Thank you." His tone was a mixture of frustration and resignation as he knew perfectly well that Caroline knew nothing of the equipment stored in the shed and could therefore have no idea what size of shed was required. He instinctively knew that her choice would be completely unsuitable and that he had wasted his time showing her the brochure in the first place.

"So what's wrong with the one I chose then? Aren't you going to order it?" Caroline asked, somewhat petulantly.

"My dearest Caroline, I clearly can't rely on your advice in the matter of a replacement garden shed."

"And why can't you? I suppose you're angry that I found you one so quickly, aren't you Julian dear?" the sarcasm was now beginning to creep in on both sides.

"Caroline, should I ever need to buy a Wendy House, I will certainly know where to come for help. However, I actually need a shed to replace the old, leaking heap, which is currently rotting away in the corner of our garden. If I don't replace it soon, my gardening tools will soon get wet and then rather rusty. My lawnmower, hedge trimmer and everything else in there, will be ruined."

"Well I thought the one I chose looked very nice, dear."

"It may have looked nice dear, but it is less than half the size of the shed we have now and that is no longer large enough. I already have things piled on top of each other and I therefore need more room. I am therefore looking for a shed of at least twelve feet by eight feet. Whereas your, delightful little 'Wendy House' might just about be big enough to house the lawnmower, if I'm lucky, but precious little else! After all, it is supposed to be for children to play in not for men to store garden implements. Now please leave me to get on with this or I'll be here all day." At that precise moment, the telephone rang prompting Julian to add. "Saved by the bell Caroline, be a poppet and answer it."

"Yes Julian, Sir!" Caroline responded with a curtsy and very false smile. "Madeline, how lovely to hear from you. How are you, and Neil, and those two beautiful children of yours?"

"Oh, we're fine thanks Caroline. How about you and Julian?"

"I was just trying to help Julian to choose a new garden shed, but you know what men are like. They don't really want our help at all because they actually seem to enjoy wasting hours reading through all that boring nonsense about dimensions, styles, roofs and I don't know what else just to make it sound as though they are the experts. The truth is, Julian doesn't seem to know what he's looking for anyway. If you ask me, Madeline, when you've seen one shed, you've seen them all!"

"I do know what you mean, Caroline. Why do they have so many in the catalogues? I find such things very confusing and, to tell you the truth, I'm happy to leave that sort of thing to Neil anyway."

"Well I'm sure Neil is very good at choosing the right thing without getting as sarcastic as our 'Mister Digwell' the bloody gardener, here."

Madeline had actually called to update them on the latest events following the séance and wasted no time in getting straight to the point, giving Caroline the latest news, including Ray's visit to Ivy Cottage, during which he told them more about his experiences. She told Caroline that he appeared to be in rather a bad way and that he wanted to revisit the whole sequence of events, even if it was only for his own clarity of mind. She also mentioned that he seemed to have his detective hat on and wanted to know more about Neil's family history. This did make sense as he was looking at how the various stories from the dinner party appeared to link into the earlier lives of Neil's parents. Madeline concluded by making the point that Ray was determined to 'get to the bottom' of this business and that he seems to be acting like a man possessed.

"He really ought to be careful," Caroline said, sounding rather concerned, "Madame Rosina did warn us of impending danger."

"But it could be equally dangerous if he does nothing. Ray's behaviour really has changed quite significantly since all this began. He appears to be really troubled by it all and is somewhat withdrawn as a result, which is not in keeping with Ray's character at all. He believes that this is all about someone crying out for our help."

"If that's true Madeline, why have they made it so difficult for us to follow? You would think they would at least give us some clues so that we could make some headway, wouldn't you?"

"Well that's all part of the mystery, isn't it? Nevertheless, I do think Ray could be right about this, you know. It does make some kind of sense to me."

"Well Madeline, Julian and I have also been discussing it all again. We have even gone through all the ghastly events of the séance. I had no idea it was going to be so scary, you know. It was so different to what I've read or heard people say about them."

"Yes I know Caroline, I now look at our dining room furniture in a very different light. Believe me!"

"Yes, I'll bet you do. I know I would. Now Madeline, listen to this. Julian has found a dilapidated old book about the occult in a sale at an old bookshop that he occasionally visits when he needs to find a book that has been out of print for donkey's years. Anyway, in this book he found some sort of ancient runes or something, which looked similar to those he saw in the timber yard. But what he found really strange was that, whereas runes are apparently normally of a Germanic origin, there were also some markings resembling pictures, similar to ancient Egyptian hieroglyphics."

"Karen would know about that, wouldn't she? Perhaps Julian should talk to her."

"He already has Madeline, he remembered being enthralled by her telling him at the dinner party that she is an Egyptologist and so he called her as soon as he found the book. They are going to spend some more time trying to piece together what he thinks he can remember of these markings. The exciting thing is that when he told Karen about some of the markings that appeared to be some sort of pictures, she said that if they were ancient Egyptian, then it sounds as though they could be messages of death or they could be depicting someone's journey into the spirit world. What's more, she knows this old retired professor who is apparently a World authority on runic characters and their meanings, so if Julian can remember enough of it clearly, she could take it to him."

"You two really have been busy haven't you, Caroline?"

"Well Julian certainly has, with Karen's help. There is something else he stumbled on which may not mean anything, but it could be worth someone following up. It was something about a sacrificial ritual, which was performed every time the thirteenth full moon fell in a leap year or some such thing, I don't really remember what Julian said too well. He wondered if the ritual that Sam and Neil saw could have been some such thing. I'm sorry Madeline, I don't remember this very well but perhaps Neil might want to talk to Julian about it."

"Caroline, my mind is really spinning now. Do you have anymore little gems for me?"

"Well, only that we now think we visited the timber yard at separate times." As Madeline listened intently, Caroline explained that she and Julian concluded that someone was murdered in the timber yard and that was why she saw bloodstains on the road after the truck moved off with its load of timber.

"We think the victim may well be the person Ray has been hallucinating about. What do you think, Madeline?"

"I'm not at all sure, Caroline because Neil thought it might be a friend of his sister, Rebecca. Her friend was from Singapore and attended the training hospital where Rebecca was a nurse and she does seem to fit the description that Ray gave us of someone with olive skin and jade green eyes. Neil said he's going to give Rebecca a call to find out if she has been in touch with her friend recently and if there is any relevant news."

"It sounds as though there is some super investigatory work going on down in your neck of the woods Madeline, please keep me posted. But unless it's really, really and absolutely necessary, please, please no more séances?"

"We're all in this together you know Caroline and we certainly will need all our joint efforts to sort it out, so I promise to keep you up-dated. Give my love to Julian."

"Same to Neil and the children, thanks for calling and bye for now."

Julian was still studying the brochures when Caroline returned.

"Come, come Julian, you must have chosen one by now, winter will come and go before you make your mind up!"

"It's not as easy as it seems, dear. There are the dimensions to consider and measuring out the space to hold the equipment I already have, plus any new equipment that I am sure I will need to buy in the future. It therefore has to be larger than the old one, but not so much larger that it won't fit on the existing concrete area. I don't want to have a new base laid as well because that would just add to the cost, wouldn't it? Anyway, I have chosen one. In fact, I already knew which one I wanted before you started choosing stupid little Wendy Houses, but it was fun watching you getting all fussed about it."

"Julian, you horror. I hate you, you rotten old bastard" she shouted in mock anger.

"And I love you to bits, my sweet Caroline" he teased.

"Madeline sends her love and called to up-date us on recent events. That's if you're still interested, you horrible man."

"How are they coming along with it?"

"Madeline says Neil's going to call his sister Rebecca to enquire about a friend who she took under her wing as a student nurse at a training hospital a few years back."

"How does she fit in then?"

"Her description fits that of the woman in Ray's vision. That is the olive skin and jade green eyes. Apparently, she came from Singapore and Madeline seems certain that she is the one. I wonder if she is the person who we thought was murdered in the timber yard."

"Only if she was murdered as a baby, Caroline. I think the year we visited that timber yard was close to the time when Neil's sister would have been born, so this friend of hers would not have grown up to be a nurse, would she? Still, we don't know that their theory is correct, the friend may be alive and well and living in Nether Wallop. Our theory could still be correct, and then again, we might all be wrong. In any event, I certainly hope we can close the chapter on this business soon, I can't wait to get back to normal life!"

"Madeline was certainly at the front when God handed out patience, I don't know how she's managed to get around Neil's pig-headed approach to all this, plus she's enjoyed more visits from Ray in one month than she usually gets in a whole year!"

"Neil is a lot sharper than you give him credit for, Caroline. He knows very well that if he goes along with Madeline, Ray and the rest of you on this, he could soon find himself simply going with the flow without thinking it through for himself, which is simply not his style. However, by digging his heels in and saying that there still has to be a logical explanation for all this, he can control the pace. I am quite sure they don't mind seeing so much of Ray either, because not only is he a great friend of theirs, but he's also godfather to the children, who he clearly adores. Furthermore, I wouldn't be surprised if Madeline hasn't already outlined her next novel from all this kerfuffle. Perhaps I'll be reading a manuscript about it all in six months time or so. I just wish I knew what happened!"

Caroline put her arms around Julian's waist, rested her head on his shoulder and enquired whether he would be much longer deliberating over the dimensions of his new shed as she had other plans for their afternoon, which did not include shed catalogues.

"Julian," she murmured, looking at him with a distinct sparkle in her eyes, "why don't you leave that for now, I've got something to show you upstairs."

Julian was by now quite well accustomed to the signals of Caroline's coy, fluttering of the eyelids and soft voice, after all they had lived together for as long as he cared to remember and he always prided himself on having an extremely good memory. Somehow, though he could never resist teasing her.

"Caroline will you push off! Can't you see I'm busy?" he feigned annoyance as he pushed her away in a rather unconvincing manner, then he grabbed her and pulled her towards him.

"Did you say you've got something to show me upstairs? Well what are you waiting for? Come on then." She loved these little acts of affection and wasted no time in taking his hand and leading him upstairs.

"Surprise, surprise!" Sam stood back to allow Karen to take up her position in the kitchen doorway with Mark grinning over her shoulder. Ray swung around, having been interrupted from chopping onions, and beamed with pleasure.

"Oh Sam, you didn't tell me they were coming over!" he cried, his eyes streaming with the tears from the freshly chopped onions and garlic that he had just prepared for the Bolognese sauce. He dropped his kitchen knife on the worktop and hugged Karen and, as she buried her head into his neck, she began to realise just how close her new circle of friends had become since the dinner party. Sam was delighted at Ray's reaction, having called Karen earlier to arrange for them to pop over for the evening. She knew that the company would be good for them both and that Ray's old friend Karen would be ideal for lifting his spirits.

"I should have guessed," Ray laughed "Sam was so keen to go shopping this morning and even suggested that I cook spaghetti Bolognese this evening." Karen chuckled her approval and automatically began to lend a hand with the meal preparations.

"It's just like old times Ray. The only difference is that you're not trying to seduce me this time,....are you?" Karen giggled.

"And, young Karen," Ray confided, getting back into his stride, "I think you'll find this sauce a little more impressive than those I used to dish up in our student days. I have picked up a few culinary tips on my travels to Europe and the Far East. It's not quite ready yet." He added, lifting a spoon to her lips.

"Umm, that's really good Ray. How long before dinner?" she asked, smacking her lips with eager anticipation.

"Just another fifteen minutes or so simmering, which will give me time to cook the spaghetti and lay the table" he replied. Sam, who had been regaling Mark with tales of some of her exploits in Spain, appeared at the kitchen door right on cue.

"Ray, you catch up with Mark over a glass of that Rioja that I brought back from Spain. Karen and I will lay the table. OK?"

"No problem," Ray replied, bending down to lower the heat under the simmering pan, "let me just start this spaghetti first." Sam handed Karen the tablemats and followed her round with the cutlery.

"Julian called me to discuss some ancient script he found in an old book, which he says looks very similar to the markings he saw in that timber yard," Karen began.

"Yes, I remember he said that he saw some weird markings on the ground there, didn't he? Does he want you to translate them for him?"

"That's the general idea and, assuming he remembers it correctly, there could be some sort of a clue here. There appear to be two distinct types of script. One resembles hieroglyphics, which I can help with, but the other is runic, and I know someone who is an expert in that field. So, with a little bit of luck we should be able to interpret what he saw. Julian and I have arranged to meet on Thursday to see how much I can decipher."

"That sounds great Karen. Good luck with your detective work." Sam replied before leaning over conspiratorially and whispering in Karen's ear.

"Guess what, I've got a great surprise for Ray. I have to tell someone before I burst. I am going to take him with me on my next modelling assignment.....to the Bahamas!"

"That's fantastic! Excellent Sam, it's just what he needs."

"It's only for a week. The idea is that he relaxes while I go off on photo shoots. The agency wants me to go out a few days earlier to help sort out some locations. We fly out next Thursday. I can't wait to get him out there, it'll be a real tonic for him. I felt so guilty when I got home on Sunday to see him looking so awful. He was unshaven, his eyes were bloodshot and he looked as though he hadn't slept for days. I knew he wasn't sleeping well recently, but I was really shocked when I saw him."

"Err, hum." Mark made sure the girls were aware of their presence as he and Ray entered the dining room. He could clearly see that they were engrossed in conversation and turned to Ray with a mischievous look in his eyes,

"Scheming are we?"

"We wouldn't do a thing like that, now would we?" Karen defended in a playful tone.

"Girl talk, something you guys would never understand." Sam added. Ray clapped his hands together loudly.

"We're just about there. The plates are warming, the parmesan is grated and we just need Mark to be a good chap and choose a bottle of wine to go with the 'Spag Bol'." He indicated the wine rack. "Unless of course, you're happy to stay with that rather good Spanish plonk that Sam brought back with her?"

"Wonderful, I'm starving," said Sam, as she took her place at the table. Karen sat opposite Sam and Mark, leaving a space for Ray next to her. Moments later, Ray emerged from the kitchen with two plates of steaming spaghetti bolognese for the girls, while Mark poured them all another glass of what he described as 'Spain's best'. Ray was quick to return with two large portions of 'Spag Bol' for the boys.

"Well chosen, Mark," said Karen, taking a sip from her wineglass, "this is lovely, cheers."

"Cheers!" said Ray lifting his glass to Sam admiringly.

"This Bolognese sauce certainly is different from our college days Ray. Perhaps a little more exotic and you have really upped the garlic too. I hope you've made a note of the recipe, Mark." Karen quipped.

"You've got to be joking! The best I can conjure up is beans on toast and, even then, the toast would probably be burnt!" The banter died away to be replaced by the clatter of cutlery on plates as the hungry diners demolished all Ray's hard work. Then Sam asked if there was any left for their guests to have seconds. Ray had made plenty, almost as if he had known about the surprise visit and everyone had second helpings except for Sam, who was always counting the calories.

CHAPTER VI –
Professor Bonsire

It was a grey and overcast morning with a few spots of rain in the air. Under Karen's direction, Julian turned off the main road and stopped in front of a heavy five-barred gate. Just to the right of the gate stood a tall wooden post bearing a rather weather-beaten sign, on which the word 'Private' could just be made out. Karen quickly climbed out of the car to open the gate, which squeaked loudly as she pushed it. She remembered from the professor's directions that she must be sure to close the gate behind them before proceeding up the rough track, which would lead to Professor Bonsire's house. Although she had never visited the professor at home before, Karen was not at all surprised to discover that his house was way off the beaten track.

The Professor had once described Karen as his star pupil and from then on, he allowed her to call him

Cecil. He was quite eccentric and always full of fun, yet in his own field of expertise, he was one of the World's leading authorities. His knowledge of ancient languages and writings was legendary. Even after retiring from teaching, he often received requests to travel around the World to help unravel the mysteries of lost civilisations. Karen kept in touch with him as best she could and he assiduously continued to follow her developing career.

When Karen first suggested to Julian that they should visit the professor, he was delighted, that was until he discovered that the old man lived nearly two hundred miles away in North Wales. However, his protestations that he could not spare the time off work were powerless against his wife's desire to spend a weekend away from home. Caroline was adamant that they should go and that she would be able to amuse herself for the few hours that Julian and Karen were visiting the professor. Furthermore, she felt that Karen's work on the previous Thursday was so encouraging that Julian could hardly refuse to complete the detective work now. The visit to Professor Bonsire was therefore quite essential.

As the track ascended the hillside, it became quite rough. Karen braced herself and held on to the car seat with both hands as she bounced from side to side.

"How much further" she enquired, "if this goes on much longer, my bum could become quite sore!" she joked. Julian gripped the steering wheel hard as they approached another hairpin bend.

"According to these directions, it's about three miles from the main road to the top of the hill and so far we've only done about a mile" he replied. As he swung the wheel back to straighten up, a large branch hanging low over the track struck the passenger window. Karen shrieked with surprise.

"It's only a stray branch, not the mad Professor's six-eyed pet monster!" Julian said with a wicked grin.

"I am amazed the window didn't shatter," she gasped, putting her hand on her chest to feel her thumping heart.

"Yes, it was quite a loud bang, wasn't it? I hope it didn't do any damage. If I had known I'd have to bring my lovely new car up a rotten old dirt track, I certainly would have thought twice about it!"

After a few more minutes of bouncing up and down along the track, Karen shouted out as they drove over the brow of the hill.

"There it is!" In front of them, nestling amongst the trees and bushes, stood an austere looking old house, sadly in need of repair. The beautiful autumnal russet colour of Virginia Creeper interspersed with dark green Ivy almost completely covered the walls. Thick bushes grew close up to the walls giving the house an overgrown and dilapidated appearance.

Parked on the gravel in front of the house was a filthy, mud encrusted Land Rover.

"At least he's got the common sense to have the right type of vehicle to come up that damn track!" Julian said with some conviction.

Karen was pleased when Julian turned off the engine and she quickly opened the car door, climbed out and stretched. Julian, on the other hand, having got out of the car, simply stood and admired the view down into the valley from whence they had just come.

"That was quite a climb," he enthused, enjoying the moment now that the hard driving was over.

"I can hear seagulls," said Karen excitedly as she began to walk round to the other side of the house.

"Wow! Julian look over here," she called out and pointed excitedly towards the sea. Even though it was damp and misty, the view from this high vantage point was quite breathtaking and they soon became absorbed by the spectacular coastline.

"Isn't it a glorious sight?" came a rich baritone voice from behind them. "I never tire of that view." They turned around to come face to face with an elderly but well-built man with long, white, shoulder-length hair and a bushy beard. The professor wore a gingery brown tweed jacket with tatty, leather elbow patches. If his jacket had seen better days, so had his corduroy trousers, which were getting rather thin at the knees. By an almost absurd contrast, he was sporting a brown checked shirt that looked brand new! The professor smiled at his two new visitors through the thick lenses of his horn-rimmed spectacles. Karen was so thrilled to see him again that she rushed up, threw her arms around his neck, and kissed him on the cheek. This made the old man blush profusely as he was not used to such shows of affection from young women.

"Dear me, let's go inside out of the wind," he said quickly, extricating himself from Karen's embrace. "That's the only trouble with living on top of a hill; the wind never seems to stop blowing" he said, hustling the two of them indoors. "Still, it can be most exhilarating up here you know. Oh yes, yes, yes. Now young Karen let me look at you." He stood back to admire his young protégé. "You're looking as radiant as ever, my dear. It's been quite some time since I saw you last, young woman. You've been neglecting old Cecil, haven't you?"

"You're looking very fit and well yourself, Cecil." Karen replied, ignoring his remonstration. "It really is lovely to see you again. This is Julian, the friend I told you about." She announced, almost pulling Julian forward into the room.

"Did you dear? Oh yes, of course you did, how silly of me. He's your teacher   chappy, isn't he?"

"No, Cecil, that's Mark, my boyfriend. This is Julian, another friend. He's the one who saw the runes on the ground in the timber yard. You remember I told you all about it on the phone?"

"Oh yes, yes, yes, of course. I remember now. A bit of a rum do that, eh? Well, we'll have to see if we can sort it out, shan't we? Now sit yourselves down if you can find a space. Just shove those papers and magazines on the table and make yourselves at home. I'll go and put the kettle on."

"No, let me do that for you while you and Julian get acquainted." Karen interjected as she slid past him towards the kitchen, which was clearly visible from the room they were in. "Don't worry, I'll find everything I need."

"Bossy as ever, I see! Leopards don't change their spots, you know. Well go on then, but just shout if there is anything you can't find," he called after her. "I can never remember where any damned thing is in that kitchen!" He added conspiratorially to Julian. "Now then young Julian, tell me about these runes you saw. Were they just markings in the dust or were they clearly written, painted or whatever?"

"Now that's the strange thing about it Cecil. May I call you Cecil?"

"Yes, yes, yes, of course you can. Now, tell me about these markings, young man."

"Well you see the thing is, they were on the ground in the corner where this pile of wood had been standing for some time and I would have expected it to be very dusty and dirty with spider's webs and so on. Now the strange thing is that the ground was actually surprisingly clean and I can't believe that imbecile of a timber merchant would have swept it out. The markings seemed to be a sort of reddish colour on a white background. Not exactly painted perhaps, but definitely colours, even if they were dull."

"Colours eh? Well red on white could be meaningful. It all depends on what else you have to tell me. Now can you actually remember any of these marks in detail?"

"Yes, I sketched some of them and Karen has already done some work on them. Ah, here she comes now with the tea. I was just telling Cecil about the excellent work you've done on the hieroglyphics, Karen." Julian said, including Karen in their conversation.

"Oh, Cecil is it already?" Karen exclaimed, almost indignantly, "it took me years to be allowed to call the professor by his first name but now you've achieved it in just a few minutes."

"Yes, yes, yes my dear but look, this is fascinating stuff," the professor mumbled, turning back to Julian.

"Where did you learn to train your memory to be able to recall shapes and script, like these runes then, young man?"

"It's my job, Cecil. I work in the publishing business and have to read numerous manuscripts, books and so forth. You soon learn to train your memory in that game."

"So, let's get back to the runes. What do you have to show me then, you two?" Karen produced a large sheet of paper on which Julian drew what he could recall of the various shapes that he saw in the timber yard. Karen had circled the items that were closer in form to hieroglyphics than runes and made some comments and suggestions beneath each one. The professor's face was a picture when he first set eyes on the sheet.

"Goodness gracious! I would never have believed it if I hadn't seen this with my own eyes!" He grabbed his cup of tea and slurped down a great mouthful. "My God, Karen, have you any idea what this means?" he cried out in great excitement. "You two have certainly stumbled on something here, you know. Oh, yes, yes, yes."

"What is it then?" Karen and Julian chorused.

"Well, where do I begin to explain something such as this? Some of these characters are very similar to the basic ancient Germanic runes, but others are of a type associated with Black Magic, Devil Worship and so forth and have an altogether deeper and more sinister meaning when used in conjunction. I will need a little time to work on this now. Please excuse me. Would you mind entertaining yourselves for an hour or so?

I should have something for you then. This is most interesting, yes, yes, yes; absolutely fascinating."

"But Cecil, before you disappear into your study, you may be interested in this old book that Julian unearthed before he mentioned the runes to me." Karen held out the thick volume with its faded leather spine and brown mottled pages.

"Well bless me, you two are certainly full of surprises today, aren't you?" the professor smiled as he took the book from Karen. "I haven't seen a copy of this since I was an undergraduate you know, and I have rued the day I handed it back to the librarian ever since. My own tutor studied under the man who wrote this book and he viewed it as the ultimate authority on the subject at the time. Of course, I have taken matters further with my own expositions since, but I shall enjoy renewing my acquaintance with this noble volume."

"Keep it, Cecil. I'll have no further use for it and it is the least we can do to repay your help, anyway" said Julian. "What's more, I came upon it quite by chance at a sale of old books and thought it might help me to unravel this mystery. I guess I was meant to have it so that I could pass it on to you."

"Are you absolutely sure, young man?" the professor stammered in disbelief at his good fortune in coming across the book again after all these years.

"Yes, of course. I shall be honoured if you will accept it as a gift. As I say, I can't help feeling that you were meant to have it."

"You are too kind. Many thanks. And now I must get to work and earn it" the professor smiled as he shuffled out of the room.

As the old man clearly wished to work alone, his two visitors decided to take a stroll along the hilltop and enjoy more of the panoramic views of the Welsh coastline, which had enthralled them so much when they first arrived. Karen was always a keen walker, having taken holidays in the Lake District, the Yorkshire Dales and the Western Highlands of Scotland with her father. She had also become well used to putting on her hiking boots to gain access to archaeological digs in various parts of the World so, although not suitably attired for a cliff-top ramble she could not resist the temptation. Julian was content to follow just as long as it was not likely to become too strenuous, as he was not really the outdoor type.

By the time they returned, the professor had laid out a modest spread of cakes and biscuits and brewed a fresh pot of tea. "I saw you coming back along the cliff path, so I knew that I would have time to make the tea before you got here," he said triumphantly. "Now, down to business" he continued, without drawing breath. "If these jottings of yours are accurate and the hieroglyphics were actually drawn at the same time as the runes in that timber yard of yours, young Julian......."

"Well, what then?" Karen asked a little nervously as the professor's tone began to sound a little more serious than before.

"Well Karen, I agree with your reading of the hieroglyphics which seem to indicate someone's journey into the afterlife, but the runes are telling me something beyond that. Oh yes, yes, yes, they tell of witchcraft and sorcery in which human sacrifices have been made. You see, it's incomplete I'm afraid. I wish I had been there to make some notes. No offence meant Julian, my dear chap."

"None taken, I'm sure, Cecil." Julian replied now in a state of some excitement. "Can you tell us any more from what I gave you?"

"It is only guesswork from here on but, I think these markings were meant to convey a message to whoever might read them. I think that someone, perhaps one of the victims of witchcraft, is asking for help from beyond the grave."

"But professor, that's crazy, I mean, beyond the grave! You mean a zombie or one of those young women who was bitten by the vampire and became – what do they call it - undead? Aren't we getting a bit carried away here?"

"It's all right Julian. Calm down," Karen soothed. "Cecil is only relating to us what he thinks the runes are telling him, and that is what we came here to find out, isn't it?"

"Yes but this is serious stuff, old girl. It's bloody scary. What the hell have we got mixed up in, for Christ's sake?"

"I'm relieved to hear you mention Him, Julian because I think you will need to call on His help before you're through with this business. Dear me, yes." The professor's deep and sombre voice seemed to underline the gravity of the situation. "If this message is from someone who exists in that twilight zone between life and death, where the body has died but their spirit cannot rest, then you seem to have been chosen for some exciting work, young man."

"Oh my God!" cried Julian in anguish, "why me?"

"I don't think it is you, Julian," Karen cut in, "I think it's Ray who needs to know about this, don't you see?"

"Oh yes, I suppose you're right. But he has just flown off to the Bahamas with Sam."

CHAPTER VII –
The Journey

Ray felt happy and relaxed as he gazed out of the window at the radiant blue sky of late afternoon still way above and the endless sea of fluffy white clouds beneath him. The plane felt as though it was hanging almost motionless in the air, increasing the serenity that Ray felt. He could not remember when he had looked forward to a holiday more than this, although on this occasion it was to be just a short break in the Bahamas with Sam. The pilot announced a short while ago that they had now reached their cruising altitude and Ray knew from experience that a meal was therefore probably not far off. He was no stranger to long distance flights as his business interests often took him to the Far East and various other destinations around the world.

Looking down at Sam's immaculate hands, he took one of them gently in his, causing her to stir slightly. She had clearly drifted off to sleep whilst reading her magazine and he gently caressed her hand and dispersed some of his warmth through it. Sam always appreciated this, as she so often felt cold, whilst Ray on the other hand, was always overheating. He frequently thought how fortunate they were to have such a close relationship and was definitely toying with the idea of proposing to her whilst they were away. The Bahamas would be the ideal location and he knew that she would love that. He would secretly arrange a meal in a very romantic setting; he would secure a bouquet of the very best exotic local flowers; then he would go down on one knee and ask her to marry him. He gazed across at her as she gently slept on, completely unaware of his plans. Ray began to feel very pleased with his surprise for Sam and could already imagine the joy he would feel as he saw her face beaming with delight when he popped the question. He knew that he would feel almost overwhelmed with happiness when she accepted him and he could hardly wait now to put his plans into action.

"Would you prefer red or white wine with your meal, sir?" Ray looked up from his reverie to see the smiling face of the stewardess looking down at him.

"Oh, err, I'll have the red wine thank you; and so will the young lady," he replied quietly so as not to awaken his sleeping fiancée to be.

The stewardess handed him two small bottles of red wine and plastic cups, smiled again and moved on to the next passengers. Sam snuggled up close to Ray and nuzzled her head into his shoulder; he turned towards her and kissed her tenderly on the forehead.

"Hmm, that's better, I must have drifted off whilst I was reading. I obviously needed it," she said, yawning.

"I was as quiet as a church mouse," Ray whispered, "and I ordered a red wine to go with our Hungarian Goulash. I hope that's alright for you."

"Perfect," she replied with a warm smile, "I need to stretch my legs and then go and powder my nose, darling. I'm a bit stiff after that little nap."

"OK Sam," Ray replied, reaching up to twiddle about with the airflow nozzle above his head. Having decided that there was not enough air coming through it to move a feather, he began to gaze out of the window again and immediately noticed that the clouds had cleared so that the Atlantic Ocean was now clearly visible far below. He felt captivated by the beauty and majesty of the sea; so deep, so mysterious and so very dangerous and he often pondered the many hidden secrets it must hold. The sky was a brilliant deep blue with just the occasional cloud drifting along when he noticed that one of the cloud formations seemed to be changing shape more rapidly than usual. He sat spellbound as the swirling formation started to head straight towards the plane, gathering pace as it came. He could scarcely believe his eyes as it began to take on the shape of something very familiar to him. It was her! He recognised the face coming at him out of the cloud. She had followed him all the way across the sea. Was he to find no hiding place from her? He braced himself in his seat and held on tightly to it. Just as the cloud seemed certain to crash into the window, it was gone in a flash and all he could see was the deep blue-grey of the sea far below him and the clear blue sky above. Ray's face betrayed his feelings of shock and disbelief, as Sam returned to her seat, now fully refreshed.

"Ray! What's the matter; are you alright?"

"Oh, yes, I'm fine thanks Sam," he stammered.

She gave him a long, hard, questioning look, leaving him no alternative but to come clean with her and tell the truth. It was a while since Ray had touched on the subject of his friendly ghost and Sam was therefore under the impression that he had finally managed to send her packing.

"You'll be just fine when we land, it's a really lovely hotel," she said reassuringly taking his hand in hers.

"You're under strict orders to just rest, relax and enjoy yourself. Promise?" she urged him. Ray nodded appreciatively, especially as he was feeling quite helpless at this precise moment. He knew that he must try hard, at least for Sam's sake, to put it all behind him especially as she booked this surprise holiday for him to rest and get over his recent ordeal.

After their meal, Sam wrapped her blanket around herself and snuggled up to Ray as the aircraft hummed its way across the apparently never-ending Atlantic Ocean.

Caught now in a different time zone, all on board dozed softly as the plane flew westward towards their tropical destination. Ray was too excited to sleep for long and soon became bored with trying. Instead, he lifted the shutter on his window to see if he could see land yet and found himself squinting at the brilliance of the clear blue sky. After a while, the pilot announced that they would be beginning their descent to Freeport within the hour and there followed the usual bustle of stewardesses rushing to serve breakfast, passengers queuing for the toilets and individual lights being dimmed as some of the passengers tried to get a little sleep before landing.

Neil wandered rather thoughtfully into the sitting room, where Madeline was sitting in her favourite armchair reading the evening newspaper, and sank into the armchair opposite her.

"Rebecca sends her love," he said pensively, "I just telephoned her."

"Oh good, how is she?" Madeline enquired.

"She's fine; still working all the hours God sent at that hospital, which she seems to love so much. I asked her whether she had been in touch with Stella recently and she sounded quite surprised that I should be asking about her after all this time." Neil paused for breath, as though he was about to deliver an important speech. Madeline looked across at him expectantly.

"Well darling? Do go on."

"Apparently, Stella has returned to Singapore because her mother died recently and so she went early to help her ageing father with all the arrangements and everything. Although Rebecca was unsure of the exact date that the old lady died, it would appear to have been about the time of our dinner party." Madeline's jaw dropped.

"You mean Stella's mother could be Ray's ghost?"

"I didn't say that, but the coincidence is rather uncanny, isn't it?"

"I'll say so. What do we do now then, Neil? Do you think we should try to contact Ray somehow?"

"No certainly not, I would hate to spoil his holiday by reminding him about his tame spook. After all, Sam took him off to the Bahamas specifically to take his mind off it. No, I think this can wait until he gets back. Besides we may have more information for him by then."

It was quite early the following morning when Sam and Ray took their first stroll along the beautiful long, sandy beach. From time to time, they would stop and talk to the local fishermen who were grouped along the beach with their huge nets still containing their night's catch. There were also numerous boxes full of colourful fish, together with crab and lobster pots. Some of the fishermen had already sold their catch to local restaurants and to the men who drive their little 'fish vans' around the villages to make their house calls, as is the custom in the Caribbean and surrounding islands. Some just simply sat around, mending their nets in readiness for the next fishing trip. The colourful array of tropical fish fascinated Ray, who stopped on several occasions to ask the names of these unfamiliar fish, which seemed to be all the colours of the rainbow. Sam tugged at his arm in an attempt to keep him moving along the beach.

"Come on Ray. Hurry up or I'll be late, and we must make a stop quickly for coffee somewhere as well." she said, dragging at the tail of his shirt.

"I'm coming!" he said playfully as he skipped to catch her up and then went running on ahead of her. Then he spun around, threw his arms up in the air and said teasingly,

"I can come back anyway. I'll have hours to kill while you're strutting up and down in front of the cameras," he said mimicking her walk with a feminine twirl. Sam giggled at Ray's awkward gyrations.

The aroma of freshly ground coffee wafting through the air attracted them as they approached the entrance to a typical 'fisherman's café' lying at the top of the beach where the sandy shore gave way to a more rocky coastline. They selected a table by the window and Sam sat down while Ray went across to the counter to order two hot, strong, steaming coffees. He wandered over to the window and peered out. The sound of the waves beating against the rocks and the squabbling seagulls fighting over scraps of food on the beach was a real tonic. He knew then that Sam was right all along and this was just what he needed. They had only been on the island for a few hours but he was already telling her repeatedly how much better he was feeling. It was as though a great weight had lifted from his shoulders and indeed, when he remembered the incident with the cloud on the plane he began to remember the face as though it were smiling at him. Sam gave him a knowing grin. "By the end of the week you'll be back to your old self again!" she enthused.

Then she looked at her watch and realised that she must get back to the hotel quickly to meet the photographers and crew who would be waiting with a hired driver and mini-bus to take them to various locations around the island for filming. It seemed a shame to have to gulp down their coffee and rush back along the water's edge but Sam was here to work after all. They walked hand-in-hand along 'Fisherman's Beach', listening to the murmur of the waves on the sand and to the sea birds crying overhead. They stopped occasionally to hug each other in this tropical paradise where it seemed to be a sin to hurry. Ray was thinking about the hours ahead of him whilst Sam would be working and remembered how she had told him simply to relax. He would certainly do so, but he thought it might be interesting to return to the beach and find some of the fishermen whom they had met earlier, so that he could learn a little more about their lives in this wonderful, sun-drenched environment.

As they reached the hotel, the photographers were busy collecting their gear together for the day and some were already complaining that the mini-bus was late. Sam kissed Ray good-bye and soon merged into the general, professional melee of the fashion world, pointing out vociferously that taxis and mini-buses were always late in this part of the World. Then by some miracle, the mini-bus arrived only ten minutes late and the crew erupted into feverish activity, recriminations and general pandemonium. With a wry smile, Ray thanked his lucky stars that he was not expected to take part in this crazy charade in which his lovely Sam was playing the central part. He somehow knew that she would soon knock this motley crew into shape and have them all 'eating out of her hand' in no time at all. As Sam and her clamorous entourage disappeared outside, Ray heaved a sigh of relief and went off to his room to freshen up and collect the rather scruffy and dented old black case that contained his treasured saxophone. After spending some time with the locals, he would find a deserted beach and blow his horn to his heart's content; life was beginning to look a whole lot better, he thought.

A little way along the beach, Ray spotted a young man standing by an old wooden cart that was laden with green coconuts. The wooden slats of the cart were either broken or missing and the rusty wheels must have been without tyres for some years now. The young man eagerly asked Ray if he wanted any 'jelly' coconuts and displayed his dexterity with a machete by neatly carving the top of the green coconut. He then expertly chopped enough off the top to leave a small, clean hole into which he inserted a straw and then handed the coconut to the big man in the colourful shorts. Ray dug in his pocket for a suitable amount of change then settled himself down with his back against a nearby palm tree whilst he sorted it out and began to suck the refreshing juice; it was delicious.

"Where's the best place to get good fish around here?" Ray asked between sucks.

"You need to be here early, man! Real early morning, before they sell off to the delivery boys and the restaurants, then you can buy direct from the fishermen, see?"

"Thanks, I'll do that." Ray replied, handing the young man the few coins he had selected, plus a little extra for his advice.

Further along the beach, Ray came across a small cluster of palm trees, under which an old upturned barrel was serving as a table for several men. They were sitting there passing the time of day together in what little shade was afforded by the trees. Ray thought he recognised a couple of the men from his morning walk with Sam and guessed that they must be some of the fishermen. One of the men leaned back on his wooden stool as Ray approached.

"What have you got in that case, man?" he enquired with a wide toothy grin.

"Oh, that's just a saxophone which I brought along for my own entertainment." Ray replied.

"They call me Joe," said the man with grizzled grey hair and sparkling eyes, offering his outstretched hand.

"Call me Ray," came the reply as Ray shook Joe's hand, "nice to meet you."

"We saw you on the beach this morning with the lovely lady. This is Arnold, and this here is Leroy."

"I'm pleased to meet you both." Ray was amazed to have struck up a conversation so soon after arriving here and somehow he knew this was going to be a day to remember.

"So where is the beautiful and delicate young lady we saw you with this morning?" Arnold asked in a very direct manner.

"Oh, you mean Sam," Ray responded with a self-satisfied chuckle, "she's at work."

"Work?" The three echoed, "We thought you were on holiday man."

"Or honeymoon?" Joe teased with a wicked grin.

"No, Sam is a fashion model; you know the ones who wear all those fancy clothes in the glossy magazines." Ray explained.

"The sexy underwear and swimming costumes?" asked Leroy, beginning to get interested in the conversation and beaming from ear to ear.

"Well, yes sometimes," Ray conceded, "but usually dresses, blouses and skirts. She came here on an assignment to model some new summer outfits in a tropical setting and I just came along with her for the change of scenery. I've had a very stressful time recently and needed a break," he added.

"I'm sorry to hear that," said Joe, "but you have definitely come to the right place to relax." He laughed, slapping Ray on the shoulder. "This is paradise, man."

"I certainly thought it could pass for paradise when we came into view of the island on the boat from Freeport," Ray agreed, "with all those palm trees and endless coral beaches. Wow, it's just so beautiful."

"Just like your lady," said Leroy, not quite able to keep up with the conversation and still obviously imagining Sam in a bikini.

"Bloody well shut up, Leroy! You must excuse him Ray," Joe explained, "it's just that we don't get to see too many beautiful fashion models around here, you see, especially white ones with the red hair."

"It's OK, I understand." Leroy's one-track mind amused Ray.

"Arnold, Leroy and me are all fishermen and so were our fathers before us and their fathers before them and that's what we do; fish!" Joe said enthusiastically. "We go out when the tide is right and fill our nets and pots and then just bring back all the fish and the lobsters and sell them to make money for our families. Then we take coffee in my wife's restaurant, where you went this morning with your young lady friend." Joe said, proudly. "We spend the morning doing a little maintenance on our boats and our nets and then our wives come down at lunchtime when we all meet up in the restaurant again. After that we play a few games of dominoes and Arnold falls asleep." Leroy fell into fits of laughter, followed closely by Arnold if only because he knew it was true. Ray took his saxophone out of its case and began polishing it up. He then fitted the mouthpiece and selected a new reed, which he wetted on his lips before attaching it to the mouthpiece.

"So when do we get to hear you blowing that horn of yours then, Ray?" asked Joe with some enthusiasm, "We could all do with a bit of music before lunch you know man."

"Just as soon as I've got this reed properly positioned and tuned up." They all quietly watched him assemble the instrument and listened in amazement as Ray went straight into one of his favourite jazz numbers, remained silent for several moments after he had finished, then suddenly burst into rapturous applause. Leroy whooped for joy, Joe grinned and whispered, "that's nice" while Arnold nodded appreciatively.

"Now where did you learn to blow like that, man?" cried Leroy, still in a state of real excitement. "It's a long time since I heard the saxophone played as good as that, man."

"I learnt while I was at school back home in England, then I played quite a lot in a jazz band when I was at university and now I occasionally play in a jazz club in London. Although I don't seem to get enough time for that these days," he added wistfully.

"Let's hear some more," Leroy encouraged, "that was real sweet."

"Yeah, what about the Blues, man." Arnold suggested.

"No, let Ray play what he wants to play." Joe cut in, "Can't you see he is using that thing to let his feelings out, man? If he wants to play jazz then that's just fine by us, eh?"

"No problem Joe," said Ray, "I'll play whatever you guys want to hear, that's cool with me, OK? Now, someone said they wanted to hear the Blues." Without another word, Ray swung straight into Basin Street Blues to the accompaniment of much foot tapping, finger clicking, nodding and the occasional vocalisation from his newfound friends.

"It's time for a drink and some lunch too, I think," Joe stated with some authority, "you must be pretty thirsty after all that blowing. I sure am just from tapping my toes." They made their way over to the café further along the beach where Joe's wife was all ready to serve lunch for the wives and anyone else who cared to join them. Joe and Ray seemed to be really hitting it off and their laughter echoed from the bushes and trees as they wandered slowly along the sandy beach under the sweltering tropical sun. Ray loved this weather but had to keep mopping his brow as he was still sweating profusely from the exertion of playing his saxophone for an hour or more. Once Leroy and Arnold had broken off into a conversation of their own, Ray took the opportunity to intimate to Joe that he was intending to propose to Sam whilst they were on the island. In fact, he intended to do so the following day and was therefore keen to seek Joe's ideas straight away. He was quite sure that Joe would know the best location and have a few interesting ideas of his own. Indeed, Joe was genuinely pleased for Ray and not only knew the right place, but also promised to catch the biggest and best lobster of the season for Sam's dinner the following evening.

A strong aroma met Ray as he entered the thatched café at the end of the beach once again, but this time it was not coffee that dominated but spice, fish and a variety of other wonderful things. Ray wondered whether it smelled so good because he was so hungry or whether the food would actually taste as good as it most certainly smelt. Although Joe's wife ran the café, there was more than fish on offer, several meat dishes were also available and Ray felt spoilt for choice. Joe went straight round behind the bar and put his arm around his wife and called out to Ray.

"This is my wife, Sylvia. She's the boss when we are in the restaurant but I am the boss at home and on my boat!"

"Just on the boat, Joe!" she retaliated, "just on the boat and nowhere else."

"She enjoys a good joke Ray, but she knows who the boss really is, eh?"

"Yes Joe and it's her, I reckon." Ray replied quickly as he did not want to cross the woman who was busily cooking his lunch, besides she looked as though she was in control anyway. They all laughed heartily at Ray's innate understanding of Joe's marital situation. Sylvia smiled at the newcomer with a look that indicated her approval. Joe explained to Ray that fishing and farming were the only way to earn a living on the island and so they worked together supplying each other with their needs and selling the surplus in the markets in Freeport.

Ray felt good at having given the saxophone a real blast and indeed having made some new friends along the way. Now he was enjoying a well-earned lunch while an old jukebox played the latest hits from the USA in the corner of the bar. He felt at peace with the World, although he was already looking forward to seeing Sam again later. After lunch, Joe invited Ray to join him and his friends for a game of dominoes and challenged Ray to win a game before Arnold fell asleep. After much teasing, Arnold decided it was time to leave as he had some 'important business' to attend to and Leroy decided to tag along with him as he so often did. Although neither Ray nor Joe had deliberately arranged it, the departure of the other two enabled them to continue their discussions about Ray's forthcoming engagement in private. They watched with amusement as Arnold and Leroy slowly meandered aimlessly up the beach, quite obviously with no pressing business engagements to attend.

"Oh man," said Joe, standing up from the table and wandering across to the bar, "that Arnold is something else. Usually, he can take a joke, but today I think he was a little bit embarrassed, what with you being here. You know what I'm saying? And Leroy just follows him around wherever he goes, just like a shadow." Joe returned to the table with two bottles of beer, dripping with condensation from the refrigerated cabinet, and put one down next to Ray's glass. As he thanked Joe for the beer, Ray began to look a little pensive as though he had something on his mind.

"I really appreciate your hospitality Joe," said Ray on a more serious note, "I feel as though I've known you for years already."

"Yeah, we're brothers, man." Joe chuckled as he poured the icy cold beer into his waiting glass. "That's just what I needed," he said, taking a long draught of his drink. Ray did the same with an appreciative grin, and then began to outline his plans to Joe.

"As I mentioned earlier, I have been under a lot of pressure recently and it was Sam's brilliant idea to come here for a short break as she was coming here for some location work anyway. Well, I have been thinking about proposing to her for some time now but I just couldn't come up with the right time or place."

"Well you have found the right place now my friend and there is no time like the present," came Joe's positive response.

"That's right. I thought about it on the flight over while Sam was asleep and I want to surprise her with a romantic evening right here in the paradise of the Bahamas."

"You are absolutely right, man! This is paradise and where better to propose to your lovely lady?" Joe enthused. "She really means a lot to you, doesn't she? She is your 'petals on the rose' and you most certainly must do the decent thing and marry her." Joe immediately insisted that he would arrange for a beautiful bouquet of flowers, which one of his friends could get for him and that Ray must let Sylvia cook for them. As soon as Ray explained how Sam adored lobster, Joe thumped the table and noisily reiterated his promise to catch the biggest and best lobster in the whole of the Bahamas just for Sam. He virtually dragged Ray across to tell Sylvia the news and to discuss with her how Sam would prefer to have her lobster cooked. Sylvia was delighted and started planning the meal immediately, throwing suggestions at Ray who suddenly felt quite bemused by all the attention he was getting.

"But Joe," Ray suddenly exclaimed in horror, "I haven't even got her a ring yet!" Joe and Sylvia burst into laughter at Ray's desire to conform to convention, especially remembering their own experience. Joe began to tell their story to a rather agitated Ray who had no choice but to sit down and listen.

"So when she climbed out of the bedroom window of her parents' house at, what was it Sylvia, about midnight?" Sylvia nodded an affirmative. "Everyone was asleep. We had no electric lights in the country districts in those days so it was pitch black, except for the moonlight, of course. We had agreed to meet up that night to talk about how we would break the news of our engagement to our parents because, although we had been courting since schooldays, it had mostly been in secret and they didn't know how serious it was between us," he chuckled. Sylvia winked at Ray in a conspiratorial way, as if to say 'listen to what comes next'. "Well sir, I am telling you, we did not plan for things to work out the way they did! We were still young and naïve, you see. Well, we laid on the beach to talk about our plans and then, well you know how it goes with the sins of the flesh; one thing leads to another and....."

"Next thing I know," continued Sylvia, "there's a baby coming. Can you imagine the upset that caused in such a strongly Christian family? Oh, man." Just then, two tourists wandered into the bar and Sylvia left the two men at the table to go and attend to her new customers. Joe took up the story.

"We took hell from our families and were disowned for what we did but our feelings for each other just grew stronger. I remember getting engaged to Sylvia and, just like you, I hadn't got her a ring. So do you know what I did? I tied a long blade of dried grass around her finger and told her that I would marry her as soon as I could." He then looked tenderly across at Sylvia, who was now taking orders for drinks behind the bar and whispered, with a glint in his eye. "After all this time I still wouldn't swap her for anyone else in the World." For a moment, Ray was lost for words but then curiosity got the better of him.

"So what's the secret to a long and fulfilling marriage then Joe?" asked Ray with genuine interest.

"Well young man," Joe started thoughtfully, "I suppose, in addition to sharing the simple pleasures of life, the most important ingredients are the little things.

Women notice the little things, for example telling her she looks good and telling her you love her every day, even when she is fearful angry with you. What's more, always let your wife think she made the final decision, even when you have already done so. Do you think you can handle that?"

"No problem!" Ray replied with a mixture of gratitude for the older man's sound advice and his determination to make Sam happy.

"So Ray, what have you been up to that has you so stressed out that your girlfriend had to bring you all the way to the Bahamas to get away from it, eh?"

"Oh, it's a very odd and quite complicated story really, Joe."

"I'm all ears, young man. Tell me all about it, we have all afternoon." Joe said encouragingly, as he always loved to hear a good story. Ray felt a little awkward about the unusual subject matter of his tale and was unsure where to begin. However, he felt sure that his new friend would not ridicule his story but would be sympathetic and supportive, so he related as much as he could remember of the dinner party and the events that followed. Joe sat listening attentively, occasionally raising an eyebrow or wagging his head in disbelief but all the time encouraging Ray to continue. Had Joe's hair not already been grey and curly, Ray thought that his story might well have had that effect on it; such was the incredulous expression on Joe's face. This was the first time that Ray had actually heard the whole story, even though he was relating it himself, and in a strange way it began to clarify in his own mind with the telling. Eventually, Ray completed the story to date and he sank back in his chair, seemingly exhausted from recounting the events that led to his current condition. Joe just wagged his head from side to side and pursed his lips.

"Oh man, I'm surprised you didn't end up in the madhouse after all that," he said, rubbing his chin wistfully and staring at the ground. "Wait a minute, though. Something is bugging me about this you know man."

"What is it Joe? You look puzzled."

"It's probably nothing at all, but your description of this woman with silvery grey hair and a sort of dusky appearance; what you called olive skin....."

"Yes, and striking green eyes," Ray interjected with some excitement.

"It just keeps ringing a bell in the back of my mind you know. Have you been troubled by her since you arrived here?" Joe enquired.

"No, not really," answered Ray, "the last time was when I was on the plane. You remember the incident I told you about when the cloud formed into her face?"

"Yes I remember but, doesn't that seem odd to you, Ray. That she's left you alone now that you're here, I mean?" asked Joe curiously.

"Perhaps it's because I am relaxing at long last and I'm now beginning to get over it."

"I'm not so sure, my friend. You see, there was an elderly woman fitting that description who died recently on The Black Island. She lived all her life on that island. You would have passed it on the ferry from Freeport about half an hour or so before landing here. I'm sorry Ray, I guess I'm rambling a bit but your description of the old wooden house with the animals outside sounds so familiar, but then that it is pretty typical of the older style houses around here. It's ridiculous anyway, why should you be haunted by somebody you don't even know?" Joe began to dismiss his own thoughts as too coincidental.

"Well I'm open to any suggestions Joe. As I told you, I've been trying to figure this out for some time now and I can't really make head or tail of it all." Ray sighed, as it seemed as though another lead had just evaporated.

"I don't really think I can help you much more, young man, even if I was right about this woman and that is very unlikely," Joe confirmed "but I do know somebody who could help you." Joe added, in a low voice.

"Then tell me more." Ray implored.

"Please keep your voice down while we discuss this. I don't really want anyone to hear me talking about him because they are very superstitious around here. Very religious but also very superstitious, and there are some things we don't talk about in public, you understand?" Joe asked.

"Yes, of course" Ray answered in a conspiratorial whisper.

"I know of an old man who lives up in the hills on that island. They say he is very mysterious and that he knows things best not tampered with, if you get my meaning. They say he practices the black arts, although he has never actually harmed anybody, as far as I know." Joe seemed to be warming to the subject but was careful to keep his voice lowered. "Although the folks round here are very superstitious and would never mention him in company, I believe some of them go to see him in secret to seek his help."

"So what about you Joe, are you nervous of this man?"

"No, I'm not scared of the old man now. I was when I was a child because I did not understand the old-fashioned ways and I believed all the nonsense people used to tell me in those days and they tried to make us kids frightened of men like him. As I grew older and my knowledge of life increased, I became intrigued by what's out there and began to open my eyes more, but at the same time I realized that we will never even begin to understand many of the mysteries we come across during our lifetime. When you go out to sea to catch fish you realize the power of nature and how small we men really are and that makes you feel very humble but not afraid of God, or of anything else."

"Tell me more about this man, Joe."

"From what I've heard he really is gifted in this way just as I have a gift for catching fish. I am told that he knows many things as well as being a healer and a herbalist. He also has a very deep knowledge of Obeah. Folks around here still follow that old religion. In fact, the local people call him 'The Obeah Man'. When I was a little boy, my father would sometimes drop me off at the jetty on The Black Island to play with some of the other boys, when he was going out for a long fishing trip. I suppose he didn't need a little whippersnapper like me getting in his way when he was out for some really serious fishing," Joe chuckled at his reminiscences of boyhood. "We would sneak off into the bush when nobody was watching to play games up in the hills. One of these games would be a dare to see who was brave enough to walk slowly past the Obeah man's gate without breaking into a run."

"How good were you at that?" Ray asked, grinning.

"Let's put it this way; I was the only one to end up with a sack full of marbles, the most colourful, flawless ones you ever laid eyes on." Joe slapped his thigh with laughter as he remembered his prowess at walking slowly past the old man's gate with his knees knocking together with fear.

"So you played marbles here as well then, Joe. That was my favourite game when I was a little boy back in England, but we didn't use them to bet with as you obviously did." Ray had really warmed to his new friend and could have listened to Joe's stories all afternoon but Joe's tone suddenly became more serious. "Let me tell you man," he continued, "many strange things have happened on that island, which is probably how it got it's name in the first place. Some of it I believe and some of it's just superstition, but if you are going to have any dealings with that man, you must be very careful. You never know where it might lead and so you would do well to safeguard yourself with some real strong protection against whatever demons you might encounter." Having experienced the terror of the séance at Ivy Cottage, Ray appreciated Joe's warning. He knew very well that he needed some specialist help and, if he could get that help from the Obeah man, then so be it.

"Joe, will you do something for me?" Ray asked.

"Of course I will, but within reason, mind." Joe already knew what was coming.

"You said that the Obeah man lives in the hills on The Black Island. Would you take me there?"

"Yes man, just so long as we keep this to ourselves, but I won't be taking you all the way to his house, mind. Here is what I will do for you. The day after tomorrow I will be taking the boat out early in the morning, as I have to go to the far side of The Black Island to check on some of my lobster pots. Everyone will think you have just gone on a fishing trip with me, but I'll drop you off at the jetty on The Black Island and show you the path to take up into the hills. I'll come back for you later on in the afternoon, at about four o'clock. How does that sound?"

"That'll be great, thanks a lot, Joe." Ray felt that he had spent a very worthwhile afternoon and that he was really onto something with this Obeah man, as Joe called him. He could feel it in his bones that this man would hold the key to the mysteries that he had so far failed to unravel. He remembered the agreement he had with Sam that they would tell each other everything about this whole saga and he could hardly wait to tell her about this latest twist.

"I tell you Sylvia, this poor man has been to Hell and back and he needs help to get rid of this presence that keeps haunting him." Joe explained to his wife that evening.

"And I tell you that no good will come of it, Joseph! That old man is dangerous and wicked. You know that very well yourself, so I don't know why are you sending this nice young man right into his lair?"

"Sylvia, Sylvia my love, that old man is just misunderstood, he's not dangerous."

"He's poisonous Joe, that's what he is. Look what he did to that poor old woman who went to him for help after her husband died. She was scared by the noises she kept hearing around the house at night and thought it must be her husband's spirit, unable to rest for some reason. I know that was no way for a spirit to behave, but then that Obeah man frightened the poor woman half to death with his chanting and the crazy rituals he used just to exorcise the man's ghost."

"It worked though, didn't it? She didn't hear any more noises, did she?"

"She was too frightened to, in case the Obeah man came back with more rituals!"

"Anyway, it wasn't the Obeah man who frightened her. It was her husband's spirit which wouldn't rest because she couldn't be bothered to give him the proper, traditional burial that he wanted."

"Why did her hair go white then?"

"The woman was eighty-three years old. The loss of her husband and his antics just made it go from grey to white a bit more quickly, that's all."

"Well I don't like it and I don't want you to go. He just might remember how you used to play outside his gate when you were a boy and then put a curse on you."

"Sylvia my sweetheart, I'm not going to the old man's gate. I will drop Ray off at the jetty and then give him directions through the village and up into the hills. It's not a difficult path to follow and he's a big, strong man who can look after himself. What's more, he's not afraid either. He just needs help and who better than the Obeah man to rid him of an unwanted spirit."

"Does his girlfriend know about this silly business, Joe?"

"No not yet, but I think he is planning to tell her tonight and I know she wants to help him with this more than anyone. He is planning to have the engagement meal with her first, before he goes. That was why I suggested we go the day after tomorrow, and anyway that's the day I need to go round past the point on The Black Island for the lobsters, so it all fits nicely."

"This will all end in tears, Joe. You mark my words; and I hope it's not that lovely girl who ends up shedding the tears."

"There won't be any tears, unless they're tears of joy because he has lost his ghostly follower. Now, what have you cooked up for tonight, my love, is that fish tea I can smell?" Joe asked as he gave Sylvia a big hug.

"Get away with you, you randy devil!"

"Oh Ray, I'm so pleased you had a good day, today. I was afraid you might be rather bored," Sam smiled as Ray began telling her how he had made some new acquaintances on the beach. "I was worried you wouldn't be able to find enough to do, but I should have known better where you're concerned, shouldn't I?" Ray laughed and shrugged his shoulders at the compliment. "So Joe is one of the fishermen we met on the beach and Sylvia is the lady who runs the restaurant, is that it?" Sam questioned.

"Yes, that's right, Sam. Joe has been a great help to me already with his recollections, his advice and knowledge of life in general. You know, it feels as though I've known him for years and, well he really is a bit of a wise old bird, too."

"What else did you get up to today then Ray?" Sam was keen to hear all about his day, as he seemed to be so happy now.

"Well, I was going to find a quiet beach somewhere to give the saxophone a bit of a workout but Joe and his pals insisted that I play for them right there and then, so I did. We had a great session with some jazz, a few blues numbers and a bit of soul as well. It was so good to be playing again, especially with such an appreciative audience. Then Ray hesitated.

"Sam, I've arranged for us to go out tomorrow evening. You don't have anything planned, business-wise do you?"

"No Ray, I don't." Sam's voice was openly inquisitive. "It sounds wonderful, I can't wait. So where are we going?"

"You'll just have to wait and see!"

CHAPTER VIII –
Jacob's Bane

The following day passed quickly for both of them, although in very different ways. Ray spent quite a long time with Sylvia and Joe, going over the plans for the evening meal until Sylvia had to shoo him away in a good-natured way so that she could get on with her work. Sam, on the other hand, tried to hurry the crew along in order to have as much time as possible back at the hotel to prepare for what promised to be a wonderful evening.

"So where are we going, Ray?" Sam asked as Ray busied himself in the bathroom, shaving and generally sprucing himself up.

"It's a surprise my darling and you'll love it. All you have to do is look beautiful, which shouldn't pose a problem for you, now should it?"

"I'll do my best to look absolutely gorgeous for you lover, now where are we going?" she teased. "After all, I need to know what to wear." Sam opened the wardrobe door to choose a dress for the occasion, but it was difficult to choose, especially as that was what her job entailed. However, she felt this was rather different as she was choosing something attractive to wear for Ray and she guessed it might include dinner at a special restaurant that Ray had found during the day. She was pleased with his progress and would agree to anything he suggested, if she thought it might aid his full recovery. "Should it be the blue or the yellow dress?" She enquired, holding them up in front of her alternately for Ray's approval. As she turned back to face the mirror on the wardrobe door, Ray came across and stood behind her, his large frame filling the full-length mirror.

"The yellow one," he whispered in her ear, then closed his eyes and kissed her softly several times around her neck. He scooped her hair up and piled it on top of her head saying, "and wear your hair high on top of your head, like this."

"Come on we don't want to be late!" This was Sam's way of stopping Ray in his tracks before he got too carried away.

Although it was only another three quarters of an hour before Sam was eventually ready, it seemed hours to Ray as he paced the floor in anticipation of this most important evening. However, when she finally glided gracefully into the room with a seductive smile, Ray's jaw dropped. She looked stunning in the little, figure-hugging, lemon yellow cocktail dress with her red her hair pinned up, just as Ray had requested.

"You look absolutely delicious!" Ray panted.

"Down boy, we have a date to go on, don't we?" she teased, blowing him a big kiss, "come on then, let's go." Ray rushed to the door and out she swept. His heart was thumping with excitement, love and anticipation and he knew that he never felt happier.

The setting was perfect for what Ray had planned for Sam and, as they walked in through the wide double doors, both Sylvia and Joe were there to welcome them. Ray introduced Sam as she had only very briefly seen the couple early the previous morning when they stopped by for a coffee after walking along Fisherman's Beach.

"Well I can see now why he's gone to town over the arrangements for this evening" Sylvia began, hands on hips, "do you know he spent at least half an hour explaining to me what you can eat and what you can't eat, fussin' here and fussin' there he was." By this time, Sam was as close as she would ever get to blushing. "Well I expect if you want to keep that hourglass figure of yours, you gotta take care of it. Still, I can't say I blame him!" As Joe showed them to their table, Sylvia took her leave of them and hurried back to her kitchen. This put Ray in mind of Madeline back home in England and he grinned to himself as he thought of her and Neil. Sam loved the restaurant so much that she was positively purring at the wonderful ambience. Their table faced straight out to sea across the wide sandy beach, framed by the arching fronds of a few palm trees. Strands of the thatched roof hung down and waved gently in the breeze. Candles on each table provided the only lighting and their flames danced as if to echo the feelings of the amorous couples around the room. A local band softly played romantic tunes in the background and on each table stood a vase of beautifully coloured tropical flowers.

Sam was thrilled that Ray had gone to so much trouble to organise a lovely evening meal for her when he was here simply to relax and do nothing. It made a complete change for her to dine at such a picturesque place, away from all the hustle and bustle of the busy London restaurants with their innate commercialism. By contrast, this was real and she was therefore very happy to be dining at Sylvia's restaurant with some of the locals. She noticed that there was no menu on the table and realised that Ray really had gone that step further by arranging with Sylvia what they were to eat. She also noticed that Ray appeared to be a little nervous as he sat there opposite, almost as though he was expecting something to go wrong.

"Oh Ray, I feel so special tonight. Thank you so much for bringing me here." Ray took her hands in his and looked her straight in the eye.

"You are special," he replied, "a very special part of my life. In fact, I couldn't live without you now, my darling." Joe, who was looking very smart tonight in his black and white waiter's outfit, was heading towards their table with a broad grin and an ice bucket containing a large bottle of champagne. Ray tried not to look too embarrassed as Joe lingered rather longer than necessary at their table with that knowing grin on his face. "Does the young lady have a favourite tune she would like the band to play?" Joe asked, as he smoothed the tablecloth out with the palms of his hands and began to rearrange the cutlery quite unnecessarily. Ray began wondering which of them was the most nervous.

"Oh I love Frank Sinatra, so any of his tunes would be marvellous, thank you." Sam smiled at Joe. Finally, Joe caught sight of Ray's expression and quickly got the message.

"I'll have a word with the bandleader, my princess." He said, almost bowing as he left the table. "Sylvia will be along soon with your first course." As he proudly strutted back towards the bar, Sylvia emerged from the kitchen bearing a large wooden tray, on which were two plates, one containing a whole butter-flied lobster and the other with a half portion. Ray noticed that Sylvia had prepared the dish exactly as they had agreed, with a watermelon and sweet pepper salad.

"It looks wonderful!" Sam squealed with delight as Sylvia placed the plates carefully on the table in front of them with a self-satisfied smile. Ray glanced across at Joe, who was busy polishing champagne glasses and rearranging the bottles on the shelves behind the bar. He particularly wanted to assist in the restaurant this evening, as he had been instrumental in bringing Ray's plans for the evening to fruition. Right on cue, he hurried across to their table and removed the empty plates, giving Ray a wicked grin, which fortunately Sam could not see from where she was sitting. The music played softly in the background, the scent of the flowers hung in the warm evening air, the candles flickered and Ray's heart skipped a beat as he stared across the table at her, looking as radiant as he had ever seen her. Sam caught Ray's mood of apprehension.

"Are you alright darling?"

"Yes thanks," he answered, as he got up from his chair and moved around the table towards her. He took her by the hand and went down on bended knee just as he had planned and smiled up at her now, his resolve strengthened by the touch of her hand. "Samantha, I love you.....will you marry me?"

"Yes my darling" she replied without hesitation and threw her arms around his neck and repeated, "Yes my darling Ray!" Joe was unable to resist the temptation to come running across to their table to open the champagne.

"The champagne is on the house!" Joe said, holding his glass up to every diner in the restaurant. His rather generous gesture made Sylvia wince, because she knew just how long it would take to make enough profit to cover such an outlay.

Once they had all received a glass of champagne, there was a chorus of "Congratulations!" as everyone toasted the newly engaged couple. Once Sylvia had brought the dessert for Sam and Ray, she took a glass, which Joe held out for her, smiled at them both and took a small sip.

"To the newly engaged couple, best wishes to you both." As she returned to the kitchen, she beckoned Joe to follow her and give his new friends a little time together as she felt that he was crowding them in his obvious excitement.

"I'll take you to the best jewellers in London to buy you a ring when we get back, but for now, will you wear this as a token of our engagement, Sam?" Ray took out a beautiful little black coral ring, which he managed to buy locally that same day.

"Ray, that is so pretty and how thoughtful of you to have bought me a ring straight away." Sam cooed. "Well, a girl can't really say she's engaged if she hasn't got a ring, now can she?" Ray explained.

"They make these locally and I had to give you a ring when I proposed, so there it is."

"It's lovely Ray. I'm so happy that my head is spinning. Thank you my darling for such a perfect evening." Later, as they strolled along the moonlit beach with their arms around each other, it would not have mattered to them if the Earth had crumbled beneath their feet; they would barely have noticed.

Ray now felt strong enough for anything and was ready for whatever fate might have in store for him. He was not afraid of visiting the Obeah man. In fact, he was now relishing the thought of meeting this enigmatic old man and finding out firsthand whether he agreed with Joe's view, and indeed, whether the old man would be able to help him. He told himself that he could only gain in strength and was well aware that, for some unknown reason, he actually felt stronger since arriving here. The last thing he wanted to do now was to spoil this wonderful evening for Sam, but he knew he must be honest with her and tell her of his plans to visit the Obeah man the following day. He stopped, turned her towards him, held her by both arms and looked straight into her eyes.

"Sam, we agreed always to be open and honest with each other, didn't we?" Ray said in a rather solemn voice, making her wonder for a moment what might be coming next. She looked searchingly into his eyes, which appeared to have been lit up by the moonlight, as he continued. "I had the opportunity to speak privately to Joe yesterday afternoon and I told him about the dinner party and the events which followed. I just felt that he would be a sympathetic listener and, as he wasn't involved, I thought he might have a different perception of it all."

"And did he?" Sam asked softly.

"Well it seems that the people around here have much more understanding of these things than we do in England. In fact, they almost seem to take the supernatural for granted." He paused for breath, as if he were preparing to deliver some serious news. Sam waited as though she already knew what he was about to say. "Joe knows a man who might be able to help me. He practises an old religion, known as Obeah, which some of the people around here still follow. Although some of them go to him for help, they all seem to keep quiet about it as though they are afraid that others might find out, but he apparently has great powers of exorcism." Ray sounded enthusiastic.

"Oh Ray darling, after all you've been through, do you think this is wise?" Sam said softly, resting her head on his chest.

"Sam, I really do believe this man can help me to get rid of this spirit, whoever she is. I must at least try."

"Just be very careful, please darling. Is Joe going to take you to see this man?"

"Yes he will. Well, only as far as the jetty on The Black Island, where the old man lives. Joe will drop me off there and give me directions to his house, which is apparently up in the hills. Please don't worry darling, I'll be fine." Ray insisted. "Oh, and Sam, please don't tell anyone where I've gone, will you? Joe doesn't want any of the locals to know that he is dropping me off there and I would rather it remained our secret. If anyone asks, just tell them that I went with Joe to retrieve his lobster pots from the far side of the island."

Ray slept fitfully that night, partly due to the emotion of the evening and partly due to his eagerness to get started on the trip to The Black Island in the morning. He was already wide-awake before the time that his travelling alarm clock was set for and was therefore able to silence it before it could wake Sam. Although the moon was still visible through the open window, Ray noticed that the sky was already becoming lighter in the East as dawn approached. Silently, he slipped out of bed and began to prepare for his journey. Remembering Joe's advice, he quietly opened the closet door and took out his leather bomber jacket, which he would need against the early morning chill. Sam stirred as be bent over the bed and kissed her.

"Be careful, darling," she murmured in a sleepy voice.

"Don't worry Sam, I will," he reassured her as he gently stroked her cheek with his fingers.

Ray felt very much at peace with the World as he walked along Fisherman's Beach. He appreciated having this space to himself and enjoyed hearing the sound of the waves gently lapping on the shore. Out to sea, he could just make out a few small fishing boats, whose dimly lit lanterns were gently rising and falling with the swell of the sea. The serenity of this simple scene stopped Ray in his tracks and he lingered a few moments to soak up the atmosphere. The moment seemed quite magical and he could quite easily have stayed there until it became light, but he knew he had to move on. In the distance, Ray could see several boats being prepared to put to sea and from one of them a hand was waving. It was Joe, who had spotted Ray's tall frame as he made his way along the beach. Ray broke into a trot as he waved back and headed towards the boat. He hurried past several groups of fishermen, who acknowledged his presence with a cheery wave and a "good morning" or "hello", even though they were busy pushing their boats into the surf and leaping aboard at the last moment. The standard form of dress seemed to be shorts, string vest and bare feet, making Ray feel quite overdressed; in fact, he was beginning to feel quite warm in his leather jacket already, but he knew it would feel cooler once they were out on the sea.

"Good morning Joe, can I help with anything?" Ray called as he drew closer to the boat.

"Hi there Ray, no it's all done thanks. We're ready to shove off now," came Joe's reply "do you want to give the boat a push for me?" As Joe stepped into the boat, Ray automatically removed his shoes and, throwing them into the boat, waded through the water as he pushed the little boat out. He had just seen it done several times and so he knew what was required of him. Nevertheless, his efforts received a look of approval from Joe who did not expect his new apprentice to be so adept at his first attempt.

Ray was captivated by the colours of the dawn as it came up from the East. An orange glow on the horizon delineated the sky from the sea and the colours graduated upwards and outwards to a dark, smoky blue overhead. Soon the Sun would peep over the horizon and the whole appearance of the sea would become at once transformed and bathed in bright light, but for the moment, all was calm and tranquil in shades of blue and grey.

A few other boats were making their way in the same general direction as Joe and the puttering sound of their little engines could be heard coming and going on the light breeze. The camaraderie of the fisher-folk was evident as they waved to each other from time to time as their boats bobbed up and down on the gentle swell. Ray soon joined in to show that he too was one of the team.

As time went on, other boats began to steer divergent courses, their crews waving as they slipped away into the distance and soon Joe and Ray were alone, on course for The Black Island.

"So you're feeling good this morning, my friend" Joe called out over the sound of the chugging engine, from his position at the tiller.

"Not bad thanks. Perhaps a bit apprehensive, but it's a task I must complete, having come this far" Ray called back from the position he had taken up in the bows where he was becoming quite mesmerised from looking down into the water.

"Sylvia asked me to give you something" Joe replied, unzipping his waterproof jacket and pulling out a small book. Ray made his way carefully towards the stern, sat down next to Joe and took the book. It was a small black, leather-bound volume with the title inscribed on it in gold leaf, 'The Holy Bible'. Ray felt touched by Sylvia's obvious concern and, as he flicked through the delicate pages, he looked up at Joe with a smile. "Thank you Joe; and thank you Sylvia. I feel quite overcome by the warmth of your friendship and your concern for my safety."

Man, she was really hard on me when I told her about the position you are in. She begged me not to take you across to that island. You see, she believes all those crazy stories people tell about the old Obeah man."

"I'm sorry Joe. I didn't mean to cause any trouble between you and Sylvia," said Ray slipping the bible into his jacket pocket where, unknown to him, it came to rest next to the piece of bloodstained material which had been there since he showed it to Sam that night in his London flat.

"You see my friend, it was one of those situations where it was much easier to agree that she was right and then to explain your desperate plight to her and, of course, why I have to help you. I feel kinda responsible, especially as I was the one who told you about him. I told her that if I didn't help you then you would have found some other way to get to the old man. If that happened and I didn't know where you were then I wouldn't be able to help you if you needed me, so what sort of friend would that make me. I think she understood then."

"Thanks Joe. I promise I'll come over and visit Sylvia myself, and personally thank her after I've seen the old man. In fact, I'll come straight home with you once you've picked me up from the island. I should be able to get back to the hotel in time for Sam's return from work."

"That sounds good, my friend. Then you can tell Sylvia how the old man is getting on, she'll be very interested in that!" Joe laughed aloud at the thought of Sylvia being inquisitive about the Obeah man, of whom she was secretly afraid. The boat chugged on relentlessly towards its destination and Ray sank deep into thought as Joe stared unblinkingly at the horizon. In his mind, Ray was rehearsing the various options for putting his case to the Obeah man to ensure that he did not get turned away. Should he take a religious approach, a scientific approach, or just tell the old man his story and wait to see his reaction? For some time now, they had been closing on a huge rock, which must have been about two hundred yards long and which rose at least three hundred feet sheer out of the sea. The narrow ledges on the rock's imposingly steep cliffs were home to hundreds of noisy sea birds whose raucous cries pierced the morning calm from a great distance. As Joe steered his boat around this magnificent obelisk, the Black Island came suddenly into view.

Although Ray had already seen the island in the distance from the ferry, it looked very different from close quarters and from the sea level vantage point of a fishing boat. There were tall palm trees just beyond the sandy beach stretching as far as the eye could see in either direction. Other taller trees further inland dominated the skyline and an almost smoky haze hung in the air above the dense woods, lending the island a slightly sinister appearance and adding to the rather sombre overall feeling of the place. Joe explained that most of the islanders still cooked outdoors, using local wood for fuel and that most of these outdoor kitchens doubled as smokehouses.

Joe cut the engine and allowed the boat's momentum to take it silently in to the jetty in the little horseshoe-shaped natural harbour and, as it slowed, he walked forward to the bows and threw a rope to a young man waiting on the harbour wall. The young man deftly tied the rope to a bollard as Joe leapt out onto the crumbling concrete structure. Joe patted him on the shoulder and beckoned to Ray who was climbing out of the boat, holding his jacket and a bag containing a bottle of water and a packed lunch for his long day on the island. Joe pointed to a rough, unmade road leading up the hillside from the far side of the village.

"That's your route my friend," he said, "although there are several turnings off the road and it is quite rough, you should find your way quite easily. I have already described the house so you can't miss it. You will know well enough when you are there." Joe added somewhat enigmatically. The two men shook hands and, as their eyes met, they smiled knowingly at each other and Ray patted his jacket pocket where he had placed the bible earlier and nodded to Joe reassuringly. "Take care, my friend" were Joe's parting words as he turned and jumped back into the boat and prepared to cast off.

"I'll see you at four o'clock." Ray replied. As he began to walk up the slight incline from the harbour, Ray turned around to see that Joe was already speeding away from the jetty on his way to the shellfish beds. Soon he was gone around a headland and Ray felt very much alone. He took a deep breath and turned to face the island again, his heart skipped a beat as he thought of what lie ahead, but he steeled himself against any misgivings and with a new resolve, set off towards the distant hills. On his way up the hill Ray saw several young boys carrying milk pails to milk the cows or goats early enough to be able to return home for their breakfast and in plenty of time to get themselves ready for school. The children would often have to walk miles to get to school so an early start was essential. Ray wondered why they all stared at him with such overt curiosity and felt a little unnerved at times. He assumed that visitors must be extremely rare on this island far away from the usual tourist haunts.

Ray continued along the path as Joe instructed and seemed to be trudging upwards for a very long time. As he went, he began to rehearse what he might say to the old man when he eventually arrived at the house, which he could now already see in his mind's eye. After a while, he came to a fork in the road and stopped to mop his brow and consider which path to follow. The path to the left was a definite fork whilst the main path appeared to be very nearly straight ahead but Ray did not want to waste time wandering off up the wrong path as it could be hours before he found his way back. Furthermore, the path was rough and dusty with sharp stones that dug uncomfortably at his feet, even through his sandals. He did not remember Joe mentioning a fork in the path when he gave him the directions, and he now found himself querying this aloud 'left or right?' A light breeze stirred along the right hand path a few yards in front of him. It was just enough to cause some of the small stones to move and catch his attention and as he looked, the hazy, translucent figure of a woman appeared on the path ahead of him. Ray felt no fear as she turned around to look in his direction and beckoned him to follow her along the right hand fork. Suddenly Madame Rosina's words began to ring in his ears, 'If ever you need help, just ask and I will guide you'. Ray recalled her chanting out these words whilst in her trance at the séance and he had indeed just asked for help when he muttered to himself, 'left or right?' He was now quite certain that he was the one chosen to undertake the dangerous mission that Madame Rosina foretold at the séance. Since that day at Ivy Cottage, Ray had been quite prepared to assume that Neil was the one who would have to undertake this mission. After all, his friends' hallucinations took place at Neil's house and several were about Neil's parents. Furthermore, Neil was with Sam when she witnessed the ritual sacrifice of the young girl. Ray felt that his own problems with the ghost that kept haunting him were co-incidental to Neil's situation, but now it was clear that he alone would have to face the dangers, of which Madame Rosina had warned them all.

Ray's mind was reeling as he began to realise that he was destined to come here with Sam in order to carry out whatever it was that this woman needed from him. Neither he nor Sam had any control over the choice of venue for her modelling assignment and some unknown force had steered them here. As he tried feverishly to fit all the pieces of the jigsaw in place in his head, he realised that he had automatically taken the path along which she was guiding him. The path led past an old, dilapidated house made of wood and corrugated iron with four or five open-tread steps leading up to the front door which, although still intact, had now lost all its paint, as had the shutters at the windows. This woman, who entered his life so recently, had appeared yet again, but this time to guide him to the man who would, hopefully, be able to answer his many questions. With his newfound knowledge and a ghost, who was now becoming more of an old friend, to guide him, Ray felt much stronger and was certain that it would not be much longer before he reached his goal.

The path now led alongside a rocky outcrop and as it curved around the rocks to the right, Ray saw a huge mango tree, the branches of which hung low over the gravel track. He recalled Joe mentioning that the rocks and the tree would be good landmarks. On reaching them, he would know that he was only ten minutes walk from the Obeah Man's house, but inwardly Ray already knew that. The sun was now getting very hot on his back and, as he approached the crest of a small hill where the dusty track led between two large boulders, Ray could feel his guide's presence even though he could no longer see her in her white muslin robe, nor see those piercing green eyes. He walked between the two grey rocks and there it was at last, in front of him and a little down the hill to the left. It was quite a large house, surrounded by a variety of different trees, putting Ray in mind of an oasis in the desert. A small copse of tall, mature trees provided some shade to the rear of the house whilst coconut palms, banana and mango trees formed a boundary around the immediate environment of the Obeah man's residence. The road passed straight by the rusty front gate, which had once been painted dark green, but which now boasted no more than a few flakes of paint that refused to be defeated either by corrosion or the bleaching effect of the sun. Wild, rambling bushes on either side of the gateposts ensured the privacy of the house, which was itself encircled by more bushes, few of which were native species. The house had clearly once been whitewashed but this too must have seen better days, as had the sun-bleached wooden shutters, one or two of which were swinging gently in the light breeze. The scene was one of peaceful tranquillity and Ray felt that the house itself seemed to have its own aura of profound peace.

Ray's hands grew clammy with anticipation as he pushed open the creaking gate. The house stood well back from the road and a short drive led up to the house, the front of which was now largely in shadow. As he approached the shady verandah, Ray could see an old man sitting there watching his approach with eyes that glinted in the shadows. He was a big man, with broad shoulders, a large round stomach and shiny bald head, but his most remarkable characteristic was a set of large, grey whiskers that stood out from his cheeks, rather like those of a cat. He stood up slowly as Ray rather sheepishly approached the verandah and, although Ray equalled the old man in height, he felt humbled in the presence of such a huge man. In fact, Ray formed the impression that this man was as broad as he was tall.

"Good morning", Ray said, holding out his hand as he stepped up onto the verandah.

"Good morning to you, young man," came the reply in a deep voice that matched Ray's own in both tone and richness, "I've been expecting you." He smiled briefly and shook Ray's hand. Ray could barely conceal his surprise as his mind raced back to Joe and Sylvia. How did they manage to get a message to this man in so short a time? He soon dismissed this idea as being absurd and reproached himself for thinking ill of Joe, even if it was only a fleeting thought. Then the realisation dawned on him that if this Obeah man were half as mystic as Joe had intimated, then he would have no problem in foreseeing Ray's arrival. Perhaps he already knew the reason for his visit as well. As the old man released Ray's hand, his smile suddenly gave way to a stern stare, which Ray found quite unnerving. Without blinking or taking his eyes off Ray's, the old man raised his arms in the air as if conducting an orchestra and then waved his hands over Ray's head and followed on down to the soles of his feet. Ray felt as though the old man was dowsing him for some reason, perhaps to see if he really was the right one for this perilous mission. Ray felt a tingling sensation run through his body from his head right down to his toes and it occurred to him that maybe he had been put under some kind of spell, or was about to be put into a trance. Panic then began to set in as he realised that he would be powerless to defend himself if the old man handed him over to the Devil Worshippers which Sam and Neil told him about in the nightmare they endured together back at Ivy Cottage. His first instinct was to run but he found himself rooted to the spot. Just then, a smile started in the corner of the old man's eyes and slowly spread across his face as though he had found what he was looking for. Ray felt the fear subside within him and very soon a feeling of calm and well-being replaced it, as the ritual appeared to be over.

"I don't believe you told me your name, young man," said the old man.

"I'm sorry, my name is Ray. And your name is?" Ray replied feeling more confident now that he felt that he had passed the old man's scrutiny.

"Please call me Jacob," said the old man, picking up his walking stick and beckoning Ray to follow him. He headed slowly and painfully towards the side of the house and began to make his way round towards the back, picking his way carefully over the dry, dusty and uneven ground. Occasionally he would hesitate as his walking stick slipped on a small rock or a stone, carefully checking his balance before proceeding. Ray was now accustomed to the rough gravel, which seemed to be everywhere and no longer worried about the stones getting into his sandals as his feet were already scratched and filthy. Now and again Jacob would wave his walking stick to point out various trees and bushes in his collection, of which he was obviously very proud. Finally, they reached their destination, which was a mound of very large smooth, rounded stones set amongst the palms, banana and other tropical fruit trees behind the house. The trees provided some shade from the late morning sun and the sound of the breeze rustling their leaves was almost therapeutic. Jacob slowly lowered his considerable bulk onto the mound and let out a long sigh as he fished in his pocket for a handkerchief, which he then used to mop his brow. He indicated to Ray that he should sit on the mound next to him.

"So," he said at length, "you've come to me for help."

"Yes," said Ray as he sat down opposite the old man, "I have." He looked up at Jacob's face and saw sadness mingled with knowledge, experience, hope and expectation. Ray felt in awe of this man and knew that he could not even begin to understand what secrets lay behind those deep brown eyes, which now and then, seemed to flash with the flame of eternal youth.

Ray's throat was dry after the long walk up into the hills from the little village that sprawled around that little harbour, which now seemed so very far away. He wondered idly whether a glass of water or some other thirst-quenching potable might be available. His wish was soon granted when a middle-aged woman, wearing an apron and a scarf tied around her head, shuffled out with a tray supporting two large glasses of iced water.

"Thank you very much," said Ray, taking both glasses and handing one to the old man. Jacob thanked him and nodded to the woman who turned and disappeared into the house. Ray drank deeply from his glass. "Thanks, I really needed that. It's quite a long trek up here from that little harbour, isn't it?"

"Yes," said Jacob with a grin, "do you walk much in England or do you go everywhere in your fancy car, young man?"

"Hey, wait a minute; is there anything you don't know about me?" Ray joked.

"That wasn't difficult, young man. I picked up quite a lot from you when you first arrived."

"So how did you know I was coming in the first place?"

"Well now, my fine young friend, this World holds many secrets and there are so many unanswered questions. Even this small island holds mysteries, many of which I cannot even answer myself. Now do you want me to answer your most recent question or do you wish to discuss your main reason for this visit?" Ray looked at Jacob apprehensively then replied.

"Jacob, I'm quite sure you must already know the answer to your own question." Jacob roared with laughter, shaking the rolls of fat on his stomach, which folded and creased as he gasped for breath.

"I admire your style, young man. I think we are going to get along just fine." As the laughter subsided, Jacob looked pensively up at his house and mopped his brow again.

"Been here all my life, you know Ray," he said wistfully.

"But surely you must have left this little island at some stage."

"Oh yes, of course I have. I travelled the great waters as a young man. America was my first port of call, the land of the free, land of hope, the place to make your fortune or so they say. My father sent me there to learn the mystic arts because he realised that from a very early age I had received the gift that his father bestowed on him through the blood. Unfortunately, not everyone knows how to use the gift and if it falls into the wrong hands all hell breaks loose!" Jacob looked straight at Ray through eyes, which now bore the yellowish hue of old age and which seemed to have lost the flash, which Ray had seen earlier. "Literally breaks loose," the old man quietly reiterated with deep feeling. As Ray looked into Jacob's eyes, he could see a reflection but it was not of himself. He looked harder and realised that he could see the woman, just as she had appeared when she guided him on the path earlier that morning. "Who is she?" he whispered to himself. Then he felt that warm glow coursing through his body again and his confusion became apparent to his new mentor. Jacob gently put his hand on Ray's shoulder and reassured him.

"Let me introduce you to our beautiful friend, the 'golden girl' who has haunted my every waking hour for many, many years." A knowing smile played about the old man's lips as he thought of her. Ray felt confused for a moment, as it never occurred to him that she might have also been haunting someone else.

"She haunts you too? But why does she trouble us both? Who is she?" Ray asked, sitting on the edge of the mound of rocks in his excitement at the thought of finally unmasking his tormenter.

"Her name is Lucille."

"Lucille? Lucille." Ray repeated, lingering over the name. "At last I have a name for her! Lucille."

"Yes, Ray, a lovely name for a pretty face and for a beautiful lady. She was the love of my life." Jacob grew distant for a few moments as his mind dwelt on that lovely face. "She could have had whatever she wanted you know, Ray. My love for her is immeasurable. I would have flown to the Moon and back for her." Ray began to feel in tune with this frail old man now and could easily understand such a deep love because he felt the same way about Sam. His mind strayed back to his beloved Sam and he wondered where she might be and what she might be doing at this precise moment. However, Jacob almost immediately interrupted his reverie, staggering to his feet with the help of his walking stick, his face contorted with pain and anger.

"But it wasn't to be, she was too afraid of what the villagers might say; not to mention her parents!" By this time, the old man was shaking with rage and Ray, fearing that he might fall, grabbed his arm. At that moment, Jacob's housekeeper came running out of the house to her employer's assistance and tried to calm him. Ray understood Jacob's pain as he could identify it with Joe's story, although that particular story did have a happy ending, whilst it was becoming crystal clear that Jacob's story was tragic.

"You don't have to continue telling me now if you would prefer to rest. I really do understand how difficult this must be for you." Ray soothed.

"I have waited so many years to tell you this," Jacob said, slowly sitting down again. He looked at his housekeeper and gave her a nod of assurance that he would be alright. She reluctantly left his side and slowly returned to the house, looking back over her shoulder to confirm that he was indeed, alright again. Having regained his composure and their privacy, Jacob continued with his story.

"Her parents were wary of my father because they knew that he was a student of the Occult and they, being simple folk, did not want to get mixed up in anything they couldn't comprehend. So of course, when they discovered that their daughter and I were in love, they forbade her to see me and tried to turn her attentions on some self-satisfied and sanctimonious idiot who they considered more worthy of her than me, the fools! Naturally, their search for another suitor from the island didn't take long because Lucille was a very beautiful young woman. She had always attracted most of the neighbouring young men without even trying, so her parents were able to make their choice swiftly in the hope that they might avoid any further complications. The pain of losing my one true love was just too much to bear, but what was even harder to accept was that she was carrying my child, our child." Once more, Jacob's body shook violently with the pent up frustration of all those years during which he was powerless do anything but watch impotently from a distance.

"Murderer, murderer!" He shouted out loud, giving vent to the passion boiling up inside him. "He stole my beloved Lucille and then my little Esther who was handed innocently into his care by Lucille, believing that he had grown to love her as his own child. Then that wicked creature led my own flesh and blood like a lamb to the slaughter, watching coldly while those demons butchered her so they could feast upon her soul." Jacob's head slumped onto his chest as he recalled the horror of those far-off days when his world had fallen apart and he tried hard to collect his thoughts before continuing with his harrowing tale.

Ray was appalled to hear that the man, whom Esther had grown up trusting as her own father was, in fact the Snake-man. He wondered who this man really was and why he chose to betray her so cruelly. Could he have hated Jacob so much for being Esther's true father that he needed to gain his revenge by bringing about her death, or was there a more deep rooted and sinister reason?

"I'm sorry you have such sad memories." Ray said softly.

"It's alright, young man. I have learnt to cope with them over the years and now, at my advanced age, I know it won't be too long before I join my beloved Lucille in heaven. She lived all those years in mourning for Esther and has now died with a broken heart, which only I can mend. You see, once I'd fully realized that I would have to accept the situation, I continued to live my life in this house, where I was born and raised, and I threw myself into my studies. My parents taught me to fear God, respect my elders and to love my neighbours and therefore I felt that there was no alternative but to sit back and watch as another man entered the life of my beloved Lucille and raised my daughter, Esther. The truth about her parentage remained our secret for some years and we honestly believed that nobody else knew, but someone else did know that the child was really mine. They knew whose blood ran through her veins and these evil creatures enlisted the aid of the man who Esther believed to be her father so they could enter Lucille's house in the still of the night and steal her from right under her mother's nose." Jacob's voice lowered and with a great heaviness in his heart, he continued. "Those demons sacrificed her innocent soul to the Devil." Ray winced as if in pain and put his hand on Jacob's arm in an attempt to console the old man.

"I am truly sorry, Jacob."

"You see, Raymond," he continued in a faltering tone, "although I am knowledgeable in the Occult and what some call the 'Black Arts', I was taught by my Father never to venture too deeply into such things as they are best left alone. However, we humans are inquisitive creatures and it is inevitable that, if we dabble in things we don't fully understand, we will eventually come unstuck."

It was fast approaching lunchtime when Jacob's housekeeper reappeared with a tray of delicious looking savoury snacks and a large bowl that was literally overflowing with a variety of exotic tropical fruits. The two men thanked her and began selecting some of the tasty morsels that she had prepared for them and in a very short space of time, their conversation died away as they become absorbed with their meal. Ray had become so entranced by the flavours of the different fruits, some of which he had never seen before, that he did not notice Jacob nodding off to sleep. Realizing how quickly time was passing, Ray began to wonder how he would rouse the old man from his slumbers when Jacob grunted as he stifled a loud snore.

"Now Raymond," he said, eyes still shut, "we have to prepare ourselves for what lies ahead of us."

"Jacob, please tell me what has to be done and I will happily do it."

"All in good time my boy, but first you must hear the rest of my story. Otherwise, you will not fully understand what needs to be done or why it is so." Jacob slowly opened his eyes and looked straight into Ray's eyes with a steely stare.

"I tried to rescue her but it was too late by the time I reached the place where they had taken her. They had already spilt her blood and devoured her soul. You see I had gone to get help…" Jacob took Ray's hand as he trembled, the tears running pitifully down his wrinkled and care-worn face, "…because I was not strong enough alone to conquer the demons that were unleashed in the woods that night!" His reddened eyes sparkled and a smile began to play around his lips. "But now my friend, my spirit is strong, although the flesh is no longer so." He said, lifting the loose skin on the back of his hand, "I was still only a student in those things then and still quite new to the practice of the religion of Obeah. They were stronger than I was and would surely have killed me too, so the best thing I could do was to go and seek help. I ran as fast as I could through the dense undergrowth, thorns ripping at my clothes and sometimes piercing my skin." He pointed to a scar above his right eye and recounted how he came so close to losing his sight in that eye in his hurry to get help. "Eventually I came face to face with some men from

Lucille's family, who were out searching for the lost girl. They were just as surprised to see me, as I was to see them. They were carrying a couple of hand-made torches, which they held high above their heads as they crept slowly through the woods. Although I was not welcomed into their group, they quickly followed me when I told them that I knew where Esther's captors had taken her. As we approached the clearing, panting with the effort and anticipation, I felt a sharp, stabbing pain in my chest, which made me wince. I knew what it meant immediately and I looked up into the sky and shouted 'NO', but even then, I knew it was already too late."

Jacob slumped forward again and Ray wondered whether the burden of telling his terrible tale was becoming too much for him, but again the old man rallied and insisted on continuing with his story. He told Ray how, on that fateful night, he felt another presence in the woods; two people, who did not seem to be of his time and who only remained there for a short while, then went as quickly as they came. He had no idea who they were or why they were there, but felt curiously comforted as though their presence would have some significance for him. Ray smiled to himself, believing that for once, he just might know more than this wise old sage.

Having regained his composure once more, Jacob went on to tell Ray how the men from Lucille's family chased the devil worshippers into the woods whilst he stayed behind to examine the wooden altar on which those monsters had just sacrificed his dear daughter to Satan. "I could only stand and watch in horror as her blood still dripped from that vile travesty of an altar onto the roots of the tree against which it was wedged. I took a penknife from my pocket, made a small incision in my wrist and squeezed out five drops of blood, which fell and mingled with hers, at the same time making a vow that one day I would avenge her death. You see Raymond, I knew in my heart that these mahogany trees would be cut down some day to produce fine quality wood and that it would be exported to a distant land where it would be used to produce equally exceptional furniture." Ray shuddered to think that some thirty years ago this man had known that by mingling his blood with that of his daughter, he would set in motion a chain of events that would culminate in Ray himself coming to this island to help him avenge his daughter's death.

"So the wood eventually ended up being made into furniture by Neil's father and was then handed down to Neil so that I would come into contact with it at Ivy Cottage. But why did it take so long to manifest itself and why did it have to be me?"

"There is much that you cannot expect to comprehend just yet and I don't have the time to explain to you right now, but you will understand in the fullness of time. All you need to know for now is that you were born at the precise moment of Esther's death and that Lucille died at the time when you were in the presence of the three pieces of furniture that were crafted from the timber over which my blood and Esther's was spilt. This was the key to unleashing the power of 'the clock', which I believe you do know something about." Ray was utterly dumbfounded and just stared at Jacob as though he was looking at a ghost.

"My God, it was you! You made all this happen. You controlled it all from beginning to end; you controlled us, all of us, the clock and even time itself!" Ray stuttered almost incoherently.

"Not quite Ray. I have told you a little of my studies and that my powers come from an understanding of how certain things are connected. It was not my power but my ability to use the power that exists all around us in the atmosphere that enabled these things to happen. With training Ray, you could do the same." Jacob smiled encouragingly at Ray who was still in shock from the old man's revelations.

"So how did the clock manage to take my friends back in time to witness those little cameos of Neil's parents and even the sacrifice itself?" Ray panted with mounting excitement.

"All in good time my friend. You must learn to walk before you run," Jacob smiled benignly now that he had Ray's undivided attention, "and I will teach you all that you need to know."

"So I was chosen because I was born at the right time and just happened to be sitting at a table, which had some of your blood in it, at the precise moment when Lucille died?"

"Yes you were chosen for that reason Ray, but it was no accident that you were in the right place at the right time. Our beautiful Lucille died that night and her spirit came to find you. The blood of both her daughter and her lover, residing in the woodwork, guided her to you and the clock acted in the manner of a beacon in the night and brought her straight to you." The memory of that night came flooding back to Ray in a flash and then he recalled the much stronger visitation at the séance.

"I have something here which I took from Lucille on the night of the séance, Jacob." Ray said, taking the piece of bloodstained linen from his pocket.

"I wondered when you would remember that little memento, young man." Jacob replied, obviously aware that Ray had brought it with him. Ray was quite stunned for a moment to hear that Jacob already knew about the piece of cloth but then thought that if Jacob could orchestrate all that he had explained in the last few minutes, it should not be too hard to accept that he knew about this piece of cloth. In any event, he remained so completely fascinated by the older man's story that he felt compelled to keep the questions flowing.

"But what if the trees had not been felled for timber, what would you have done then, Jacob?" Ray asked doubtfully.

"We would have found another way. Remember Ray, good will always triumph over evil no matter how long it may take, be it years, decades or even centuries."

"So how did the carpenter, Neil's father, know that he had to make a clock?" Ray was still confused, but utterly fascinated, and that was just what Jacob needed.

"It was inspiration my boy, pure inspiration. However, had those trees been cut down sooner, then the clock would have been made sooner and perhaps Lucille would have died sooner. Perhaps someone else, who was born at the right time, might have come to me instead of you. You see Ray, all the events had to link together chronologically and the clock of course, being a rather special timepiece, held the record of events, which it simply played back just as a film projector does in a cinema. To tell you the honest truth, I have no idea what other secrets it might hold," Jacob muttered as an afterthought, "but that's another story, I suppose."

As Joe's little boat rounded the headland on its way back towards the Black Island's only harbour, Joe began rehearsing his excuses for arriving late to pick Ray up at the appointed hour. The day had been very successful and he was preparing to boast about his record catch of lobsters, including a massive one he had earmarked for Sam. He cut the engine and began coasting up to the jetty where the same young man was still loafing about since early that morning. He lazily pulled himself up and deftly caught the rope, which Joe tossed to him, and tied it fast to a bollard. Joe leapt out of the boat and looked around.

"Remember the man who I dropped off here this morning?" Joe began.

"Haven't seen 'im since man," replied the languid youth as he flopped back down onto the coiled rope he had been sitting on when Joe arrived, "he went up into them hills this morning. He was lookin' for trouble if you ask me, man."

"Well I wasn't asking you, boy!" Joe snapped, feeling guilty at letting Ray down. He looked at his watch: a quarter past five. Perhaps Ray had got into some deep conversation with the old man and lost all track of the time. He decided to start walking up the path and wait on the brow of the hill that overlooked the harbour. There was a good view of the path ahead from there and he would be able to see Ray coming from at least a mile away. It took Joe ten minutes to gain his vantage point above the harbour but there was still no sign of Ray. By six o'clock, Joe began to feel a little concerned and wondered whether to carry on up the path or return to the boat where he had a torch stashed away in a locker together with blankets and a first aid kit, although he hoped the latter would not prove to be necessary. He decided to return to the boat and make his final decision then, but as he walked back towards the boat, he began to think about Sam and wondered how she would react if he returned without Ray. He therefore decided to stay on the boat and so he lit a hurricane lamp and settled down to wait. After a long, hard day hauling in lobster pots, he soon dropped off to sleep. When he awoke at seven o'clock, he began to panic, partly because Ray had still not shown up and partly because he knew that Sam would start to get worried that Ray was so late getting back. However, his main fear was that Sylvia would lay the blame on him and she would kill him. He quickly put off and began to sail back with a fair following wind and favourable tide towards the two women who would be waiting anxiously for his return.

As Joe approached Fisherman's Beach, he could see a knot of people waiting with torches and oil lamps. Theirs was a close-knit community and if any of the boats came home late, a group would soon form on the beach, consisting of other fishermen and their families, ready to help the latecomer or put to sea if they saw a distress signal. Sylvia was the first to Joe's boat to see if he was alright and was quick to spot the anxiety on his face. Sam then pushed through the assembled throng to greet Ray, but the look of joy and expectation on her face soon turned to concern when she saw that he was not on board.

"Joe, where's Ray?" she questioned him anxiously.

"I don't know Sam," he replied, "he wasn't there when I went back for him. I waited for a long time, but there was no sign of him."

"What have you done, Joseph?" Sylvia wailed. "Why did you leave him there?" The others began to murmur amongst themselves in low tones, several had knitted brows as a few questions were formulating in their minds and some forming almost under their breath. "Why did he go there in the first place?" "Joe, man you should know better than that?" Nevertheless, Joe was in no mood to enlighten them. In a flash, Sam was in the boat, yelling at Joe to take her straight to The Black Island immediately.

"Go on Joe, take her back with you as quickly as you can in case there's been an accident or something. I'll try to get in radio contact with the folks over on the island and let them know you're coming. Hurry now for Heaven's sake!"

CHAPTER IX –
Deliverance

Jacob stood up uneasily and rested wearily on his gnarled and ancient looking walking stick, looked Ray straight in the eyes and said, "Well young man, it's time. Are you ready?"

"Yes Jacob, I certainly am ready," replied Ray eagerly, "What do you need me to do?" Jacob held up his hand and without another word, led Ray into the house via the back door. He turned into the long passageway leading to the front of the house and shuffled along with Ray in hot pursuit, but then halfway along he paused and turned to face his young visitor.

"Ray, I am quite sure that you trust me by now and so I am equally sure that you will accept my word when I tell you that I have to blindfold you before you enter the room in which our mission, and indeed our journey, will commence. It is for your own protection that I must do this. You do understand, don't you?"

"Yes that's fine Jacob," Ray replied, "I quite understand."

"Thank you. As you are not accustomed to the powers contained within this room, I am aware that you will experience an emotionally overwhelming sensation as you enter. The blindfold will help you to acclimatise more quickly to your new surroundings in this very special room, which has actually become a shrine to my life's studies." Jacob reached out, opened the door of a small cupboard built into the wall at about head height and took out a neatly folded piece of thick, black cloth, which he then carefully tied around Ray's head as a blindfold. The old man then proceeded to lead Ray carefully down the remainder of the passageway towards a large, ornate and heavy-looking door. Although the varnish was peeling off the wood in places, its dark colour was quite striking, as were the elaborate carvings on the panels. A large ornate, spherical brass knob dominated the middle of the unusually wide door, whilst a smaller, equally ornamental brass handle at the edge of the door afforded access to the room. Jacob fumbled in his pockets for a moment or two before producing a large brass key, which he then inserted noisily into the lock. Ray could hear all that was taking place, followed by a long creaking sound as Jacob finally opened the door. Jacob then guided him through the doorway and into the room.

Although his blindfold was of thick cloth, Ray was instantly aware of an intense light that seemed to penetrate his darkness, causing him to squint involuntarily. He also felt quite giddy and at one point almost lost his balance altogether, causing him to tighten his grip on the old man's arm.

"I do apologise again for the need to blindfold you Ray, but you may well find it all a bit too much to take in at once and I don't want you to feel disorientated at this critical point in our venture together. Now, I have to insist that you swear to me that you will never reveal the secrets that I am about to share with you, to anybody at all. You must tell absolutely nobody, as long as you live. Do you understand me, Ray?"

"Yes Jacob, I do understand what you're saying because I can actually feel it in the air. There is something here way beyond normal understanding and I consider myself extremely privileged to be here." Ray said with great humility. Jacob smiled with pride and invited his visitor to remove the blindfold, but Ray did so slowly, keeping his eyes closed for a while in order to allow them to adjust to the light. He then half-opened them slowly but quickly closed them again, because the brightness was just too much to take. Once his eyes grew acclimatised to the whiteness of the light in the room however, he began to look around him in awe and wonder. At first glance, the room appeared to be a cross between a library and one of those old apothecary's laboratories seen in period films, but it was much more than that. In fact, it was unique. As Ray looked around the room, his first impression was that it was completely out of character with the rest of the house, not only in terms of its furnishings, but also its whole ambience was quite different. Although the room was bathed in white light, Ray could see no windows, electric lights or any other form of artificial lighting. It was apparent to Ray that this room was right in the centre of the house with no outside walls, yet there was that bright light radiating from somewhere unseen. He also noticed that the floorboards, which were polished black to match the door, were rather uneven because they were made of roughly hewn local timber. Furthermore, unlike the door, the floor had a number of large knots and the odd crack here and there. In the middle of the floor was a beautiful square-shaped Persian rug, cream in colour, with patterns depicting the moon and stars in the centre whilst the signs of the zodiac adorned its margin. The walls were clearly the work of experts in their trade, beautifully panelled with wood and bore the patina of age, whereas the floor appeared to have been rather crudely fashioned. Purple drapes hung on either side of a large mirror and echoed the patterning of the rug, although here the patterns were of a golden hue. A rather fine Victorian washstand stood in one corner of the room, its bowl and jug decorated in dark red vine leaves, revealing clusters of both white and black grapes. Beside the washstand, two shelves were stacked with neatly folded white towels, which Ray assumed must have been laundered and stacked by Jacob's attentive housekeeper. There were shelves with several rows of beautiful leather-bound books, their titles engraved in gold leaf. Coloured-glass bottles of all shapes and sizes, containing a large selection of potions and elixirs, stood in rows along other shelves and Ray noticed that, as some of these were the same colour, Jacob had clearly labelled them all. Another shelf was full of brass, clay and wooden drinking goblets of assorted shapes and sizes, some with interesting decoration. There were bunches of both fresh and dried herbs, neatly tied with string, hanging from hooks on the dark-stained ceiling and several glass cases contained stuffed animals and birds. A large, lifelike monkey in a tall glass case behind the door caught Ray's eye, as its own eyes appeared to be following Ray around the room in a most disconcerting manner. A real tribute to the taxidermist's art Ray thought. The skulls of various animals lay on a table on the far side of the room and Ray was uncertain as to whether one or two of the bones might even be human in origin. Incense burners and candleholders were randomly dotted around the room, adding to the general air of ordered chaos. Apart from one or two stools in front of a couple of small tables, Ray could only see one chair and that was quite clearly Jacob's chair. In fact, its well-worn appearance was that of an old friend.

"This is a wonderful place, Raymond." Jacob said enthusiastically as he closed the door and made his way across to the large wooden chair, the seat and arms of which were smooth and shiny with age. He turned and beckoned Ray to join him. Ray felt almost overcome by a wave of humility as he began to realise the rare privilege Jacob had bestowed upon him by allowing him to enter his private sanctuary. He was still feeling quite giddy when he eventually walked over to join Jacob in front of a very large, ornate mirror. Ray saw a stool in the corner of the room, picked it up and set it down next to his mentor's chair. Jacob picked up a bottle labelled 'Sacred Water' and poured some into each of two brass goblets, which he had just taken down from the shelf that Ray was admiring a little earlier. Taking a sharp knife from the ledge beneath the mirror, Jacob reached out for Ray's right hand and quickly pricked the top of his thumb.

"Ouch!" cried Ray, speedily withdrawing his hand. Jacob patiently took hold of his hand again as if dealing with a child.

"Trust me, Ray, it's my turn next." He said as he held Ray's hand over one of the brass goblets and squeezed hard enough for a few drops of blood to drip into the sacred water. Ray immediately pulled his hand away and stuffed his thumb into his mouth just as a child would. Without hesitation, Jacob repeated the procedure with his own thumb, dripping blood into the second goblet. He then mixed the contents of the two goblets, putting some of the mixture in each, and then placed them in front of the mirror. Ray wondered what this fascinating old man was going to do next.

"Raymond, I want you to be strong and to listen to my every command. We are about to embark on a dangerous journey, a journey that will take us out of the world we know, through the twilight zone to the place where this all began many years ago, but I will be with you every step of the way, even if you cannot see me. You will always be able to feel my presence. Fear not, Ray."

Jacob then instructed his apprentice to light the many candles that were dotted around the room whilst he concentrated on lighting two large round black candles, which stood right in front of the mirror. As soon as the candles were all alight, he reached up to the shelf to his left, lifted down a very large leather-bound volume and blew the dust off it before thumbing through to a page that he knew well. Placing the ancient tome in front of Ray, he indicated a small paragraph and asked Ray to read it out aloud. Jacob joined in reciting the words as if it were poetry flowing freely from his lips. He needed no book to help him remember, as he knew the words perfectly well after so many years of study. They then recited another paragraph and again Jacob led the reading as if it were poetry and Ray soon slipped into the rhythm of the words until he felt as though he were being carried along by their chanting. As Ray watched the reflection of the candle flames dancing in the mirror, he caught sight of a scene that was slowly unfolding deep in the forest, but as soon as he realised it was there in the mirror, it was gone again. Ray had no idea by what means this great adventure would begin or how he would travel from this world to wherever it was that they were bound for, but he knew he would put his trust in this strange old man.

Suddenly a cold draught swept through the room! Twirling as it forced it's way through, whisking a few papers off a table and causing the larger candles to flicker and the smaller ones to go out completely. Jacob abruptly stood up, gathered his staff and picked up one of the goblets. "Come Ray", he said hurriedly "drink and then we will be ready to begin our journey". The two men drank from the brass goblets and then returned them to their place in front of the mirror. Jacob began to recite the final verse of his readings now more urgently than before and encouraged Ray to do the same. Soon their voices joined in harmonious chanting, growing louder and louder until Ray's head began to spin. Looking at the changing scene around him, it quickly became apparent to Jacob that their journey was to be strewn with dangerous obstacles. He was also well aware that the demons would try to take them into the twilight zone and destroy them both before they could reach their destination, but he was ready to face his old adversaries and to meet them in spiritual combat. Unfortunately, Jacob had no alternative but to use the black candles, which he found at the scene of the sacrifice more than thirty years before, because they alone would have the power to transport him back to the exact spot where the evil deed had taken place. However, he was also well aware that these candles would still be under the commanding power of their original evil masters, they would use them in any way they could to prevent him from returning to the scene of the sacrifice.

Ray looked into the mirror again and could see that his surroundings were changing intermittently, and then they would return to normal. There was an enormous struggle going on between the opposing forces of Jacob's desire to transport himself and Ray to the sacrificial site and the candles' attempts to drag them into the twilight zone. Ray could feel himself levitating above the ground as an electrifying force swept through the room, engulfing the two men who continued to chant whilst every object in the room appeared to be swirling around them. Even the ceiling spun enthusiastically as it joined in the general melee. The flanks of the two black candles suddenly ruptured and began to ooze crimson blood as the black molten wax ran down their sides and trickled across the shelf to join forces with each other and then gather speed across the floor. The two men felt themselves drawn inexorably towards the ceiling, slowly spinning round and round as if caught in an inverted whirlpool, while the magnetic force in the room dragged artefacts from all four corners of the room, giving Ray the impression that he was caught up in some enormous kaleidoscope, moving ever faster.

Some of the most highly prized volumes from Jacob's vast collection hurled themselves through the air, one of them only narrowly missing Ray's head. The 'Ancient Book of Broken Spells', which they had been reading from earlier did not escape the mayhem either as its pages flipped over and over, backwards and forwards, as though in search of something. Amidst all the confusion and unseen by the two men, the picture in the mirror was resolving itself into a sombre scene of dank, humid desolation. Suddenly the vortex, which had so recently elevated the two men up towards the ceiling, reversed and sucked them down with a rush straight towards the mirror. Their chanting stopped abruptly as this latest turn of events took them both completely by surprise. Ray braced himself for the crash that he knew must be imminent and feared that they would both be cut to shreds on the broken glass. However, to his utter amazement they simply flew straight through the mirror and tumbled over, and over, eventually coming to rest on the warm and dusty ground.

All was suddenly still and silent and the air was hot with a thick, musty smell. Ray's vision blurred for a few moments but as he managed to focus, he could feel dry, dusty soil beneath the palms of his hands. He looked around and saw that they were in the middle of a deep valley and, although there were trees and bushes as far as the eye could see, they appeared grey and lifeless. The soil was so dry that it rose in clouds of ash as he began to walk. He looked around anxiously for Jacob and then caught sight of him staggering along through the bushes, clutching his trusty staff. Ray leapt to his feet and ran to the old man's aid.

"We don't have a moment to lose Raymond," Jacob panted as he tried to get his breath back after struggling to his feet, "come on, this way I think" he added as he desperately tried to pick up his pace. Ray looked on in bewilderment and admiration for the determined spirit of this venerable old man. Ray's first impression was of surroundings laden with gloom and foreboding and he wondered why the old man had brought him here rather than to the forest where he expected to be able to free himself of his bane. Jacob, on the other hand realised that the black candles had done their master's work in transporting them to this place of doom and destruction. He realised immediately that, although he had used their powers to bring him and his young companion this far, a difficult and dangerous journey now lay before them. He dare not tell Ray what tasks might lie ahead of them before entering the forest, nor would he be able to explain this unfortunate twist of fate in case it frightened Ray into deserting him. Jacob had waited for this day for most of his life and he could not now entertain the prospect of losing the chance to free his daughter's soul now, at the eleventh hour.

If he were to fail now, her soul would never be free to rejoice in heaven, nor to rest in peace, but would remain enslaved to the powers of darkness for all eternity. He had to make this final journey now, he had to be successful and he knew that Ray was the right one to help him to free, not only his daughter's soul but also the other tormented souls which existed in the same twilight zone. With Ray's help, he would rid this barren forest of the curse, which the powers of evil had brought down upon it and he would return it to an area of great beauty where flowers and wildlife would return.

Ray yelled out in anguish as something struck his neck and then proceeded to give him a nasty nip. He waved it away as one would a persistent wasp, when the tiny creature, resembling a bat with long spindly limbs, whirled round and struck again. This time it landed on the side of his head and the pinprick sensation that followed told Ray that his ear was under attack. He soon learnt that these little needle-sharp teeth were to be avoided at all costs. These irritating little monsters flew around in an apparently drunken stupor, biting anything into which they happened to crash. As they flew towards him out of the dim light of this unearthly place, Ray was reminded of the fireflies that he saw a day or so ago around Sylvia's restaurant. However, they were both pretty and harmless, whilst these little horrors came fully armed with sharp teeth and claws.

"What in Hell are those damned things, Jacob?"

"That's a very pertinent question Ray, if I may say so, when you consider where we appear to have landed. I believe they are related to the zurloos, although they are usually slightly larger creatures, about the size of a pigeon. These little horrors are permanent residents of the twilight zone. We outsiders know them simply as 'tormentors' which certainly does seem to be an appropriate name, doesn't it?"

"Ouch, another one's found me now. Get off you little bastard!" yelled Ray "Can we go now Jacob, I've just about had enough of your zurloos, or whatever the little buggers are called." Jacob laughed and agreed that they really should be making haste and the valiant pair moved off quickly, hoping that their speed would be enough to outwit these rather comical little flying rats with their vicious teeth.

They had been walking for about ten minutes or so when the ground began to tremble beneath their feet and Jacob hurried on as fast as his old legs could carry him. The atmosphere had grown denser with the heat and Ray could clearly see that Jacob was now desperately trying to reach the nearby thorn bushes, which he knew would provide them with some cover. As he followed Jacob towards the bushes, Ray suddenly felt his body jerk violently backwards without any warning. He struggled forwards with mounting panic as his feet merely scratched at the dry soil, producing clouds of dust, as he tried desperately to gain some grip, but to no avail. Then Jacob saw them rising up out of the ground between his vantage point in the bushes and Ray, who had failed to close the gap between the two of them. Evil, repulsive looking beasts from the very depths of Hell itself were unravelling themselves from the dust and turning their gaze towards Ray. Jacob knew that Ray could not see these creatures but that he would certainly feel the ferocity of their violent attentions. Although little more than half Ray's size, these grey, scaly, crouching fiends used their sharp claws to terrible effect as they darted in and out in a frenzied attack on their unfortunate victim. Jacob could clearly see their huge, pale yellowish eyes and their wide mouths with pointed, razor-sharp teeth, which seemed to protrude at all angles. Numerous spikes jutted out of their long tails and the scales on their backs stood up similar to a dinosaur's armoured defences. The noise was deafening and Ray felt the blood drain from his face as his energy began to desert him. He just stood there frozen in fear as a mighty, unseen force grabbed him and began to lash at him. It threw him from side to side like a rag-doll. He felt the repeated stabs of pain as sharp claws scratched at his face time after time and he felt their cold, clammy touch as he reached out in a vain attempt to defend himself. Ray gasped for air as the stench of hot, foul breath seemed to envelope him and he tried to cover his ears with his hands before his eardrums exploded with the terrible noise of the attack. Ray was now quite certain that death was near and he knew he could not take much more of this fearful pounding, when suddenly the ground seemed to shake, followed by a sudden and total silence! He looked down and saw that there was blood all over him and his shirt hung in tatters. The only evidence that these awful creatures had been there was a broken and bloodied claw, which had fallen from its owner in the fury of the attack. It lay on the ground nearby, now clearly visible to Ray, who stared down at it in disbelief and horror. Finally, he looked up and saw Jacob standing by the thorn bushes with his staff outstretched in the manner of a medieval magician. Ray's heart pounded so hard that he thought it would burst from his chest and he slumped to the ground, utterly exhausted.

"Jacob," he cried out at last, "what in God's name was that?"

"They were Sentinels, Ray. Guardians of the Underworld sent up here to destroy us. Our arrival here will have been no surprise to our enemies, my friend." Ray staggered to his feet, wearily crossed the few yards to where his elderly companion still stood, looked him straight in the eyes and thanked him for saving his life. "Jacob, I don't know what happened just then or how you defeated it, or them, but I'm very grateful for whatever you did to get them off me. In fact I couldn't even see who, or what, they were."

"That's just as well Ray, they were not a pretty sight. You did very well, young man and I am proud of you."

"Thanks Jacob, but I'm really exhausted after all that effort. Is there somewhere we can rest and have a drink or something?" Ray asked wearily.

"Are you out of your mind?" came Jacob's stern reply, "we have no time to lose, especially now they know exactly where we are. Anyway, this is only the beginning, the first hurdle, the first real test of my powers."

"Heavens above, how many more tests of your powers will there be Jacob? I'm not sure I can take much more of this; and what about my powers?"

"Nonsense, you are a big strong man; much stronger than you know in fact, you have an overwhelming physical and mental strength. Now listen Raymond, you must trust me. If you put your trust in me, I will be there wherever you turn and whenever you need me. As I said before, this was never going to be an easy journey but we have no choice but to endure it. What's more, our purpose is clear and we know our destination. Now, there are another two obstacles for us to overcome before we can pass through the portals of the Underworld and on to our appointment with destiny." Ray composed himself and, with a feeling of inevitability, followed as Jacob picked up his staff and shuffled across to where the ugly-looking grey claw lay in a pool of blood. "We may well find a use for this later," he muttered, picking it up hurriedly, "come along now Ray, there's no time to lose." He hurried off and Ray followed along dutifully behind, amusing himself by mimicking the old man under his breath, "no time to lose, no time to lose, we'll be late Raymond, come along now, come along." As he followed the man whom he now saw as both his mentor and his saviour, he decided that if this journey was going to help liberate the spirit of Jacob's daughter, Esther, as well as freeing him of Lucille's ghost, then he must go on and complete the journey. However, after his recent terrifying ordeal, he realised only too well that he was taking a grave risk and that there would be plenty more dangers in store for him. He thought of his beloved Sam and his new-found friend Joe, and of Neil and Madeline back home, and realised that the sooner he got through this nightmare with Jacob, the sooner he would be able to see them all again. Jacob stopped beside a large-leafed succulent plant, broke off one of its thick, rounded leaves, and squeezed the juice into his mouth to quench his thirst. "Come along Ray, I thought you were thirsty." he jibed. Ray was unsure to begin with but he needed to slake his thirst so he took the plunge and found that, after the somewhat acrid first impression, it did not taste too bad and he was very thirsty, after all.

Although weary, Jacob knew that they must press on; not knowing when their next test might manifest itself. He knew that he would need to search for the strength within, that strength which he had been carefully nurturing for so many years now. He had spent those years garnering knowledge and assimilating the teachings of the most erudite scholars of magic and the occult from his travels around the World and he had used all of this to formulate his plans for revenge. He knew well that the time was now very near and he would need to call upon all that he had learnt if he was to face the terrible ordeal that he must endure for the sake of those he loved the most. The coming test would be the culmination of all he had worked for and prepared for and he must not fail.

They wandered along the dusty path and it seemed to Ray that Jacob knew exactly where they were going even though he kept on checking the route and pondering the possibilities at each turn along the way. From time to time Jacob would point his staff straight out in front of him and Ray was quite certain that the staff was, in some way, guiding them towards their goal and he was sure that it was Jacob's use of the staff that had so recently saved his life. From time to time Ray thought he could hear a faint tinkling sound carried on the breeze, a sound similar to wind chimes perhaps, or maybe they could be panpipes. Perspiration trickled down the old man's face as they plodded for some time until Ray felt the earth tremble slightly beneath his feet but, assuming that it was due to the fatigue he felt from his recent experience, he continued on his weary way without giving it too much thought. Jacob, on the other hand, became ever more alert as he was now sure that their next test was imminent. He did not have very long to wait however, as a large crack appeared in the ground ahead of them and began to open up rapidly, snaking towards them with a mighty roar. Jacob was a little way ahead so Ray started running to close the gap, but the deep fissure shot between them and widened with incredible speed so that Ray could not possibly jump across. As he wobbled uneasily on the brink and then stepped back, he realised with mounting horror that another fissure was opening up behind him. He called out in desperation to Jacob, who was now a long way off on the other side of this ever-widening barrier. The cracks were now opening up around them in all directions, giving the appearance of a maze. Then, as the noise died away, Ray could hear a wailing sound coming up out of the ground and then once again became transfixed with fear as he saw the strangest-looking creatures he had ever set eyes upon, climbing up out of these bottomless pits. They appeared to him to be some sort of parody of the human form but with translucent, colourless flesh and large lifeless eyes that reminded him of a fish on the fishmonger's slab. Their moaning was quite pitiful and while Ray became mesmerised by the sound, he felt a cold and damp sensation around his foot, looking down he saw an almost transparent, pallid strand curling around his ankle. Its grip tightened alarmingly as it began to drag him towards the edge of the awful chasm. Then another crack appeared beside him and, as he lost his balance and crashed to the ground, another translucent fin-like limb looped around his other ankle and began dragging him mercilessly towards oblivion.

"Jacob, where are you?" Ray screamed in panic, his heart pounding harder than ever in his chest. He reached out to grab at whatever he could find. Some quite solid-looking dry roots protruded from the soil and he tried frantically to grab hold of them. If only he could anchor himself on one of these, he may be able to gain some purchase on the soil with his feet and try to kick these foul creatures off his ankles. However, his assailants were determined to pull him down into the depths of Hell. With his painful, bruised and bloody fingers, he grasped at another root that was slightly larger than those onto which he had tried so hard to cling a moment or two before. Then at last, he managed to secure a firm grip. Pulling with all his strength, he began to make some headway this time, but he realised that he was pulling the combined weight of his own body plus that of these disgusting creatures, which were now firmly attached to him like limpets. He dug his hands into the soil for leverage and slowly began to edge his way up out of the chasm. As he could see the light above him now, his resolve grew ever stronger until finally he managed to pull himself out of that dreadful place. Just as he did so, the little Bible that Joe had handed him on the boat, fell from his pocket and the pages flipped over to The Psalms. Ray grabbed the Bible and began to read with great difficulty from Psalm 27, although his voice was trembling with fear and some of his words were barely audible, 'The Lord is my light and my salvation; whom shall I fear? When the wicked, *even* mine enemies and my foes, came upon me to eat up my flesh, they stumbled and fell...' At these words, the pallid creatures screamed and slid back into the fissures, shielding their eyes as though the sun were shining too brightly for them and they shrank away and slid back into their pits as quickly as they had appeared. It was nonetheless a difficult struggle for Ray to free his ankle but he felt his strength returning not only physically but also spiritually. He felt that he was beginning to know what was required of him automatically now and this gave him much-needed confidence, although he still had to pinch himself now and again in an attempt to wake himself up from this unbelievable nightmare.

As if by magic, the earth beneath their feet swiftly returned to normal, the cracks fitted back together again like a jigsaw puzzle, sealing themselves up as rapidly as they had opened. The ground now looked perfectly safe again, as though the cracks had never existed.

"Well done Ray," Jacob enthused, "you managed that test all by yourself, without any assistance from me at all. You are learning fast my boy."

"It wasn't anything I've learnt Jacob, it was Sylvia's Bible that saved me that time. It was difficult at first, but I guessed that reading holy words to those disgusting creatures would make them shy away and slip back down their holes." Ray said triumphantly.

"Those disgusting creatures, as you call them, were the lost souls who have been looking for a final resting-place since their painful deaths at the hands of the High Priest and Priestess of Darkness and their evil accomplices. Now that your spiritual strength and understanding is growing to match your physical strength, I think the time has come to explain a little more of our mission. Raymond." Jacob sat down on a large rock and beckoned Ray to join him. "We are not here simply to exorcise the ghost of Lucille, neither are we here only to release Esther's spirit so that it may roam free and join her mother's in paradise. We are also here to free all those tormented souls whose earthly bodies were sacrificed to the Devil over the years and, at the same time, to free this island of the evil that pervades these hills and forests and puts fear into the hearts of honest men and women. That is our mission Ray." Jacob preached, banging his staff down violently on the ground.

"I have come this far, Jacob," Ray said quietly, looking at the old man with great respect and determination. "You have taught me a lot in a short space of time and now that I'm feeling stronger again, and strangely at peace with this situation, I am ready to see it right through to the end and I damned well will." Ray no longer felt as scared as he did after the first attack and also realised that he was no longer as tired as he was earlier, although he could not explain why he felt the way he did. But Jacob held the key, because he was slowly becoming weaker as Ray's strength increased but he feared that if he told Ray that, the young man's confidence might take a tumble, so he decided to bide his time.

The skies darkened and were full of foreboding as Ray looked up at the gathering storm clouds, he shuddered with apprehension at whatever evil deeds might lie ahead of them, although he was now totally resolved to face whatever their enemies may throw at them. Jacob wearily rested his arm on Ray's shoulder as if to underline his reliance on the younger man's physical strength. "The time has come now I think, young Ray." Although he knew what the old man meant, Ray stubbornly refused to accept that he might have to face Jacob's enemies alone. He turned and embraced the frail old man and assured him once again that he had not come this far just to turn back now. He looked up at the angry sky and, full of nervous apprehension, began to recite the Lord's Prayer to himself as beads of sweat rolled down his face. Whilst awaiting his fate with all the equanimity he could muster, he looked back at Jacob, but was quite astonished to see something he had never experienced before. This amazing old man had performed the ultimate illusion of invisibility. He could still feel Jacob's arm on his shoulder and could hear his measured breathing but could no longer see him at all. The very air about them grew still and palpably thick and heavy. The faint clamour of distant voices slowly rose up out of the very ground itself and the taunting, whispering of a voice that sounded uncannily reminiscent of Sam's told him that he was about to die a horrible death. The voice then trailed off into maniacal laughter as the clouds began to race ever faster and a cold wind screamed through the trees in the madness of the moment. He felt enveloped in hatred and his body became icy cold as the powers of darkness began to prepare him for the despair that would precede them taking his soul into eternal damnation. Ray stared up at the clouds, which had now turned a deep purple as they swirled across the embattled sky, resolutely telling himself that he would not submit and that, as Jacob's ambassador, he would see this thing through to the bitter end. It was at that moment that he felt a reassuring squeeze on his shoulder as Jacob prepared to release his grip and slowly move away from Ray. It was difficult to see anything now as darkness was falling very quickly, adding to the feeling of loneliness that was pervading his senses, but he took comfort from Jacob's words that he would always be there when Ray needed him and after all, Jacob had saved him from a terrifying and painful death not long ago.

Nothing could possibly have prepared Ray for the sight that greeted him at the precise moment that the darkness became total. Out of that inky blackness he could just make out two tiny points of light coming slowly towards him from the far distance, now small, now growing at great speed and then suddenly mutating into two huge, macabre and unearthly figures with massive dragon's wings and cold, staring, lifeless eyes which seemed to bore right through him. Ray's heart stopped beating for a moment as he looked in abject terror at the High Priest and High Priestess of Darkness. Their heads resembled goats with huge coiled horns and black fur covered their shoulders. In the silvery light emanating from their bodies, Ray could see blood dripping from their slavering mouths onto their long white robes, which draped the rest of their bodies. The High Priest raised a large, scaly hand, adorned with long, vicious talons and Ray could well imagine this hellish monster swooping down on those dreadful wings and ripping into its unfortunate and terrified victims with those eagle's talons before devouring their flesh. Fire crackled around their feet and they began to grow visibly as Ray stared at them still dazed with fear.

As they gradually grew larger, towering above Ray and staring down unblinkingly at him, Jacob realised to his horror that these demons had grown dramatically in size and power over the years since they took his daughter's life. He guessed that this must be the result of gathering a large number of souls in that time. Indeed, it occurred to Jacob that they had devoured every living thing in the forest and now had such power that no other living creature could enter the forest without facing certain death. Jacob himself felt cold and a little unsure of his powers against such violent adversaries, but then he thought of Esther, Lucille and the other poor souls suspended between life and death. His whole purpose in being here was now crystallising before his eyes in the shape of Ray standing perfectly still and defiant before these harbingers of death towering above him.

Jacob concentrated his thoughts and spiritual energy on Ray and a soft halo of light began to grow around his young apprentice as a beacon glows in the darkness. Ray immediately recognised this gift as a tool, not only of defence, but also of truth, life and revenge against enemies more powerful than his worst nightmares could ever have conjured up and he concentrated his thoughts on his mission. Retaliation was swift as the huge black wings grew in size, blotting out the skies and any remaining vestige of light from above. Then Jacob's voice rang in Ray's ear. "Look out Ray, jump to your left!" Ray threw himself to his left just as a long silver shard fell from the sky and thumped into the ground where he had been standing. Without Jacob's warning, the sharp missile would have sliced Ray in two. As Ray scrambled to his feet, Jacob's voice rang out again in his ear and again Ray leapt aside as another of the immense icicles slammed into the ground where he had been sprawled after the first salvo. Then another and another were unleashed but Jacob's warnings and Ray's agility defeated each attack. Again and again the attacks came but with Jacob watching from a clear vantage point and transmitting his warnings into his protégé's ears, Ray was able to move quickly enough to avoid certain death on each occasion. The demons were clearly not pleased with the way things were going, as they must surely have expected to finish Ray off quickly and take his soul with their first missile. The High Priest moved his head from side to side as though listening for something or trying to ascertain how Ray was able to sidestep these ferocious attacks. He seemed to be aware that someone or something was warning his intended victim but was unable to intercept the signals. Jacob knew that the demons would now unleash indescribable fury to destroy Ray, whose goodness and honesty offended them deeply in this desolate landscape where they no longer tolerated even life itself. He quickly set about transferring all the power that Ray would need to withstand the next attack, even though it would have a weakening effect on him. As the two friends prepared for the next onslaught, the circle of light surrounding Ray became ever brighter and he began to believe that, with Jacob's magic, nothing could touch him now. Indeed, Jacob was creating a force field of virtue around Ray, which no evil would be able to penetrate, but in so doing, his own powers and strength were quickly waning. Angered by his continued defiance, the demons rained balls of fire down on this human upstart but the protective field of light that Jacob had conferred on Ray held firm. Eventually the attack ceased and smouldering rocks surrounded him. Then Ray felt Jacob's hand on his shoulder once more.

Before Jacob could speak or Ray could acknowledge the old man's presence, the High Priestess rose up higher into the air, her eyes now glowing red in the reflected light of the fire still surrounding the two companions. Higher she rose, her huge black wings spread yet wider, now looking more fearsome than ever as she rocked from side to side in the way that a cobra does as it prepares to strike. Long plaits hung from her head almost to the base of the white robe, on which Ray could just make out some strange black patterns, and swung from side to side in a mesmerising motion. Ray knew that she was readying herself for the attack that he had feared ever since the two demons came into view, but although he now felt stronger and wanted so much to be sure of Jacob's protection, the terror of what was clearly about to be unleashed was almost taking control of him. He understood that this was her intention and boldly stood firm and insolent in the face of insuperable odds. He could still feel Jacob's hand on his shoulder and steeled himself to believe in the old man who had already brought him safely through untold dangers.

As she swayed back and forth, the High Priestess began to transform into a huge serpent, extra limbs in the form of smaller snakes emerged from her body and writhed around, their forked tongues lashing out as they sought their prey. A little below the creature's cold serpentine head, Ray was chilled to the very bone to see Sam engulfed in its slithering coils. He looked on in horror, Sam cried out to him, her face contorted with fear and as she reached out towards him, another coil grasped her wrist and held her fast. Ray immediately began to weaken, fearing that all was lost now that they had Sam. Jacob realised in an instant that if Ray let go now, the force field of virtue around him, and indeed everything that Jacob believed in, would crumble in an instant and they would be powerless before these terrible spectres of evil. Jacob abruptly bellowed a thunderous reminder in Ray's ear, just as he was losing his grip, almost bursting his eardrums in the process.

"Remember your mission, Ray!"

"But, Jacob, they've got Sam. Can't you see? They will kill her if I continue to defy them. I'm beaten. I have to give in to them," Ray wailed.

"This is only an illusion, Ray. They *don't* have Sam at all. You must trust me, Ray." These were Jacob's last words as he left Ray's side again to draw on his last reserves of spiritual strength.

With a blood-curdling shriek, the High Priestess swooped down and hit Ray with the speed of lightning and a force quite beyond his comprehension. The ground shook and there was a deafening explosion, coupled with a blinding flash as she hit Jacob's field of light. In an instant, this fiendish creature from Hell transformed into a prodigious source of energy, which flowed through Ray and Jacob like a great tidal wave of raw power.

"Now Raymond, we attack NOW!" Jacob yelled in Ray's ear. The force field suddenly dropped and they were immediately elevated high into the air, taking The High Priest completely by surprise as they came face to face. "Strike now!" shouted Jacob as both men lifted their arms up high above their heads and then, with their fingers pointed, aimed their outstretched hands towards this ghoulish ambassador of Hell and struck with all the welled up emotion they could muster from deep within themselves. Ray felt the power surging up from the soles of his feet, up through his whole body and out to his very fingertips and he could feel the tingle and crackle as it leapt like an electric spark in the direction of the unsuspecting target. The spirit of goodness and life had filled their entire bodies and was now unleashed in a great torrent of pure white light and power. Nothing evil could possibly withstand its force, nor stand in its path without being instantly ignited by the purity of its energy. Their adversary shook violently as the light struck him full in the face and sparks jumped crazily between his horns. His face contorted with rage and pain as the white light continued to flow straight into his eyes. Then at length, his whole frame lit up and glowed with an incandescent light before exploding in a gigantic fireball and finally crumbling to ash as it gave up the titanic battle. A painful screeching, reminiscent of the wailing of a banshee, permeated the forest as the beam of light found its way into all the nooks and crannies and all the other hitherto dark places of this barren land. The sky itself lit up as Jacob and Ray continued to disgorge their magical energy until they were sure that their mission was complete. Eventually, Ray looked around, sensing that Jacob was no longer there by his side but he could neither see nor hear his companion. What he did see however, brought tears of joy to his eyes; hundreds of smiling faces floated around in the sky and all were looking at him. The innocent faces of boys, girls, young men and women whose lives had been cruelly taken as sacrifices to Satan, now smiled down at him from beautiful blue skies as they drifted slowly up towards the fluffy white clouds which were waiting to embrace them. Ray was not sure whether he was dreaming or whether this was how it felt to die but the tempestuous events of the last hour or two finally proved too much for him and he passed into unconsciousness.

It was getting dark when Sam and Joe found the place where Ray's body had come to rest looking pale, washed-out, dishevelled and bloodstained. Sam collapsed to her knees, threw herself across Ray's motionless body, and sobbed pitifully. "Wake up Ray, you can't die. I won't let you die, Ray, Ray!" With her diminutive body, she tried to cover Ray's great bulk to warm him through and get his circulation going again.

She thought she could hear a faint groan coming from deep within his chest and raised her head to look at his face, and then instinctively she kissed him tenderly on the lips. Although his eyes remained closed, there was definitely some movement beneath his eyelids. Sam grabbed him by the shoulders and shook him with all the strength she could muster.

"He's alive, Joe!" she yelled excitedly. "Ray, are you alright? Are you hurt Ray, please answer me." She pleaded. Slowly, Ray's head lolled from side to side.

"Sam, thank God you're alright." He whispered. "What happened? Where's Jacob?"

"Lay still my darling. I'll go and get help."

"But Sam, where's Jacob? I must find him." Ray turned his head slightly as he was in great pain and could see his friend Joe some way off, bending over someone lying on the ground. He recognised Jacob's robes as he lay crumpled up on the soft green grass where so recently there had been only dust. He wanted to get up but the pain was so great that he could not even raise his head.

"What is it Ray? You're badly hurt, please don't try to get up, you'll only make it worse" Sam cried.

"I must get to Jacob, Sam. I must." Ray implored her.

"Please keep still Ray. I'll go and see if he's OK." Sam ran across to Joe to find out what had happened and saw an old man lying motionless on the ground. She had no idea who he was but could see that Joe looked very upset. Joe was mopping his brow with a handkerchief when Jacob moved his lips to speak but no sound came.

"He's trying to say something, Joe." Sam said excitedly.

"We need to get closer." Joe put his ear close to Jacob's lips and realised that the old man was calling for Ray. "Come on Sam, help me get Ray over here." With all her might, Sam helped Joe to lift Ray up off the ground and support him as he limped weakly across to where Jacob's twisted body lay on the grass. Ray then collapsed on the grass beside his new friend. The two men regarded each other with complete admiration and both managed weak smiles. Neither Sam nor Joe could possibly understand what had taken place here today between these two great men, nor would they ever be able to fully comprehend how Ray's life had changed irreversibly forever. Joe intuitively rested his hand on Sam's shoulder and guided her away for a few moments so the two men could commune once more. Jacob's weak laughter had the ring of triumph as he whispered to Ray.

"Thank you, young man. Thank you for setting Esther's spirit free. My mission is now complete."

"You're going to be fine, Jacob. Joe is incredibly strong and he will be able to carry you to the nearest house where we can get some help." Jacob smiled at Ray again.

"No my good man, I'll not be requiring your friend's help, but thank you again, Ray. They are waiting for me and I have kept them waiting quite long enough already."

"They who, Jacob?" Ray asked quizzically. Jacob lifted a finger and pointed up to the sky and Ray instinctively allowed his gaze to follow where Jacob was pointing. Looking up, he saw the beautiful face of the woman with whom he had become so well acquainted over the last few weeks. She held a little girl's hand and they were walking slowly, happily through an orange grove and were heading towards green fields and meadows.

"Lucille. Lucille and Esther." Jacob muttered. Lucille was chatting to her daughter and pointing to the different, pretty flowers and trees. Jacob gripped Ray's arm firmly and winced in pain whilst Ray comforted him as best he could. Joe walked back and handed Ray a water bottle which he had been carrying and motioned Ray to give the old man a drink. Jacob sipped from the bottle then Ray gently rested his head back but kept his warm hands there to cushion him.

"Remember young man, call me if ever you need my help and I will always be there."

Ray watched with almost unbearable sadness as Jacob departed this World and crossed over to the next. Ray looked upwards and saw Jacob's face smiling down at him and waving as he went to meet Lucille. The happy old man lifted Esther up in his arms and kissed her. Ray stood watching as they slowly disappeared into the sky and all that remained were shadows in the gathering gloom of late evening.

CHAPTER X –
Epilogue

"Wow, what a story! That is absolutely incredible, Mum! Is it all true, about Uncle Ray and the old man, I mean?" Sarah asked in sheer amazement.

"Yes my dear, every very single word of it; and I don't mind telling you after that our lives were never the same again," Madeline mused as she stared into the dying embers of the fire. "Your father always used to 'pooh pooh' anything to do with the supernatural but after that episode with Ray, he changed and since then has been inclined to keep his own counsel."

"I'm surprised Uncle Ray survived at all after taking such a beating."

"Well, he was still physically in very bad shape when he got home from the Bahamas, and he did take quite a long time to recover, but being Ray he was very philosophical about it all. Nevertheless, you know it did change him mentally and spiritually as well. He seemed to get stronger with more inner confidence, bless him." Madeline smiled at the memory of those whirlwind days and found it hard to believe that it all took place nearly forty years ago.

"Why did you keep such a fascinating story away from me all these years Mum? And more to the point, why haven't you used it as a basis for one of your novels?" Sarah demanded.

"I did!" her mother responded, much to her daughter's astonishment. "We just never published it. You see, Jacob passed on a great gift to Ray, who made a promise to Jacob that he would study to develop his newfound power. When Ray and Sam returned from the Bahamas, they obviously came straight here to tell the rest of us what had taken place. Everyone who was present at the dinner met here and that was when Ray explained how important it is to keep the knowledge of these powers secret. He had no desire to live through the same type of heartache that poor Jacob endured. Every year since then, the eight of us, Ray, Sam, Karen, Mark, Julian, Caroline, your father and I, meet up specifically to discuss any spiritual events we have experienced throughout the year. At the same time, we take the opportunity to renew our oath when Ray performs a special ceremony and this is followed by an 'open forum' permitting us to share our spiritual experiences with each other".

"But, Mum what would you do if you needed to discuss anything urgently"?

"Oh, that was another strange thing that happened. It was as though Ray was telepathically linked to each one of us, if any of us had the need to contact him, he would already be aware. We all agreed, from that day onward, what happened here in Ivy Cottage should remain a secret until we have all passed on. You see my dear this is a legacy! Now it seems to me that my account of these adventures should be published one day, and that is precisely why I have told you the whole story, but you must promise me that you will honour our pact and not tell a living soul until we have all departed this world.

"Of course Mum, you have my word."

The next few days passed slowly until the morning when Neil was to be discharged from hospital. Madeline and Sarah busied themselves all morning with their preparations for his homecoming after David and Ray left to collect him. It did not seem long before they heard the crunching of the car's tyres on the gravel drive and the two women could no longer contain their excitement and rushed to the front door of Ivy Cottage. The door was wrenched open with much enthusiasm as David parked the car as close as possible. Ray quickly opened the door and leapt out to help Neil to get out of the car, but Neil already had the door open and was halfway out before Ray got to him. Neil stood up, breathed deeply and said,

"It's good to be home"

Madeline walked into the lounge carrying a tray of afternoon tea for Neil and the others. She looked across the room to see Neil standing by the mantelpiece, his fingers gently stroking the clock. Madeline placed the tray on the coffee table and went to join her husband.

"David thought it would be a lovely surprise for you darling," she said.

"Yes" he replied quietly as he continued to stare at the clock. Then he turned round slowly and looked thoughtfully at Madeline for a long time.

"I am sorry" he said softly "but I'm afraid it cannot stay here".

That night, Madeline tiptoed to the dining room and waited for the clock to strike the hour. She listened to the familiar deep, rich sound before carefully lifting it down from the mantelpiece, opening the back and removing the pendulum. She wrapped the clock in a soft cloth and placed it on a bed of straw in a wooden box, then slowly closed the lid. She carefully hid the key in a cupboard until she would be alone in the house when she could return The Clock to the loft where David had found it.

About the Author

Janet Dove was born in West London and as a young child lived in the Caribbean with her parents for four years before returning to the UK to commence full-time education. Janet is married with two children, one having graduated and the other still at university. She currently works as a Personnel Manager for a global bank in London. Since her school days, Janet has had a passion for writing stories of fantasy, culminating in The Clock. The sequel is currently in the process of gestation but will soon follow The Clock into print.

Printed in the United Kingdom
by Lightning Source UK Ltd.
108200UKS00001B/23